TRUTH IS A WHISPER

A CHRISTIAN COWBOY ROMANCE

WOLF CREEK RANCH
BOOK ONE

MANDI BLAKE

Lindi,
I hope you
love the cowboys.
Mandi
Blake

Truth is a Whisper
Wolf Creek Ranch Book One
By Mandi Blake

Copyright © 2022 Mandi Blake
All Rights Reserved

Published in the United States of America
Cover Designer: Amanda Walker PA & Design Services
Editor: Editing Done Write

CONTENTS

PROLOGUE

Jameson

Jameson pulled up at the hay barn and jumped off the UTV. If he could get the attachment hinges greased and the hayride trailer put together in the next thirty minutes, he might make it back to the dining hall before everyone else gathered for dinner.

That way, he could spend a minute with Ava without everyone and their mother watching them.

Actually, it was just *her* mother that Jameson didn't want watching. Linda Collins didn't care one bit for him, and she wouldn't be afraid to make her opinions known—again—if she caught him with Ava.

He hung his hat on the hook by the door and grabbed the grease pump. He'd made it through four hinges when quick, pounding footsteps echoed in the barn behind him.

Ava was running toward him with her dark hair flowing behind her, and boy was she a sight for sore eyes. The image of her hadn't left his mind all day, but he still got that shot of adrenaline every time he saw her.

Jameson laid the pump on the tractor tire and wiped his hands on a grease rag before jogging to meet her. She was beautiful even on a bad day, but she was gorgeous in the summer sunlight. And that smile—the one that somehow made his own lips turn up at the edges—was the image he couldn't get out of his head.

When Ava was close enough to make out her facial features, Jameson jerked his jog to a halt. She wasn't smiling.

"I'm so sorry." She stumbled to a stop, nearly barreling into his chest.

He wrapped his hands around her arms to steady her. Those eyes. Fear and confusion greeted him instead of the happiness he'd come to expect. "What? What happened?"

"You almost didn't make it back in time, and I —" Her sentence fell, and her hand rose to cover her quivering chin.

"Ava, what's wrong? Tell me." He rubbed his hands up and down her arms, begging the worry in her eyes to subside. Seeing her upset always ripped a hole in him. All the grieving for her grandmother had been hard on her lately, but she'd been smiling more these last few days.

"We're leaving. Now. Mom got a call about breaking news, and they want her back tonight."

A weight settled on his chest, and his hands stopped moving. "I thought we had more time."

"Me too," she whispered. Moisture glistened in her eyes, and she bit her lips between her teeth. Her phone was ringing, and the robotic noise pierced the quiet around them.

It was her mother. It had to be. Linda Collins wasn't the kind to be left waiting, but Jameson prayed Ava wouldn't take the call. In the two weeks he'd been getting to know Ava and growing closer to her, her mother had been a constant blade slicing between them, and he'd kept his distance—for the most part. At least around her mother. Ava had been the kind of beauty meant to be admired from a distance—captivating but untouchable.

Now that their time was up, he wanted to consume every detail about this moment that might be their last.

Jameson wrapped his arms around her the way he had all those times she'd mourned. She cried as her cheek rested against his chest. A damp sweat clung to his shirt, but she didn't pull away.

Her words were broken and shaky through her

sobs. "I know she's hard on me, but I don't have anything without her."

Jameson's hold tightened, and he swallowed the retort in his throat. Ava didn't have anything without her mother because Linda was a controlling monster.

But Ava had him. She had all of him, but that wasn't enough, was it?

"I won't be able to go to college if I don't go with her."

"Shh." He rubbed a rhythmic circle on her back and tried to calm her shaking. The fact that Ava brought up staying at all soothed the ache just a little bit. At least he wasn't the only one trying to rearrange the world so they could stay together.

"I know what that means to you." He did, but it still left him feeling cold and empty.

Ava had confided a great secret to him when she'd told him of her hopes to go to college. On the surface, her decision to further her education was one that was expected and applauded. To her mother, it was a sign that her devoted daughter wanted to make her proud. But to Ava, it meant a chance to one day gain her freedom and make her own way—away from her mother's manipulative hand.

Ava hadn't used those words, but Jameson knew exactly what was going on between the Collins women. He'd grown up with a narcissistic mother, and he knew the unfair hand Ava had been dealt. He wanted her out of her mother's grasp more than he wanted his next year's worth of paychecks.

Why couldn't Ava have grown up here at Wolf Creek with the grandparents who loved her?

Ava's phone began ringing again. She lifted her head and wiped her cheeks. "I don't want to leave. The ranch. You. Grandpa."

This was his chance. He could ask her to stay. If he could say anything, what words would make her want to stay here? What could he offer her?

Nothing. Her mother's snide comments from the past few weeks rang in his ears. Linda Collins was sure and loud about Jameson's inability to live up to the lifestyle expectations the Collins women were used to.

But Ava didn't seem as materialistic and pampered as her mother. Ava had been eager to jump on the trail rides, dance by the bonfire, and lie in the back of his truck watching the bright Wyoming stars.

"She won't let me come back. She said so," Ava cried.

Jameson wrapped his arms around her again, unable to say or do anything to alleviate the brokenness in Ava's voice.

Could he go to Denver with her? He could find work there. No, he'd worked too hard to get this job.

Then there was his mom. She didn't have

anyone else to care for her, and her health had been going downhill fast and teetering on the point of no return for months now. Felicity refused to have anything to do with their mother, and he couldn't ask his sister to help the woman who'd neglected and abused her for years. He hardly blamed Felicity for giving up on their mom. He despised her himself.

What about his firefighter certification? He was only days away from passing, and he'd be one step closer to his plan to build a better future. But what would be the point if he wasn't working for something bigger than himself?

But he knew about Ava's future plans, and her next step was getting a degree. Her mother had offered to pay for college and allow Ava to live with her while she studied. That was an offer that was hard to refuse.

She could keep her head down and work hard for four years. That was what he was doing, wasn't it? Did he need to let Ava go for the greater good? So they could both stay on track for the future they'd planned?

Too bad they'd planned those futures separately. Two weeks wasn't enough to change a life's worth of dreaming.

Ava's phone rang again, and she huffed. Frustration and tension wrapped in her every muscle. "Why do I feel like I should plant my feet right here and grow roots so she can't take me away? I just met my grandpa, and he's been so good to me. I already lost the grandma I never knew, and I *hate* that!"

She was screaming now, and Jameson couldn't do anything except hold her and breathe. In and out. It had taken the death of the matriarch of Wolf Creek Ranch to bring Ava and her mom back here, and from where he stood, the whole trip out here was a slap in Ava's face. She would have loved Lottie Chambers. Mrs. Chambers had taken Jameson in and been like the grandma he never had, but Ava hadn't gotten the chance to know her real kin.

"Ava!" Linda's piercing yell jerked Ava out of his arms.

She turned, and they both watched her mother stomping toward them in her heeled boots. They had to be uncomfortable, and they looked ridiculous as Linda marched into the barn. Her cheeks were red, and her jaw was tight as she came near. Without thinking, Jameson stepped in front of Ava. It was an instinct.

"I had to drive all the way up that dirty trail chasing you. What were you thinking? Why aren't you answering your phone? We're going to miss our flight!"

Ava's tears renewed, slicing through Jameson's chest like a hot knife. All he could hear was the roaring in his ears and Ava's sobs.

Why was this happening? He'd finally found

someone he liked, and she was being ripped away when things were going so well.

Well, not anymore.

Linda's scowl wasn't deep. She probably Botoxed the ability to frown out of her face years ago, but he could feel the rage coming off her in waves.

"Let's go!"

"Give me just a minute. Please," Ava sobbed from behind Jameson's shoulder.

"You've had your minute. Enough. Get in the car."

Ava stepped forward and turned to look at him. Was she waiting on those words he hadn't said? What were they? He despised her mother, and he cared about Ava, but he was smart enough in his twenty years to know that wasn't enough, and it wouldn't get either of them far.

"I—" Ava began.

"Come on!" Linda cut Ava off, grabbing her arm and pulling.

Jameson stuck his arm between Ava and her mother. "Don't treat her like that."

Linda rounded on him, but he wasn't afraid of the fire in her eyes. He had a flame of his own burning inside him.

"Get out of the way," Linda growled, low and tempered like a warning.

"You can't jerk her around like that," Jameson said.

"Stop," Ava whispered through her quiet sobs.

The word was meant for both Jameson and her mother, but Linda wouldn't give in.

He'd forgotten how much Ava hated confrontation, especially when it came to her mother. He hated that fear in her eyes, and the last thing he wanted was to be the cause of it.

Prepared to do anything Ava asked of him, he pulled back his hand. If he fought Linda, she'd only make things worse for Ava later.

Linda turned without hesitation, pulling Ava along behind her.

Pulling her away from him and Wolf Creek Ranch.

Ava's sniffles lingered until he watched the last of her shadow disappear around the wall of hay squares stacked against the solitary wall of the pole barn.

Injustice swirled in his gut, but his shortcomings kept his boots cemented to the dirt floor.

She was gone, and the barn was quieter than ever. He exhaled a shaky breath. How had it happened so fast? In just a few short weeks, he'd gotten to know her and had developed feelings for her. Now she was gone.

Jameson rested his forehead against the cool metal

of the nearest tractor. There were so many reasons Ava should've stayed. She'd never get to know her grandpa, who happened to be a great boss and one of the best men Jameson had ever met. Selfishly, Jameson would never get to find out what could've been between Ava and him. He'd never wanted to know a woman as much as he wanted to know Ava. Two weeks hadn't been enough time to pour over the millions of opinions, ideas, likes, and quirks that made Ava Collins the incredible woman he'd been getting to know.

Jameson lifted his head when he heard footsteps and wiped the dirt from his forehead.

Henry Bowman, the foreman of Wolf Creek Ranch, stepped around the side of the tractor. "Hey, you okay?" The furrow in the older man's brow said he knew the answer.

"Yeah. Fine." Jameson picked up the grease pump and got back to work. The lie tasted rotten on his tongue.

He wasn't okay, and everything inside him said to run to Ava and catch her before she left Wolf Creek Ranch for good.

CHAPTER 1
AVA

Present Day

Ava sidestepped a producer without looking up from her tablet. Where was Katrina? She was on in less than five.

Ava tapped the Bluetooth in her ear. "Jeremy, I need Kat."

"She's on her way."

With a few taps on the screen, she'd confirmed the order for Linda's wardrobe for the next three weeks. Lowering her tablet, Ava scanned the studio and caught sight of her mother instantly. Kat might be perpetually late, but Linda didn't allow so much leniency.

Linda chatted with her co-anchor, Tyler Rossman. Ava's jaw tensed as Rossman touched her mother's elbow. The two had great on-screen chemistry, mostly because they'd been casually seeing each other since Linda got the job at the station five years ago. It was a part of her life Ava chose not to think about often. It was strange seeing her mother flirting with men all the time since her dad died. Sure, she wanted her mother to move on and find love, but Linda had only found affairs and one-night stands.

Her phone rang, and she tapped the earpiece to answer before the first ring ended. "Ava Collins."

"Ava?" The man's crackly voice was robust, despite the shake that foretold his age.

She raised her hand, ready to quickly end the call. "I'm sorry. I—"

"It's your grandpa. Ronald Chambers."

Ava lowered her hand and cut a glance at her mother, who was settling into her seat at the anchors' table.

"Hey. How are you?" There were so many things Ava wanted to say and an endless list of questions she wanted to ask, but every coherent thought seemed to fly out of her brain.

Her grandpa was on the phone. She hadn't heard from him in years.

"I'm okay. Been better. Listen, I know your mom might not like me talking to you. Well, that's not the truth. She told me not to call you, but I figure this once won't hurt."

"She what?" Ava gritted her teeth. The outburst would go unnoticed in the busy studio, but she didn't want to catch her mother's attention.

"She doesn't like me talking to you, and I want to respect that." Her grandfather sighed. "Seems as though I had a stroke or something, and—"

"A stroke or *something*!" Ava shouted. She no longer cared if she attracted attention, and she made a beeline for the offices.

"Yeah. All that medical jargon is way too fancy for me. Those doctors said a lot of things."

"Is Henry there?" She had no idea if the old foreman was still working on her grandpa's ranch, but she needed details. "Is anyone there with you?"

"Henry's here. Although I tried to run him off. He's like an old dog."

Ava's chest constricted. *A stroke*. She couldn't lose another family member without getting to know him. The first time she saw her grandmother was at the funeral. "How bad is it? Is he helping you?"

Her grandpa's voice was strained but clear. "I think I'll hang on just one more day."

"One day! I'll have to see if I can get a flight. I—"

The old man laughed until he coughed. "Ava, Ava. I was messin' with you. I plan to pester these folks around here for at least two more decades. No one's gettin' rid of me that easy."

Ava pushed open the door to the small cubicle-style office she shared with five other assistants. "Grandpa, how bad is it, and do you need me?" Efficiency was Ava's middle name. Any other day, she would have chuckled at her grandpa's tenacity. Today, she was worried he was dying, and she wasn't there with him. The guilt tightened her throat.

Why hadn't she been there all along?

Linda. That's why. Ava's mother had a personal reason for pushing their family out of their lives. She'd just never shared the secret with Ava.

She was already on the travel agency website when her grandfather responded.

"It was a month ago. Water under the bridge now."

"You had a stroke a month ago? And you're just now telling me?"

"Well, it took me a while to track you down. Not having your number and all."

"I thought I gave it to you." She was sure of it. She remembered putting her contact information in his old flip phone the one and only time she'd visited her grandpa's ranch.

"You did. And your mother told me not to contact you. So, I didn't for a while. Then my phone got crushed."

"Crushed?" Ava asked. The cursor hovered over the button to continue her flight search.

"Horse stepped on it. That's not the point."

"How did a horse step on it?" Of all the things. Wyoming was a strange place.

"Bucked me off and tried to step on me. Thankfully, the phone was the only casualty."

"When?" How many times had her grandpa come close to death in the six years since she'd seen him?

"Oh, 'bout three years ago."

"What were you doing on a horse?" He'd been pushing into the upper seventies the last time she'd seen him.

"Training."

Ava propped her forehead in her hand. "Are you okay?"

"I'm hanging in there."

"You don't sound so certain."

"Well, I don't want to lie to you. I'm really fine. Henry isn't convinced, and he won't quit pestering me."

"He's probably just worried about you."

"He retired a few months ago, but he's been hovering around my house instead of taking that cross-country trip with his wife he's always talked about. I know you're busy, but I was wondering if you'd consider coming up for a little bit. Just until Henry and his wife get far enough away that he won't turn around if he finds out you've gone back to Denver. A few days? Just pretend you'll be staying to take care of your invalid grandpa, and Henry will run off into the sunset with his bride."

"Did he just get married?" Ava asked.

"No. They've been married for coming up on forty-three years, but what good is retirement if you don't get to spend a bunch of time with your family and pester each other to death?"

Ava stared at the screen with row after row of flights that could take her to Wolf Creek Ranch within the next twenty-four hours. What would it be like to go back to Wyoming? She'd loved it there, and she missed her grandpa.

"Let me get the approval from my supervisor." Thankfully, her mother wasn't in charge of making those decisions, or she'd never get the go-ahead to leave. Although Linda would definitely try to stop her, Ava didn't want to think about that just yet.

"Take your time. Henry will be here clucking like a mother hen until you get here."

Ava's voice dropped to a whisper. "I'm glad you called. I'm sorry she doesn't want us to talk. I don't know why."

"It's okay, baby girl. Your mama has her reasons, even if we don't know what they are."

He didn't know either? The revelation caught Ava off guard.

"Well, I've gotta run. Those horses don't feed themselves."

They didn't? She'd always thought they ate grass. "I—"

"See you soon. Love you," her grandpa said in farewell before the call ended.

Ava's eyes widened, but she wasn't seeing the monitor of flight schedules in front of her. Her grandfather had said he loved her the last and only time she'd seen him, and she'd thought it strange then. How did he know if he loved her or not? He knew so little about her.

She could count on one hand the number of times Linda had said "I love you," and they'd all been in the midst of a disagreement. Linda said those special words, and Ava felt rotten for even thinking of going against her mother.

Love was strange and confusing. Who knew what it really meant?

She checked the time. She had an hour before Linda was off-air. If Ava could catch Jordan now, he might approve her vacation time before her mother found out.

Ava pushed away from her desk and was down the hall in seconds. She had to do this quickly, before she had a chance to chicken out.

Remember Grandpa. Don't think about Linda's reaction. This is about Grandpa. He had a stroke. He called asking for help.

She continued to list her reasons until she knocked on Jordan's door. The optimistic train of thought she'd been on decided to crash and burn in those few seconds while she waited in silence.

Finally, Jordan called, "Come in."

Ava brushed a hand down her black pencil skirt and tugged on her suit jacket before opening the door. Jordan sat behind his desk, pecking speedily on his laptop.

Once he finished his typing, he looked up and smiled. "Ava." He stood and walked around the desk. "To what do I owe this visit?"

Jordan had always been kind to her, but she'd overheard too many conversations in the offices. His made-for-TV face afforded him lots of attention, and he indulged whenever possible. Ava was friendly whenever their paths crossed, but she maintained a healthy distance. She wasn't sure what she was looking for in a man, but "popular with the ladies" wasn't on the list.

"I'm sorry for such short notice, but my grandpa just called. He needs my help in Wyoming for a few days. I was wondering if I could take a vacation."

Jordan's smile fell as he rested his backside against the desk. "Your grandpa? You mean Linda's dad?"

Ava wrung her hands. Working with her mother meant everyone at the office knew a little more about her than she liked. "Yes. She doesn't know yet.

I just got off the phone with him. He had a stroke, and he needs help for a few days."

"Will Linda want to go too? I don't think I can lose you both. How many days are we talking?"

"No. Linda won't want to go. I was thinking a week."

Jordan's eyes widened, and he crossed his arms over his broad chest. "A week. That's more than I expected."

"It's more than I expect to be gone. I may be able to come back sooner."

"Is Brianna up to speed? Can she and Kelsey take over for you while you're out?"

"I'll meet with both of them right away. We stay in touch, so we all know everything that's going on. There are some things I can do off-site, so I'll fill them in on the things I'll be working on while I'm gone."

Jordan brushed the neatly trimmed beard on his chin. "Sounds like I don't have a good enough reason why you can't go."

Ava smiled. She'd never taken time off work, but this was something she wanted to do—needed to do. Her grandpa needed her, and she didn't want to miss this chance to be there for him and get to know him. He was getting so old, and her time was running out.

"Touch base and let me know when you expect

to be back," Jordan said as he pushed off the desk and walked back around to his seat.

"Thank you. I'll be back soon."

Jordan's grin returned as he sat down. "I'll hold you to it."

His wink was probably meant to be playful, but it evoked an icky chill in her spine. Jordan was a good fifteen years older than her, and Ava was probably the only woman in the office who didn't clamor for his attention.

A pretty face meant nothing if the man didn't care about her, and no one had cared about her the way Jameson had the last time she'd visited Wolf Creek Ranch.

The sudden memory had her breath catching in her throat. Did he still work there?

"Um, thanks again. I'll stay in touch." Ava spun for the door and bolted into the hallway. Thoughts about Jameson Ford always left her feeling empty.

But as she sprinted down the hall, careful not to stumble in her heels, those thoughts bloomed with hope. It was crazy to think he'd still work there, right? Her grandpa had joked that cowboys were meant to ride away, following the wind to the next ranch every few seasons. Jameson had probably moved on long ago.

Why hadn't Ava moved on? Why was Jameson the only one who hung around in her thoughts? She'd dated, but they'd all been so forgettable.

Not Jameson. He'd lit a kindling in her heart and stoked a wildfire. All in just a few weeks.

Back in her office, she grabbed her purse and shut off her computer. She could pack a few things and be back before Linda's next air time. She shouldn't be thinking about Jameson. Her grandpa needed her. That was the reason she was going to Wolf Creek.

Even as she pushed through the series of doors on her way out of the station, she couldn't shake the hope that Jameson might still be at the ranch.

CHAPTER 2

JAMESON

Jameson walked into Deano's Diner a little after ten in the morning. He'd been up since before dawn and hadn't had breakfast yet. After speeding through all his off-day errands, it was time for a sit-down.

The bell above the door chimed as he stepped inside. The warm coffee smell greeted him, causing his stomach to rumble.

Jameson always felt out of place on off days. He'd been working three jobs for years, and the empty time made him jittery—the reason he'd skipped coffee this morning. He filled some of that extra time helping Mr. Chambers out at the main house, but his boss usually ran him off after a few hours.

Jameson tipped his hat at Kendra as he stepped up to the counter. "Morning."

She pulled a pen out of the bun of curls atop her head. "Morning. What can I get for you?"

"Double biscuit and gravy with sausage. A coffee, too, please."

Kendra scribbled the order on a pad and handed him a ceramic mug. "I'll have it right out."

"Thanks." Jameson poured his coffee and followed the robust laughter into the adjoining room.

The group of older, blue-collar men that everyone in town called "The Round Table" was in session and as riled up as always. The group took up almost every seat of the long picnic-style table that ran the length of the dining room. Jameson lifted his mug in greeting. "Morning, gentlemen."

Grady stood, scraping his wooden chair across the tile floor and clapped a hand on Jameson's shoulder. "How's the boss this morning?"

"If I was any better, I'd be you. What about you? Working hard or hardly working?"

"Hardly working," Grady said as he lowered back into his seat and tucked his thumbs underneath the straps of his overalls. He'd worn the same uniform for as long as Jameson could remember.

Jameson took the seat beside his friend. "Retirement looks good on you, but I have to say it's weird not seeing you at the feed and seed."

"I'm still around. I can't give it up completely. Hey, you know someone looking for a round baler?"

Grady jerked his thumb toward the far end of the long table. "Jerry's trying to get rid of his."

"You talked to Micah or Silas about it?" Jameson asked.

Jerry shook his head. "Not yet, but I'll stop by there on my way home."

"That'd be my first guess." The Hardings might buy the baler from Jerry, even if they didn't need it. Blackwater Ranch was booming, and Silas never hesitated to help out a neighbor.

Kendra set a steaming plate of gravy and biscuits in front of Jameson. "Enjoy."

"Thank you, ma'am." Jameson closed his eyes and inhaled. "Man, Kendra makes the best gravy."

Grady hummed in agreement. "If she wasn't married, I'd kiss the cook."

"Might want to keep your lips to yourself, old man," Jameson said.

"Speaking of lips, who are you kissing these days?" Grady asked.

Jameson lowered his fork and swallowed the bite he'd barely chewed. "What is this, kiss and tell?"

Ted lifted a mug to his lips. "Might as well be." The old man's skinny frame was deceiving. He lifted heavy furniture every day at Blackwater Restoration, and Jameson hadn't ever seen a single bead of sweat on the man's brow.

The bell above the door chimed, and Officer Asa Scott strolled in.

Grady threw his hands up in the air. "It wasn't me."

Asa chuckled. "At ease, old man. I'm here for coffee."

Jameson stood and held out a hand to his friend. "What do you know?"

Asa shook his hand. "Not enough. How's Mr. Chambers?"

"He's back to good. Tired of Henry fussing over him."

"Good. Tell him he owes me a cup of coffee."

Jameson's phone rang in his pocket, and he pulled it out. "Speak of the devil. Let me take this." Jameson answered, "Hey, boss."

"What are you up to?" Mr. Chambers asked.

Jameson sat down in an empty booth near the front window of the diner. "Just catching up with the guys. How can I help you?"

"I don't need any help."

Jameson grinned. His boss was tired of being coddled after the stroke he had a month ago. To be fair, Mr. Chambers had made a great recovery, despite his age.

"I just need you to come by if you get a chance today. Not for work. Just a personal call."

Jameson stood and walked back toward his half-eaten plate of food. "Sure thing. I'll be there in half an hour."

"See you then," Mr. Chambers said before he ended the call.

Asa was back with a steaming mug of coffee. "What'd he want?"

"I don't know yet. He hardly ever calls me on my day off, but I've been stopping by to help out with some odds and ends at the main house."

"He misses you," Grady crooned.

Jameson sat back down to his biscuits and gravy. "Probably wants me to kick Henry out. Those two are going to cat fight if Henry doesn't leave the poor man alone."

Jerry piped up at the other end of the table. "Send Henry my way. I could use an extra worker around the farm."

"I think Mr. Chambers would appreciate you taking his babysitter off his hands," Jameson said before digging back into his meal.

Within minutes, Jameson had cleared his plate, and Kendra had shoved a Styrofoam cup of coffee in his hands on his way out the door.

A few minutes later, he was turning beneath the tall sign at the entrance to Wolf Creek Ranch. It still surprised him sometimes to think he was the foreman here. He'd worked here off and on since high school, and dozens of workers had come and gone since then. A few from his first days were still around, but Jameson was the one Mr. Chambers and Henry chose to promote when the old foreman announced his retirement.

All those years of loyalty counted for a lot in this business.

He drove slowly past the baling fields with one elbow resting on the open window. The earthy smell of dirt and hay welcomed him home. He'd been living in the wranglers' quarters for a few months now, and home was a fitting name for the old cabin.

A few of the wranglers were chatting with some guests beneath a tall evergreen tree at the archery range. Jameson lifted his hand, and they all waved back, including the little girl and boy chasing each other around the field.

He parked in front of the main house, noting that Henry's truck wasn't around. At least Jameson hadn't been called to break up a fight. Henry had been the foreman at Wolf Creek Ranch for thirty years before he retired and handed over the reins to Jameson. He got the sense the old cowboy didn't know how to have a life outside the ranch. Despite Mrs. Bowman's constant begging to tour the country, Henry couldn't leave his friend after the stroke.

Maybe that was the reason for this meeting. Was Henry finally sailing off into the sunset? Whatever it was, it had to be time-sensitive. Jameson stopped by the main house every morning to talk through the day's workload. What did Mr. Chambers need that couldn't wait until tomorrow morning?

Jameson toed off his boots on the porch and stepped inside without knocking. Mr. Chambers never locked his door, and ranch workers were in and out all day. He'd made the decision to put his office in his house, and that made for blurry personal and professional boundaries.

It also meant Mr. Chambers had welcomed Jameson into the main house for years, and he'd come to think of the man as family. It was easy to do when Jameson's own family had been so scattered and dysfunctional. Mr. Chambers didn't have anyone else left either. They made a perfect pair.

The main house was the opposite of Jameson's childhood home. Well, homes. His mom had moved him and his sister around from shack to trailer to apartment when he was growing up, and he didn't remember much about any of them. They all smelled and had bugs and mice. Any cleaning and cooking had been done by his older sister, Felicity, and she'd been too young to handle a household when Jameson came along.

He should probably send Felicity flowers more often. He wouldn't have made it out of diapers without her.

Jameson moved through the house toward the living room. Mr. Chambers didn't step foot in his office until after lunch. He used to spend his mornings with Lottie before she died. Now, he told people he spent his mornings with the Lord. No one could fault him there. Jameson could always use a little more one-on-one time with the Big Man upstairs.

In the living room, Jameson looked around for any sign of life, but the room was quiet.

"Boss?"

"In the kitchen!"

Jameson followed the voice and found Mr. Chambers pouring a cup of coffee into a brown mug.

"Don't start your fussing. It's decaf," Mr. Chambers said with a scowl.

Jameson lifted his hands. "Have caffeinated if you want."

"Stupid doctors say I shouldn't. What if someone told them they couldn't have coffee? Huh? I bet they'd start some kind of newsworthy protest and—"

"Hey, um, let's just pour this out and make a new pot of *real* coffee." Jameson took the carafe from the old man and poured it into the sink.

"You're the only one around here with sense, you know that?"

"Maybe don't tell Henry this pot is the real deal. I don't like it when he gets all strung up."

Mr. Chambers tossed the last spoonful of coffee grounds into the maker and flipped the lid shut with too much force. "He gets this whiny, high-pitched tone that grinds my gears."

"You ever think you and Henry need a break from each other?" Jameson joked. The two friends were thick as thieves, even if they got on each other's nerves.

Mr. Chambers passed a mug to Jameson. "You read my mind. That's why I called."

"Why do I have to be brought into this?"

"Cause I said so. Now I have a guest coming, and I need you to show her around." Mr. Chambers turned to Jameson and raised one brow. "Did you have plans today?"

"No. You said her? Is this a lady friend of yours?"

Mr. Chambers grinned. "You'd like that, wouldn't you?"

Actually, Jameson hadn't heard a peep from anyone about Mr. Chambers dating again. Lottie had been gone for six years, and while they all loved her, Mr. Chambers had love and devotion for that woman like no one else on the ranch could understand.

A man didn't spend fifty years with the love of his life and just forget about her, right? It wasn't like Jameson knew much about love. The only real love Jameson knew was for his sister, and he'd do anything for her. Anything.

Mr. Chambers pulled the carafe out of the coffeemaker before it had finished brewing and poured a cup. "Actually, it's my granddaughter.

She's coming from Denver, and she should be here any minute now."

Jameson froze. Mr. Chambers's granddaughter.

"She was here a long time ago. You won't remember her."

"Ava?" Jameson whispered. Her name on his lips felt heavy. He hadn't said it in years.

"Oh, you do remember her." The old man's false surprise was high pitched.

Jameson straightened. "You know I remember her, you old coot. Is she okay? Why is she coming?"

"Oh yeah, you two had that little tryst when she visited before." Mr. Chambers grinned over the top of his mug.

"It wasn't a tryst. That word makes it sound like we were just playing around."

"Well, kids tend to do that." Mr. Chambers waved his hand in the air as he mimicked young folks in love. "They're all 'I love you' one day and 'I never want to speak to you again' the next day."

"I was never like that," Jameson said.

"Not you, per se, but other kids are like that."

Jameson's tone deepened to a serious one. "I wasn't like that about Ava."

"I know. That's why I called you. I know you liked Ava, and she could use a friendly face when she gets here. I kind of sprung this on her."

"What do you mean?" Jameson asked.

"I told her I had a stroke and I needed help."

"You didn't."

"Okay, fine. I didn't. I asked her to come stay until Henry leaves. I want Henry to get out of my hair and on the road with his wife."

"That makes a little sense. I can't believe she's coming back."

Mr. Chambers rested his mug on the counter. "You and me both, son. If her mother lets her make it all the way, it might be a miracle."

Jameson's blood ran cold at the mention of Linda Collins. There were few people in this world he disliked, and Linda was one of those that made his jaw tense immediately.

A light knock rapped on the front door, and both men stilled. A bead of sweat raced down the back of Jameson's neck.

"That must be her," Mr. Chambers said. "Why don't you get that."

CHAPTER 3

AVA

Ava slowed as she drove beneath the wood-framed entrance to Wolf Creek Ranch. A howling wolf silhouette rested at each of the high corners. It had been so long since she'd seen the ranch, but even the drive in was familiar.

A rustic sign told her to continue on Mountain Meadow Lane to the main house and stables or turn left to go to the archery and trap ranges. She followed the steady incline of the lane until she reached the crest of a hill where miles of the mountain valley stretched into the distance. The foothills of the Bighorn Mountains lay ahead and to the left, standing guard over the old settlement.

Ava had seen this place before, but that didn't stop her from gasping in awe. It was strange to think her mother had grown up here. A ripple of injustice twinged in her heart. Linda didn't appreciate the home Ava had never been allowed to know.

She continued on the path until the main house came into view. Grandpa's place had all the comforts she'd wished for in a home growing up in Denver. She'd lived in a suburban townhome when her dad was alive, but her mother had moved them to an upscale loft in the city a few months after her dad passed. Ava had much preferred the townhome, but growing up in a place like this would have been a dream.

The squeals of children playing on the playground were muffled inside the car, and she rolled the window down to hear them better. Why hadn't she driven with the windows down since she picked up the rental at the Sheridan County Airport? The fresh air would have been good for her.

Her phone dinged with a text notification as soon as she parked in front of the main house, and her throat constricted. Linda had been messaging her since last night, and the thread was one gut-ripping statement after another. Ava had woken to six unread messages, each meaner than the last.

Should she check the message before going inside? It would only dim her excitement to see her grandpa, but what if it was an emergency?

She unlocked the screen. There were three waiting messages from her mother.

Linda: I really hope you decided not to go. This will be the end of my career.

Funny, her mother wasn't worried about Ava's job, only her own.

Linda: Just don't come back. I'll have them replace you.

The pine-sweet air from a moment ago now settled in her lungs like mud.

Linda: It's me or him. If you choose him, you can start looking for a new place to live.

Ava swallowed hard. Her hands shook the phone she held. Why did her mother hate Grandpa so much that she didn't care that he'd had a stroke?

Linda was always over the top, and they both knew that those extremes always meant Ava would concede to her mother's will. This time felt different. Ava's determination was strong, and there was no way she could turn around and leave Grandpa.

Ava: Grandpa only needs help for a little bit. I'll be home soon. Please don't be mad. I don't want you to think I'm choosing one of you over the other because I came to help him.

She sent the text and lowered the phone to her lap. Her life had been a series of challenges to please her mother, and for the first time, Ava felt like she might lose.

She looked up at the main house. A porch ran along the front where a wind chime blew in the gentle breeze. A few pairs of dusty boots were lined beside the front door, and a set of rocking chairs swayed, waiting for someone to enjoy the peaceful day.

She needed to get out of the car. That was the next step. It was frightening and exciting at the same time. She wasn't sure if Linda's threats were set in stone or meant to pressure her into doing what her mother wanted. Her chest ached when she recalled the hurtful things her mother had said in the last eighteen hours.

Guests and ranch employees were everywhere. No less than a dozen people stood just outside the dining hall next to the main house, children of all ages played and ran, and a white-haired couple walked out of the check-in office. No one would notice if she just sat in her car for the rest of the afternoon.

She could sit out here and be a coward, or she could get out of the car and do what she came here to do. Her grandpa could be inside needing help with something right now.

No, she wouldn't sit here. She had to do this, with or without her mother's approval. Linda was four hundred miles away, and this was Ava's chance to do something on her own terms.

She opened the door and stepped out of the car. Putting her foot down had never felt so good. Straightening her shoulders, she stepped onto the porch and jerked when something zipped by her face. Ava grabbed at her chest and sighed. A hummingbird flitted around a bright-red feeder hanging nearby.

What did it say about her that she'd been startled by a small, harmless bird? Just because there was a storm brewing in Denver didn't mean she couldn't enjoy her time in Wolf Creek. She raised her fist to knock when a sign beside the door caught her attention.

"Unless the Lord builds the house, those who build it labor in vain. Psalm 127:1."

It was an interesting greeting. Not one she'd seen anywhere else. But her grandpa's place was different, too, in a good way.

She rapped her knuckles against the hard wood and turned to look around while she waited. Everyone wore similar clothing. Diamond and triangle patterns in deep reds, turquoise, and browns were everywhere. Ava looked down at her plain, navy-blue sweater. She'd jumped at the chance to wear it, since her mother would have wrinkled her nose at it. She'd also worn jeans for the first time in at least a year. Linda hated jeans and claimed they were common and unflattering. Ava disagreed, but she'd never actually voiced the opinion.

The door opened, and she jerked her head up. Jameson Ford stood in the doorway. The same

Jameson she'd thought about for years was right in front of her, in the flesh.

No, not the same one. This man was an older, more handsome version of the one she remembered. Her lips parted slightly, and she stood paralyzed. His dark hair was tousled, and his skin was the same tan skin she remembered in her dreams. With one hand on the doorknob and the other on the frame, his body took up the entire width of the opening.

The word "Wow" came to mind. He'd done some fantastic growing up in the last six years.

She'd been foolishly telling herself that she'd built Jameson up to be this superhuman.

He was just a man, and she was just a woman— no better than any other.

He'd probably found someone else by now and had three kids and a minivan.

He'd definitely gotten over her, and she could get over him, too.

These were the lies she told herself in her attempts to forget him and put the memory of that summer behind her.

The real truth was that she'd met and dated other men in college, and no one had come close to Jameson. No man had looked at her the way Jameson had since she left Wolf Creek.

Until now. That same blazing intensity was in his eyes now the way it had been that day when she'd been ripped away from him. Years ago, that look had ignited a fire under her skin and branded her heart.

Burns left the ugliest scars.

"Hey." His voice held the same timbre she remembered in her dreams.

Ava closed her drooping jaw. Maybe it hadn't been slow motion as much as a long, uncomfortable silence while she got swept up in memory lane.

"Hi, I'm—"

"Ava," he finished in a deep rise and fall with the syllables.

Something pieced together in her mind, fusing to connect the past and the present.

"Jameson." She smiled as she whispered his name.

"It's good to see you." If his expression was anything to go by, he truly was glad to see her. His thin lips parted to reveal that gorgeous smile she'd always loved.

"It's good to see you too. You look great." That was the watered-down truth.

His gaze stayed locked with hers. "And you're beautiful as always."

Her cheeks grew warm. Those were the sweetest words she'd ever heard.

Jameson jerked his head and stepped to the side. "Come on in. Mr. Chambers is waiting for you."

Ava stepped inside the house and looked around. Everything was exactly the same as it had been six years ago. She remembered sitting with her grandfather in front of the rock fireplace as he whispered stories about her grandmother. Linda had gone to bed, and Ava had snuck back downstairs for some time with her grandpa without the stressful watch of her mother.

The wooden staircase featured photos of Linda when she was a little girl. She'd demanded Grandpa take them down the last time they'd visited, but it seemed they'd been hung back up in their original places since then.

Even the smell was the same—smoky wood and a hint of citrus.

"He's in the kitchen," Jameson said behind her.

She'd actually remembered where it was from her last visit. Now that she was here, everything felt familiar.

When she stepped into the kitchen, she didn't see her grandfather.

"Maybe he went to the living room," Jameson suggested.

She followed him to the large community room that she hadn't spent much time in during her last visit. Her grandpa sat in a recliner with a crocheted throw covering his legs.

"Grandpa." Ava tempered her greeting. He looked the same, but what if the stroke symptoms weren't all visible?

"Ava." He leaned forward slowly and groaned as he pushed off the arms of the recliner.

"Give it a rest, old man," Jameson said.

"What?" Ava turned to Jameson with wide eyes.

Her grandpa chuckled. The raspy laugh eased her discomfort.

"I'm just pullin' your leg." He stood quickly, throwing the blanket onto the nearby couch. "I'm fine and getting better every day."

Relief flooded her body, filling to the top where tears might soon spill over. "Grandpa." She wrapped her arms around him and breathed in the comfort of his arms.

"It's so good to see you, sweetie."

"It's good to see you too," she whispered in his ear. Did she have to let go? She'd spent so much time without him that she wanted to make up for lost time.

He patted her back and gestured for her to sit on the couch. "What do you think of the place?" he asked.

"It's just like I remembered it."

"Maybe you'll get on a horse again."

Ava grinned. She'd been fascinated by the horses before, but there really hadn't been much time for fun. Planning a funeral and getting her grandma's affairs in order had taken up most of her stay. What little free time she had was spent with Jameson, mostly talking after she slipped out of her room at night. They'd talked on the porch for hours, watched the stars from the bed of his truck by Wolf Creek, and she'd finally gotten on a horse for a sunset ride with him.

Too bad there would be less of that kind of fun on this trip.

But maybe she could. She cut her gaze to Jameson, who looked back at her with a knowing smile. He was definitely single because the look he gave her was hot enough to make her blush in front of her grandpa.

"Jameson here is gonna show you around today. Looks like the two of you have some catching up to do."

Ava jerked her attention back to her grandpa. "I thought I'd spend the day with you."

Her grandpa waved a hand. "You know I don't need any help. I really wanted you to come because I missed you."

She smiled. "I missed you too."

"But you and I will have plenty of time to catch up when the sun goes down. Plus, I have some boring paperwork to do. Go enjoy the sun while it's out, and we'll talk this evening."

"I'm sorry I wasn't here to help sooner," Ava said. He'd done all his recovering from the stroke without her, and she was hardly needed anymore. "I want to help however I can while I'm here."

"I'm glad to hear that," her grandpa said. "Speaking of, how long are you staying?"

"Probably a week." She'd made the decision to use the full week she'd requested off work instead of rushing back. She needed the time off, especially since she wasn't ready to face Linda's wrath.

"In that case, you two better get going."

Ava stood and turned to Jameson, but his smile from earlier was gone.

CHAPTER 4
JAMESON

A week? He wasn't sure how long he'd thought Ava would stay, but a week wasn't long enough.

There'd been a time when he hadn't thought twice about taking her into his arms. Now, those few words had crushed his hope of ever touching her again.

Only a week. He couldn't do it.

Jameson waited until Ava stepped out of the living room before he gave Mr. Chambers the "Are you kidding me?" face. The old man just shooed him away as if the one-week expiration date was no big deal. It wasn't a big deal if Jameson didn't have any skin in the game. Unfortunately, he did, and he knew from the past that it wouldn't take him long to get caught up in Ava's charm. That is, if she'd let him. She might be a different person now.

With a resigned huff, he followed Ava through the sitting room to the front door. She stopped next to him on the porch while he slid on his work boots. He pointed to his truck parked near the shiny rental that had to be hers, and she walked quietly beside him until he opened the truck's passenger door for her. He walked around the front of the truck as if Ava Collins dropping back into his world was something that happened every day.

It wasn't.

As soon as he slid behind the wheel and closed the door, Ava broke the uncomfortable silence.

"I was sure you'd have forgotten about me."

Jameson slowly turned to look at her. She looked too perfect sitting in the passenger seat of his dirty truck. It was the exact image he'd dreamed of dozens of times since she left. It was like they'd pressed pause on things six years ago, and she'd just hit play.

Could they pick up right where they left off?

They sure could.

Was it a good idea?

Nope. But that didn't stop him from wanting it.

"How could I forget you when I think about you all the time?" It was the sad truth—one he hadn't shared with anyone.

Seconds passed in silence. He couldn't look at her even though he wanted to. He wanted to memorize the changing colors of her eyes and the way her hair framed her face.

He couldn't win this fight. When he cut his gaze toward Ava, her smile was as wonderful as he remembered. The last time she'd been here, he'd watched all trace of happiness drain from her face every time her mother was around.

But when he had her alone? That smile alone had been enough to bring him to his knees.

Ava laughed, biting her lip to temper her reaction. "What a line!" Her mouth said "joke with me," and her eyes said, "please."

He could do that—for her.

Make Ava happy. Mission accomplished.

That had been his goal the last time she'd visited. That and assure her that her mother's crazy mind control games weren't normal and she was perfect with or without that woman's approval.

Hearing Ava's laugh prompted Jameson's grin. Not much had changed if they could joke and laugh like they'd been together just yesterday. "You can laugh all you want, but it's the truth." He looked over his shoulder as he backed out.

"This feels like old times," Ava said. Her tone was relieved.

"It's not old times. This is now time. Much better than old times."

"You think so?" she asked playfully.

"I know so. Stick with me, and we'll make it

happen." He winked at her and waited for her shy smile. He was a glutton for punishment. Nothing good could come of this in six days.

"I missed you," she whispered.

He stared at her for a second too long. Those words validated the heartache he'd gone through when she'd left so suddenly. That fire had taken a long time to get under control, but it never went out.

"I missed you too."

"I feel like we missed so much."

Regret. She was talking about regret, and that soothed some of the what-ifs he'd been turning over and over. He had a pile of regrets of his own.

"Let's get going. We've got a lot to see and not a lot of time." He shifted into gear and pulled out of the lot.

Ava stared out the window as he drove past the playground. "You don't have to entertain me. I remember all this. It doesn't look like anything has changed around here."

One thing for sure hadn't changed: he still wanted Ava.

He didn't have to show her around, but he wanted to. If he intended to use Mr. Chambers' request as an excuse to stay close to Ava, so be it.

"We added a new dance hall and a fire pit. We have about a dozen more horses, and we have an archery range too."

"I stand corrected. You're changing with the times. Looks like you have a little bit of everything."

Time. That was one thing they didn't have. He gripped the steering wheel and focused on the road ahead. "Is it really just a week?"

She didn't answer right away, and he forced himself not to look at her.

"I'm sorry," she whispered.

"Nothing to be sorry about." He was a big boy and could keep his attraction to a pretty woman in check, right?

Probably not, but he'd do what he could. "You want to see the stables first?"

"Please. I could use a little horse therapy."

He parked in front of the stables, and Ava was already climbing out before he could get around the truck to open her door for her.

"Do you ride in Denver?" he asked.

Her brow quirked up when she met him in front of the truck. "You remembered I live in Denver?"

"I remember everything about you."

Ava laughed again, and the goofy grin he hadn't been able to shake since he laid eyes on her widened again. There had been a sadness hanging over their time together last time, but this time, happiness followed her everywhere.

Maybe that was his own happiness. Seeing her again was a dream that had felt so far from reality these last few years.

"I forgot what a sweet talker you are."

He stopped just outside the stables. "Listen, I don't think Jess was here last time, but she's the stable manager. This is your warning: She's a little bit forward."

Ava frowned. "Like how?"

"Not in a bad way, but let's just say she's a boss. Most of the time, that's a good thing. She's friendly, but if she's trying to make you do something you don't want to do, tell her to back off."

"Oh-kay," she drawled. "Thanks for the warning."

"She's harmless, and she'll be your friend. She probably won't take no for an answer on that one."

Ava shrugged. "I can't hate that."

"You'll like her. Just set your boundaries, and you'll be fine." As soon as he said the words, he realized setting boundaries wasn't Ava's strong suit.

He jerked his head toward the entrance, and Ava stuck close to him. Hopefully, he'd said the right thing about Jess. Most everyone got along well with the spunky stable manager, but no one wanted to get on her bad side.

He pointed to the big chalkboard on the wall near the offices. "Here's the schedule for the day. Jess is in charge of horse care and training. Her brother, Brett, is in charge of rodeo activities."

"Rodeo? What kind of rodeo activities?"

"Mostly games for the kids. They practice and

learn during the week, and we have a rodeo on Friday night where they can show off their new skills for their parents. Brett and Colton do a little bronc riding and cattle roping for the grand finale. It's always good for a few laughs."

Jameson scanned the stables and indoor arena. "I don't see Jess. She might be in the feed room." He walked around the arena, slowing his steps so Ava could look around.

He had no idea what her life in Denver was like. If she was still in contact with her mother, Ava might be some high-profile local celebrity or something by now. He'd gotten the impression that's where Linda had been steering her daughter, but the limelight didn't fit Ava's personality at all. Hadn't her mother noticed?

Jameson introduced Ava to a few stable hands mucking out the stalls. There were hundreds of moving parts to the ranch, and he knew every one of them. It was still strange to think it was his job to supervise the entire ranch. He remembered all too well the months he'd spent mucking stalls, stocking up for pack rides, and scraping the arenas.

When they'd reached the far end of the stables, he indicated the door to the right of the large opening leading to the outdoor arena. "This is the feed room."

Jess was right where he'd expected—bent over a

large, metal barrel with the top half of her body disappearing into the hole.

"Jess, you got a minute?" Jameson asked.

She popped her head up. Stray hairs that had slipped from her blonde ponytail stood in all directions on her head. "Hey. Sup?"

"I wanted you to meet Ava. She's Mr. Chambers' granddaughter."

Jess's eyes widened, and her mouth formed a perfect O. "You're the Ava I've heard about!"

Ava looked up at Jameson with wide eyes that mirrored Jess's. "You've heard about me?"

Jess dusted her hands off on her jeans. "Oh yeah. Mr. Chambers and I are like this." She crossed her fingers. "He's always bummed that he doesn't get to see you much."

Ava's shoulders drooped. "I guess that's on me."

"Well, you're here now!" Jess slammed the metal lid down on the barrel. "You're here now. That counts. How long you staying?"

"A week." Ava nervously shifted.

"Aw, man. Mr. Chambers is gonna be bummed about that. He misses you."

Maybe introducing her to Jess first wasn't the best idea. Coming on strong was Jess's middle name. She was one of the nicest people anyone could meet, but he'd forgotten that she was an acquired taste.

Jameson leaned closer to Ava and brushed his

pinky against hers. It was a small gesture and a reminder that he wasn't steering her wrong.

"We need to run. This was our first stop, and she still has a lot to see."

"Have fun. See you at supper." Jess smiled and waved before ducking back into the barrel.

"It was nice meeting you," Ava called toward Jess's backside.

"You too!" Jess shouted into the barrel.

Jameson sighed when they stepped out of the room. "I promise she wasn't trying to make you feel bad about not visiting. Jess isn't... Sorry, I really don't know how to explain it."

"It's fine. She was just honest. I should have come around more. I don't really have an excuse."

"You don't have to defend yourself. Jess might not know why you haven't been here, but I think I do."

She turned to him with a look of gratitude. "You do. Some things haven't changed."

"I was hoping you wouldn't say that."

A scream pierced the quietness around them, tearing them from the heaviness of their conversation.

Jess came running out of the feed room, a rare look of concern on her face. "Was that Brett?"

CHAPTER 5
AVA

Ava's heart beat hard and quick. There had been pain in that scream, and Jess's expression said they all had reason to worry.

Jameson ran to the opening leading to the outdoor arena. "It's Brett."

"He's training Thunder," Jess said.

Thunder had to be a horse, and Ava didn't want to know how many different ways a horse could harm a man, so she kept her feet planted while Jameson jogged the few feet back to where she'd been standing, unable to see the outdoor arena where Brett was training.

Jameson looked at her, and the determination in his expression said the words before his mouth did. "I have to go."

"Go!" she shouted, shooing him toward the exit.

"Ava can stay with me," Jess said. "Tell him I said he's an idiot."

Jameson gave Ava one last look before running off to check on Brett. He didn't look worried as much as focused. How common were injuries around here?

Jess ruffled her ponytail when Jameson was out of sight. Pieces of hay and what must have been feed pellets rained from her thick hair. "Well, I guess you're my assistant now."

Ava grinned as her heart rate eased. "Jameson said you'd be bossy."

"He said that?" Jess said, posting her hands on her slender hips.

Seriously, Jess had a lot of confidence for a woman who looked like she could pass for a pre-teen.

"I'm sure he didn't mean it in a bad way," Ava said.

"No, he's right. I'm the boss," Jess said as she brushed her ponytail over her shoulder. She looked at her watch. "Have you met the ladies in the office yet?"

Ava shook her head. "I just got here. The stables were our first stop."

Jess stuck out her elbow. "Let's go. I need to see how many signups we've had for rides tomorrow."

Ava linked her arm with Jess's, remembering Jameson's warning. So far, Ava didn't mind going along with Jess's plans, and it would be nice to meet more of the women who worked at the ranch.

Outside the stables, Jess unhooked her arm from Ava's and pointed to a dirt-covered truck. "That's me."

Ava slid into the passenger seat. The interior looked cleaner than Jameson's, but it smelled worse.

Jess started the loud engine. "Sorry 'bout the smell. Horses."

"Have they been in your truck?" Ava asked through the hand she used to cover her nose and mouth.

"No, but my boots have. Don't worry. It's a short ride."

Jess didn't waste a moment, even if the ride was short. "So, you know Jameson?"

Ava twisted her fingers in her lap. Every place, every meeting, and everything that had happened since she arrived was completely out of her comfort zone. Casually chatting about Jameson Ford was so far out of that zone that she didn't know which way was up.

"Just a little. I met him last time I visited."

Jess kept her attention focused on the dusty road ahead. "Jameson's a good one."

Tension filled the cab of the truck like water pouring into a barrel. Ava's lungs constricted as if they were full of water too.

"Um, are y'all a thing?" Ava asked.

"Heavens no," Jess spat. Her nose crinkled. "He's cool, but there are no kissy vibes there."

"Kissy vibes?" Ava asked with a grin. She could relax a little bit if there were no kissy vibes.

She might still be trying to figure Jess out, but Ava was getting the feeling that Jess was the upfront and honest type.

"You know. There's no spark. But he's cool. We hang out and stuff."

Ava had known Jess all of fifteen minutes, but she knew already they were going to get along. She needed more honest friends in her life.

"I just heard you say you're staying a week, but Boss was giving you a look back there. He might be in over his head."

Ava's eyes widened. "What kind of look?"

"I don't know what it's called. He just looked like he liked you, which seems weird since you just got here."

Hope bloomed in Ava's chest that had no right to be there. "Yeah, we hung out a lot the last time I was here."

"Interesting," Jess said, as if that's all it was —interesting.

Jess parked in front of the building beside the main house. Ava remembered it was the dining hall. It was just a few steps to her grandpa's front door.

"You seen Mr. Chambers yet?" Jess asked as they met in front of the truck.

"Yeah. He said he had some work to do and we could catch up later."

"He's a morning and evening kinda guy. I think he takes a nap in the middle of the day."

The long building looked like it had two entrances. The one on the right side had double doors and the one on the left was a single. A porch with a wooden railing ran the length of the front of the building. Jess walked straight to the door on the left side labeled "office" and walked in, holding the door open for Ava to enter behind her.

The room had a rustic look with small figurines made of horseshoes on various surfaces. The burnt-red curtains were pulled back beside picture windows that looked out toward the porch.

A young woman with a bright smile waited at the check-in desk. Her blonde hair hung in loose waves over one shoulder, and her light-blue eyes seemed to fit the excitement in her tone.

"Howdy! Welcome to Wolf Creek Ranch."

Jess rested an elbow on the counter. "Ava, meet Everly. She's the welcoming committee. Everly, this is Ava."

"Collins," Ava added.

Jess leaned over the counter a little. "She's Mr. Chambers' granddaughter."

Everly's eyes widened, and her mouth formed a wide O. "You're kidding! Stella!" she yelled toward the adjacent room.

Everly turned back to Ava and spoke softer. "It's so great to meet you. I've always wondered about his granddaughter."

"You have?" Ava asked. Every time she heard that her grandpa had talked about her, it tightened that knot of shame in her gut.

The woman Everly had summoned clomped into the check-in office. She looked to be in her fifties or sixties, with wide hips and a posture that came with ingrained confidence. Her round cheeks were rosy, and she brushed a hand over her short hair as if taming it after her jog into the office. "Where's the fire?"

Jess grinned as she jerked her head toward Ava. "This here's Mr. Chambers' granddaughter, Ava. And this is Stella Guthrie. She runs the gift shop."

Stella opened her arms. "Well, I'll be. I've heard talk about you."

Ava felt her cheeks heat. "Oh?"

"Yeah, he thinks the world of you. Been waiting to see when you'd show up."

Jameson had warned her Jess might be forward, but no one had prepared her for the friendly candor of the others. Ava held out her hands and forced a grin, hoping to smooth things over. "I'm here now."

"And it's a good thing!" Stella sang as she wrapped her arms around Ava.

Oh, what a greeting. Ava couldn't think of any

instance when she'd hugged someone she'd just met before, but Stella acted as if it was normal.

Just go with it.

Stella had just released Ava from the welcoming hug when Jameson walked in. His gaze met hers immediately, and her stomach flipped like she'd just shot down the first big hill of a roller coaster.

"Morning, ladies. I see you met Ava."

"It's almost suppertime," Jess quipped as she picked up a clipboard from the desk. "Brett okay?"

"He's fine. Rolled his ankle when Thunder knocked him off-balance. I got him a boot."

Jess shook her head. "He's asking for trouble with that one."

"I'm with you, but he's determined. Though I'm not sure how much he'll be worth the next couple of days. He rolled that ankle pretty good."

"He'll be fine," Jess assured without looking up.

Jameson turned to Ava. "These ladies being good to you?"

Ava opened her mouth to answer, but Stella piped up first.

"Of course we are!"

Jess laid the clipboard back on the desk. "My work here is done. See you later, Ava."

Ava waved. "Bye, thanks for the introductions."

Everly rested her elbows on the desk and propped her fists under her chin. "So, how long are you staying?"

"A week?" Ava said. Why had she made it sound more like a question? She cleared her throat and tried again. "I'm staying for a week."

That sounded better. Stronger.

"She's staying at the main house," Jameson said, jerking a thumb over his shoulder.

"Let me show you to the guest room over there," Stella said in her sweet, high voice. "I don't think Mr. Chambers can walk up the stairs anymore."

Everly walked around the desk. "I can show her."

Stella waved Everly away. "Get out of here. These old legs need exercise."

Ava chuckled. Stella couldn't be over sixty-five. Could she? She had a few wrinkles around her eyes and laugh lines beside her mouth, but they didn't make her look old, just friendly. Her hair was a dull sandy-blonde, but it wasn't gray or white.

"Everly, watch my shop," Stella said, pointing to the area.

"Yes, Ma'am," Everly called, resigned to her post.

When they stepped outside, Stella snapped her fingers. "Jameson, get her bags."

A quick, "Yes, Ma'am," came from behind them.

Ava chuckled. It was nice to be around someone and know there weren't any high expectations to live up to. Stella was so casual, Ava instinctively relaxed and leaned in to whisper, "Can you show me how to do that trick?"

"Oh, honey, it takes years of practice. Thankfully,

I was extremely qualified when your grandpa hired me. Forty-five years of marriage gave me a lot of experience."

"Your husband is a lucky one," Ava said. She couldn't resist peeking over her shoulder at Jameson as he pulled the luggage from her trunk. Whoever ended up with Jameson Ford would be a lucky one too. She would be lying to herself if she didn't admit she wished it would be her.

Stella looped her arm through Ava's and patted her hand. "My beloved is gone, but he lives on in my heart."

Ava gasped. "I'm so sorry. I didn't know." She'd known the woman for five minutes and was already sticking her foot in her mouth.

"Now you know. And it's okay. He likes it when I talk about him."

Ava wasn't sure how Stella knew that, but she might know the man more than he knew himself after being married to him for almost half a century.

Stella pointed at Jameson as he hefted Ava's luggage up onto the porch. "Now, that man's a keeper. One hundred percent eye candy."

Ava's cheeks heated. Jameson stood less than ten feet away. He'd definitely heard Stella's comment, but his expression stayed neutral.

"Lead the way, ladies."

Stella kept a hold on Ava's arm as they entered the main house. "I've always admired this house.

Chuck and I lived in a townhome in Indianapolis, but I always wanted something like this."

Ava let her fingertips drag along the worn wooden banister as they ascended the stairs. She slowed her steps when she saw the photos hanging on the wall. Frame after frame showed her mother smiling in school pictures, riding a horse, and in a family photo with her grandpa and grandma.

Her mother looked so happy then. What happened?

At the top of the stairs, Stella pointed left. "These rooms have the best view. Which one?"

Ava peeked her head inside the first room. The bed was topped by an ivory down comforter, and the window was open to the valley behind the main house. The next room had the same view, but the colors were bold blues and greens that paired well with the mahogany in the wood, giving it an earthy tone.

"I like this one." She did like it, but the soft whites of the other room were her safe space. Here, she wanted to step out of that comfort zone, if only for a few nights.

"Good choice. This one is my favorite. You know, I decorated these rooms."

"Really? You have great taste."

Stella wrapped her arm around Ava's shoulders, pulling her close. "I knew I liked you."

Jameson leaned against the wall with his arms

crossed over his chest. His grin was knowing, yet playful. "You sure that's the one?" he asked.

"Yes. That one." Ava pointed to the colorful room.

Jameson picked up the bag and carried it into the room. No one would guess that the bag had barely passed the airline weight restrictions. Jameson carried the fifty pound bag like it weighed nothing at all.

He set the luggage beside the bed. "It's almost time for supper, but you have a few minutes before the bell rings."

"I'll unpack these later," Ava said.

Jameson's grin quirked to one side. Did he know she wasn't ready to end their time together yet?

Stella threaded her arm with Ava's again. "Then let's get back down. We're wasting daylight."

Ava looked over her shoulder at Jameson. She was pretty sure any time spent with Jameson wasn't wasted.

CHAPTER 6

AVA

Grandpa was toeing off his boots at the door when Ava, Stella, and Jameson came downstairs. Her grandpa seemed to be getting around well for a man who'd recently suffered a stroke. Actually, Ava wasn't sure how recovered he should be by now. She'd had little time to google since she heard the news and rushed to the ranch.

But she could see subtle changes in him since her last visit. He moved slower, almost as if he was pushing against an invisible force. He seemed to be going and doing the things he wanted. Had Stella been serious when she said he couldn't climb the stairs anymore?

A smile spread across his face when he saw the three of them. "You getting settled in okay?"

Ava barely had time to open her mouth before Stella spoke.

"Of course she is. She chose the Frontier Bedroom."

Her grandpa hung his hat on the rack. "Ah, I forgot you'd given them names."

"A house like this has character. It deserves to be named," Stella touted.

"As you wish. I have some chores to catch up on, but I'll see you three at supper." He pointed to Jameson. "Thanks for showing my Ava around."

My Ava. What did it say about her that her grandpa's claiming warmed her from the inside out?

"It was my pleasure. We didn't get very far this afternoon. I might have to steal her away again to finish the tour."

Her grandpa chuckled. "Boy, it'd take months to show her every corner of this place."

"That's my plan," Jameson said. He turned and winked at her.

Ava's smile grew wider. How did that simple movement cause her knees to weaken? She'd smiled more today than in the last three months combined.

"Save me a dance," Stella called as Ava's grandpa walked off. Pretending to lean in and share a secret, Stella said, "He likes me."

Jameson laughed, short and loud. "Everyone likes you. You don't give them much choice."

Stella patted his shoulder. "It's good you know that, son."

It seemed Stella had adopted Ava as well, and

Jameson was right. It was hard not to like the spunky woman. She was a lot like Jess when it came to speaking her mind, but she didn't seem pushy or brash.

Ava continued walking beside Jameson and Stella, but she couldn't help glancing back toward the main house.

"You okay?" Jameson asked.

"Yeah. He just seems different than the last time I saw him."

Jameson brushed the side of his hand against hers as they walked. "Don't worry. He's a strong man. He'll likely outlive us all."

Ava looked up at him. "I missed your optimism."

He leaned in to whisper, "I missed you."

Oh boy. Was her stomach going to flip every time he whispered sweet words in her ear? She definitely wasn't complaining.

Stella playfully bumped Ava's shoulder on her other side. "Cheer up. I've known that man most of my life, and he hasn't changed in the last ten years."

"You've known him that long? I don't remember seeing you here the last time I visited."

"Chuck and I came here every year, usually in the fall. We were regulars. When Chuck died, I came back hoping to rekindle a little bit of that magic we always found here. It wasn't the same, but it reminded me so much of some of our best times.

That time I came here after Chuck died, Ronald offered me a job, and I stayed."

Ava noticed that most of the other workers called her grandpa Mr. Chambers, but Stella seemed to be on a first name basis with him. Those formal lines didn't seem to be her style.

"Like, you just didn't go back home?" Ava asked.

Stella lifted a shoulder. "Pretty much. He needed someone to run the gift shop, and I needed something to keep me busy instead of pining over my husband. I went home to pack up, and I moved here."

If Stella could move here on a dime, why couldn't Ava? Stella's job had been waiting for her, but Ava could surely find something around here. She was much younger than Stella. It wasn't too late to start over.

Ava had missed out on the chance to build her own life away from her mother when she dropped out of college. Was this a second chance?

A surge of boldness swelled in her chest. She could do it, couldn't she? Learn to fly or figure it out on the way down.

"I'm glad you found happiness here," Ava said.

Jameson opened the door to the office, letting Ava and Stella enter first. "Yeah, now we can't get rid of her."

Stella swatted Jameson's shoulder as she passed, and he feigned hurt. "You love me."

"That I do," Jameson said.

In the office, Everly stood at the desk where they'd left her, but a dark-haired cowboy leaned against the counter talking to her. They both looked up when Ava, Jameson, and Stella entered.

"Hey, boss," the cowboy said, extending a hand to Jameson.

"You can't find anything to do on your day off?" Jameson slapped the guy's hand instead of shaking it.

The greeting was casual in a way Ava assumed the workers around here might use when they saw each other every day. At the studio, her colleagues often walked past her without even a nod or hello.

"I could say the same for you." The guy looked at Ava with a friendly smile. "I'm Blake."

Ava shook his hand. "I'm Ava."

"Ava is Mr. Chambers' granddaughter," Jameson said.

"Oh, that's awesome. He's a good guy," Blake said.

Jameson pointed a thumb at Blake. "This here's our trail manager. He makes sure the hiking trails, pack trails, and campsites are clear and safe for guests."

"That sounds interesting and important," Ava said.

Everly laughed. "Don't make too big of a fuss

over him. He won't be able to get his big head out the door."

"I am important!" Blake said, exaggerating disappointment that Everly didn't seem impressed by his skills.

Stella patted his arm and crooned, "Yes you are, son. I don't care what everyone else says about you. I think you're *important*."

Blake's eyes widened. "What is everybody saying about me?"

"We took a vote last week. You're most likely to overachieve," Jameson said.

Blake laughed. "Yeah, sounds about right."

The office door opened quickly, and an older man who looked like a cross between John Wayne and Clint Eastwood barged in.

Maybe those were Ava's only references for cowboys. She should really broaden her horizons.

The man stood in the doorway and jerked his thumb over a shoulder. "Need your help at the outdoor arena."

Jameson stood at attention. "Again? Everybody all right?"

"Brett just needs a hand with the new stallion."

Jameson turned to Ava, and she read the indecision in his expression.

"Go on. I'm fine."

"You sure?" he asked in a whisper.

"Of course, she's sure!" Stella barked. "The woman said go on. Do you have ears?"

Ava covered her smile with a hand in front of her mouth. She hoped to one day be as bold as Stella.

"Okay. I'll be back soon." Jameson glanced back at Ava as he left the office.

Once he was out of sight, Stella sighed. "I hate to see him go, but I love to watch him leave."

"Stella!" Everly cried. Her outrage at Stella's comment was overshadowed by her playful smile.

Blake laughed as he backed toward the door. "Well, it's been fun. See you later." He tipped his hat and closed the door as soon as he was out.

"That one knows how to rain on my parade," Stella said, pouting.

Everly resumed her place behind the desk. "Don't worry. His brain is bigger than his behind."

Stella narrowed her eyes at Everly. "You'd know."

"Is he your boyfriend?" Ava asked.

Everly straightened her shoulders. "I don't know anything about his behind, and he's not my boyfriend."

Stella rolled her eyes. "This one has a fiancé, and it ain't Blake."

Everly turned her attention to the computer, and her tone was flat and stern. "I've known Blake for over a decade. He was my... never mind. I've known him a long time, and we're friends."

A bell chimed, and Stella tugged on Ava's arm. "Suppertime. Let's get going. I don't like to be last in line."

"You coming?" Ava asked Everly.

"I'll keep an eye on the gift shop now and grab a plate when Stella gets back."

Stella waved a hand over her head as she headed out of the office. "I'll hurry back!" She pulled Ava toward the connected dining hall. "We take turns going to meals first, but Everly usually likes to wait until the crowd thins out."

"She doesn't *seem* shy."

"It's not that. It's more that she lived most of her life in crowds, and she'd rather be alone or with a few close friends."

"That's understandable," Ava said as they walked along the porch.

A crowd had gathered outside the dining hall, and the quiet from only minutes ago had been replaced by laughter and chatting. Ava wove through the crowd behind Stella on their way to the entrance.

Inside the dining hall, the voices were louder and happier. The tall ceilings with exposed beams and rustic chandeliers gave the place a casual atmosphere. Guests of all ages dotted the room, sitting down to eat and talking as if they all knew each other.

"Don't be shy now," Stella said. "We'll end up at

the end of the line if we don't get to goin'."

Ava laughed. "Did you skip lunch?"

"No, but I've lived long enough that I earned my place at the front of the line. These young people can move it or lose it."

Ava dodged a kid as he ran past. "I'm young."

"Yeah, but you're with me today. You can tell me all about yourself over supper."

Ava's face felt cold as her blood ran to her toes. Stella seemed nice, but Ava wasn't ready to be grilled about her absence. Not that she had an excuse now or later.

A high-pitched whistle pierced the buzzing air, and Ava turned to see where the noise had come from. She looked over her shoulder, but nothing unusual caught her eye.

It was probably a parent trying to get a kid's attention.

Satisfied that the whistle wasn't intended for her, Ava turned around and walked straight into the chest of a man. She stumbled backward and tripped over the person standing behind her. Her grip on Stella's hand slipped, and Ava's backside and hand hit the floor, jarring every bone in her body and sending pain radiating up her spine and wrist.

Before she could catch her breath, the man's heavy boot crushed her fingers. "Ow!"

The man knelt beside her, creating a barrier between her and the crowd. The pain overrode her embarrassment for a moment until she was able to inhale the first deep breath.

"Are you all right?" he asked as he offered her a hand.

It was dirty, but she took it, grateful for the help.

"I'm okay." She cradled her throbbing hand, testing small movements.

Everyone around had stopped to either help or see what the fuss was about, but Ava still hadn't gotten her bearings. She was still shifting her weight from one side to the other and trying not to rub her backside.

"Good grief, child. Is this your first time walking?" Stella joked.

"Seems like it. I wasn't looking where I was going, and I..." Ava looked up at the man she'd bumped into. He could have been her age or a little older. He was about a foot taller than she was, and he was built broad and thick like a linebacker.

The pounding in Ava's fingers and backside had her stomach rolling, but she faced the man she'd walked into and swallowed the lump in her throat. His expression told her little about what he might be thinking.

"I'm so sorry I bumped into you. I wasn't watching where I was walking."

The man looked her up and down before responding. "No problem. Sorry I stepped on your fingers."

Ava forced a grin. She wasn't sure if her apology was well received or not. "It's okay."

The man's gaze lingered on her a few seconds before he turned back to the other men standing around him. He reentered the conversation as if her apology was less than a wrinkle in his smooth-sailing day.

Well, that talk was over before it began. She didn't even get his name or have a chance to introduce herself.

Stella wrapped a hand around Ava's arm. "You sure you're okay?"

"Yeah, I just wasn't paying attention."

Stella humphed. "Dane could have been a little nicer."

"Dane?"

"Him." Stella pointed over her shoulder at the man Ava had walked into.

When Ava looked his way again, his attention was focused on her. She still wasn't sure what to make of his expression. He hadn't been outright rude, but he hadn't been overly apologetic either. Granted, Ava had run into him first.

"It's fine. There was a lot going on, and I was in the way."

"He's not the kind you can expect anything extra from anyway. Dane is here for a paycheck."

Ava cut a glance at Dane again. "He works here?"

"Yeah, he's the new ranch hand, and he hasn't

impressed me much."

Stella obviously had a strong opinion of the man. Maybe Ava wouldn't see him anymore this week. Neither of them had made a great first impression.

Stella introduced Ava to almost everyone as they made their way through the food line, but the names and faces were starting to run together. She'd been here for a few hours, and between the flight, the stress of seeing her grandpa, the nervousness of seeing Jameson again, and meeting dozens of new people, Ava didn't want the food as much as she wanted a warm bed.

The noise in the dining hall grew louder, and Ava felt the first pangs of a headache in her temples. She let Stella do all the talking, and ate small bites of the baked chicken on her plate.

Stella leaned close to Ava but didn't whisper. "Hey, you okay?"

Ava squinted, trying to dim the light "I'm fine. Just getting a headache."

Stella stood and grabbed both plates. "Let's get you to your room. You must be exhausted."

Ava sighed. Shutting herself in a quiet room and sleeping until the sun came up was at the top of her to-do list.

She followed Stella to the office where she peeked a head in. "I'm takin' Ava to the main house. I'll be right back."

Ava shuffled her feet through the gravel lot connecting the main house to the dining hall. Stella didn't fill the silence with chatting this time, as if she knew Ava needed the break.

"I'm sorry to bow out early. I really enjoyed meeting you. And thanks for introducing me to so many people."

Stella wrapped an arm around Ava's shoulders. "It's been a pleasure. I'll let you rest and see you tomorrow."

They both waved friendly good-byes as Ava stepped into the main house. With the door closed against the bustle outside, she rested her back against the wood and took a deep breath. She'd made it. She'd successfully left her mother, her job, and her home. She'd arrived safely at Wolf Creek Ranch to a warm welcome. She'd done a lot of things she never expected to do. All out of her comfort zone and all risky, at least when her mother's wrath was involved.

"Ava?" The shout came from the kitchen.

"It's me." She followed the voice and found her grandpa in the kitchen pulling a heaping plate of something she couldn't identify from the microwave.

"I didn't expect you back so soon," he said as he stirred the brown-and-white mixture. "Want some beef tips and rice?"

"It smells good, but I actually just came from the

dining hall. You don't eat over there?"

"Sometimes. I worked long hours today, and I needed some quiet time."

Ava smiled as she rested on the barstool and propped her arms on the counter. "Me too. I felt a headache coming on, so Stella brought me back."

"I know why you have a headache. You spent half an hour with that loud woman." He rummaged in a high cabinet and handed Ava a medicine bottle.

Ava chuckled as she took it. "She's friendly."

"She's bossy and opinionated," he said as he filled a short glass with tap water.

"That too," Ava agreed. Despite Stella's outgoing nature that was so different from Ava's reserve, she'd enjoyed hanging out with the woman.

"But she's a good worker, and a good friend. If I didn't think so highly of her, I'd have stood up to her a long time ago. Plus, she brings me food." He pointed his fork at the steaming plate.

"She made that?"

"She keeps my refrigerator stocked with something I can easily heat and eat if I don't feel like mingling at mealtimes."

"That's sweet of her."

"Don't call her sweet. She'll take offense."

Ava laughed and swallowed the pills.

Her grandpa grabbed a napkin and a tall glass of water. "Come on. I like to eat on the back porch."

CHAPTER 7
JAMESON

Jameson picked a clump of mud out of Thunder's shoe. Brett had his hands full when it came to this one. Thunder was the newest addition to Wolf Creek's stable, but Jameson was starting to think this stallion might not ever be fit for a guest to ride.

Brett handed Jameson a tube of ointment for the horse's hoof. "Thanks for the hand."

"No problem. Ready to say you were wrong about this one?"

Brett leaned back against the wall and hefted his booted foot onto a bucket. "Never. I can't lose the bet."

Jameson looked up from the horse's hoof. "What bet?" There was a warning in his measured tone.

"Colt said I can't do it. I'll have to grow a mustache if I can't train Thunder."

Jameson looked back at Thunder's hoof to hide his grin. "But you'd look so good with a stache. Are you thinking about the Alan Jackson or handlebar?"

"Shut up." Brett shifted his booted leg and winced. "But if he messed up my ankle, I'll sell him myself."

"Glad it's you and not me." Jameson hadn't said much about Brett's ankle yet, but he'd been rearranging schedules in his head trying to figure out how they could manage without him if he couldn't keep up for a few weeks.

Henry stepped out of the tack room holding a frayed halter. The old man was always the first to get into everything going on at the ranch. He'd made a good foreman because he wasn't afraid to get his hands dirty. "Anyone else having nightmares tonight?"

They'd all been pushing Henry to leave since he retired, but now they could actually use a hand around here when he was set to leave soon.

Jameson shoved a shoulder against Thunder's flank when the horse tried to crowd him. "I know I will." In truth, the stallion's dark eyes had a sinister look that chilled Jameson's blood. He'd never feared a horse before, but Thunder was a beast.

Paul walked into the barn carrying a saddle. The older cowboy's wolfdog, Thane, kept pace beside him. "You still hung up on Thunder?"

"I can't give up on him," Brett said.

Thunder jerked his leg from Jameson's grip and thrashed. The horse's back hooves were pounding the ground one second, the next, they were flying through the air dangerously close to Jameson's head.

He hadn't made it this far without learning how to duck, but this time he'd felt the wind off the flying missile. He hit the ground with a thud that rattled his teeth.

Brett hobbled to Thunder's right side, and Henry took the left, tugging the horse into submission.

"Dude, that was close."

Jameson looked up at Dane. If he'd walked up while Thunder was thrashing around, why hadn't he jumped in to help? Instead he was standing around like he didn't know hands were for working.

With a huff, Jameson was back on his feet and helping the others settle Thunder.

He could be enjoying the sunset with Ava right now. Probably best not to think about what he'd rather be doing. Most everything was better than getting pounded on by a horse that weighed as much as his truck.

After another fifteen minutes spent wrestling Thunder until he was minimally groomed, Brett led the stallion outside. The collective relief was palpable in the stables.

Henry lifted his hat and wiped his arm across his brow. "I'm too old for this."

"Me too," Dane said. "Glad I missed the worst part."

Henry slapped the back of Dane's head. "You're too stupid to know what to do anyway."

"Someone's grumpy. You miss supper?" Dane asked.

"Headin' over there now. Jameson, you heard anything about Ava Collins coming in today?"

Jameson's attention perked up at the mention of Ava. "Yeah. She got in early this afternoon. I left her with Everly and Stella when I ran over here."

"Shoot. I bet that was the girl I ran into in the dining hall," Dane said. "Who is she?"

As much as Jameson would love to talk about Ava, he didn't want to hear what Dane thought about her. In fact, his blood heated just thinking about Ava meeting Dane and what he might have said to her. The guy didn't have the best social skills, and he had no filter, which often got him into trouble with the guests, and the other ranch hands, and, well everyone.

"She's Ron's granddaughter, and you better keep your distance." Henry leveled Dane with a look that dared him to even think about bothering Ava.

Henry just moved to the top of Jameson's best friend list.

Dane scowled. "Granddaughter. What's she doing here? She ain't staying, right?"

"What's it to you?" Henry asked.

"Nothing I guess." Dane looked back and forth between the other men. "Am I the only one curious about a family visit? I mean, he's not trying to hand things over to her, is he?"

Henry huffed through his nose. He'd been transitioning to retirement when Mr. Chambers had hired Dane, and it was clear the old foreman wouldn't have given the young dufus a chance. "Once again, none of your business."

"It kinda is my business if she's taking over. That old man can't live forever, and why did I not know he had any family left? I ain't working for a woman."

"You've got three seconds to get out of my sight," Henry warned.

Dane huffed and rolled his eyes as he turned to leave, swiping his hand through the Bible verse Jess had written on the information chalkboard.

Jameson shook his head. It was like the guy didn't know Henry and Ron told each other everything.

Paul stepped out of the tack room with Thane. "Thunder gone?"

"You just missed him," Henry said.

"I wanted to keep Thane away until the horse calmed down." Thane was well trained, but a riled up horse was enough to challenge any other dominant animal's control. "You need a hand?"

Henry wiped his hands on his jeans. "No, but I think we're due at the back porch. I missed supper.

Ron's granddaughter is here. Maybe we'll catch her this evening. You in?"

Paul stretched his neck to one side and then the other. "I think I'll pass, but thanks for the offer."

Henry shrugged. "Suit yourself. You need to meet Ava. She's a good one. You weren't here the last time she came around, were you?"

Paul looked toward the outdoor arena, and Thane brushed against his leg. "No. I haven't met her yet."

"Just be glad you missed her mother this time." Henry whistled. "That woman is a handful. Ava, now, she's a good one. Sweet just like Lottie was."

Paul turned and started toward the exit. "I need to get going if I'm going to get the packs unloaded before the sun goes down."

Henry raised a hand in a casual wave. "Jameson, you in?"

"Right behind you. My truck is out front." He tossed the ointment and curry comb into the bin.

They passed Brett on the way to the main house, and Henry yelled out the window, "You want to see what we can round up for supper?"

"I'll pass. I'm kinda hoping Jess made me a plate."

Jess might have been Brett's younger sister, but she looked out for her brother as much as he did for her. Actually, they made a pretty good team when they weren't bickering.

"I'm sure she did," Henry said. "See you tomorrow."

The lot in front of the dining hall was packed as usual in the evenings. Guests usually migrated from the dining hall to the fire pit or the dance hall out back. Jameson parked in the alley between the main house and the check-in office.

The sunset was a vibrant orange when they stepped around the house to the back porch. Jameson perked up when he spotted Ava sitting next to her grandpa. He hadn't noted any physical similarities between the two yet. Maybe Mr. Chambers had once had dark hair like Ava's before it turned white. It certainly didn't match her mother's, but Linda probably dyed her hair that light-blonde color.

When Ava saw him, her tired eyes lit up like she'd just caught sight of a room full of presents on Christmas morning. Not that Jameson had ever experienced that happiness, but that's the kind of joy he thought of when she was smiling, especially at him.

"Well, look what the cat dragged in," Mr. Chambers said as he stood. "I thought you'd forgotten me."

Henry laughed. "Only 'cause I knew Ava was coming." He removed his hat and stuck out his hand to Ava as she stood. "It's good to see you again."

Ava beamed. That's the only way Jameson knew

to describe it. Her eyes were bright with genuine eagerness to see Henry again. "It's good to see you too. Grandpa was just telling me about how you've been taking care of him."

"You hush. I didn't say anything like that," her grandpa huffed.

Henry left well enough alone, but pride lifted his chin. After managing a ranch and keeping things running smoothly for thirty years, the man needed to know he was still doing something important with his newfound free time.

"I hear you already met Jameson," Henry said as he jerked his head toward Jameson.

Ava was already looking his way, and he'd never wanted to soak up every ounce of attention from a single person so completely in his whole life as he did right now.

Ava's cheeks darkened, and her gaze held his. "I did. He showed me around a little bit too."

Henry eyed an empty plate sitting beside Mr. Chambers' rocking chair. "Well, I'm here for food. You got any scraps in there?"

"Come on in. Jameson, you coming?"

"I'm fine, but thanks." He hadn't come for the food. He had his eyes on something much better.

"I thought you said you missed supper," Henry said.

"I'll survive." Jameson had never been good at any of the facial expressions that gave someone a hint without having to actually say the words. He darted his gaze toward Ava and back to Henry.

Get the hint or you're moving down a few pegs on my best friend list, old man.

"Suit yourself," Mr. Chambers said as he led Henry inside.

Once he was alone with Ava, the quiet peace that he loved about the ranch settled around them. He wanted a million moments alone with Ava because he'd never get enough.

Too bad he had a limited number of days to cram in every second he could get with her. Six days was just enough to make him wish for more. This one day had been enough to rattle his common sense and make him forget everything except her and that subtle grin that made his fingertips itch to touch her hair. He knew it was soft. His hands remembered the feeling like he'd touched her just yesterday.

The dim sunset wasn't bright enough. The precise details of her face were harder to make out when shadows fell over everything in sight.

He stepped closer and wished he could redo the last hour and a half. It was his day off. He could have called another ranch hand to help with Thunder, but it was his instinct to get up and go when someone needed a hand. Now, he missed that time he'd rather have spent right here.

"You get settled in?" he asked.

"Not really. I went with Stella to the dining hall for supper, but I got a headache."

"Was it the noise? Are you tired?"

"Probably a mix of both. It got better when I took some medicine and came out here with Grandpa." She propped her arms on the porch railing and looked past him to the sun sinking over the distant Bighorn Mountains.

He leaned on the railing beside her. "There's more to see tomorrow." At least he hoped so. He wanted to show her everything, but their days were numbered. He had work up to his ears, and a full night's sleep around here was rare. Still, he could sleep when he was dead, or at least when Ava left.

When she left. It felt so final and unfair. Again. But when had his life ever been fair? Well, God had given him a strong sister and a better job than he deserved. He should be content with that.

But he wasn't. He wanted Ava—the one who got away and was leaving again.

And that hopeful glint in her eyes wasn't helping.

"Are you off again tomorrow?" she asked.

Jameson shook his head. His day off hadn't really been a day off. Not that it ever was, but he liked it that way. Except today, he'd wanted all that time with Ava.

Her attention turned to her feet.

"Hey." He gently lifted her chin. "Will you come with me?"

"To work?"

"It's not like we have to go far. And Mr. Chambers usually hangs around with me during the day."

Why was he trying to convince her to spend more time with him? His heart demanded he seek her out whenever possible, but his brain said that was stupid. He was heading for a train wreck when she left, and he'd be left wondering why he'd lost her—again.

He should have begged her to stay the first time. He wouldn't have amounted to anything in Denver, but she belonged here. He saw it in the way she looked at the sunset and in the way she looked at him.

Yeah, he was a goner.

"You think he can do all that? I mean, is he getting around that well?"

"He's fine. Plus, it won't really be all day. He likes to take a nap after lunch and catch up on things in the office. I have to be in the kitchen for an inspection at two, and I have a meeting with our contractor at three."

Ava tucked her arms around her middle as a gust of wind picked up her hair. "Are you always so busy?"

"Never busy enough." That had been the truth

until today. He liked filling every hour with something to do. He worked hard because...

Well, he worked hard because he wanted to earn his keep. And he never wanted to be a burden, at least not since he stole the majority of his sister's childhood because she'd been the only one who cared if he lived or died.

He wasn't helpless anymore. In fact, he could take care of a family—his family. And no one made him want that more than the woman standing in front of him.

"Thank you for showing me around today. I loved it."

Her smile disappeared, and she looked out at the far reaches of the ranch.

"What's wrong?" he whispered. Her hesitation made him wish he hadn't asked.

"Nothing I hadn't expected."

"It's her? Is she giving you a hard time?" He'd been pushing thoughts of Linda out of his head all day. She somehow had a way of ruining his mood from hundreds of miles away.

"She sent some texts."

Jameson's hands fisted at his sides. "You know you can throw that phone in the creek."

That got him a small grin. "I wish I could sometimes."

"No, really. I could throw it from here." He

pointed at Wolf Creek that snaked through the valley.

Her tired eyes had his gut twisting. Was Linda still as bad as she used to be? Or worse? Either way, he wasn't going to stand by while Ava took her mother's verbal beatings. Not this time.

"Don't bring your phone tomorrow."

"What?"

"Leave it in your room. Turn it off. Whatever. Just don't let her ruin your day again. I'm glad you're here. Your grandpa is glad you're here. You have a week here, and I can't watch you be sad all week."

She was looking at him as if the thought had never occurred to her before, but the wheels in her head were turning—hopefully in his favor.

Finally, that crease between her brows softened, and she whispered, "Okay."

It was a small victory, but it was one step toward winning her happiness. Ava didn't deserve to be hounded all the time, and maybe she'd realize how happy she could be if her mother wasn't filling her head with abuse all day.

"Will you meet me in the morning?" he asked.

She took a step toward him and smiled. "I wouldn't miss it. If it's anything like this sunset, I'll be getting up early every morning."

If the rest of the week was anything like today, he'd be working double time to get that extra time with Ava.

The words he wanted to say bubbled up his throat and rolled over his tongue before he clamped his jaw closed.

It's a date.

But it wasn't a date. It was another day he was too eager to spend with a woman he had no business hanging around.

Too bad that wasn't a good enough reason to leave well enough alone where Ava Collins was concerned.

"Where and when?" she asked.

"There's a bench behind the stables, near the south pasture."

Ava grinned. "I know the one."

The bench had been their meeting place the last time she'd visited. When he came in from the trail rides, he'd dusted off his clothes and met her to watch the sunset. She'd brought sandwiches and water, and they'd stayed away from the main house until her mother called.

Jameson wiped the back of his neck. "Sunrise too early?"

"Not at all. I'm used to waking up while it's still dark outside."

"Good. There's something I want you to see."

The dimming sunset lit up her expression, and her eyes seemed to sparkle. He loved seeing her happy. He made a living taking people on adventures, showing them the beauty of nature and giving them a vacation to remember, but he was sure no one had ever been as happy to be here as Ava was today.

"I'm sure Grandpa can manage a little bit without me in the morning."

Jameson laughed. "Trust me, that old man doesn't need your help."

"What do you mean?"

"Just what I said. He's fine, and it's driving him crazy that Henry won't leave him be for two minutes."

"I know. Maybe I can just hang around and get to know him without making him feel like I'm coddling him."

"I think that's exactly what your grandpa wants."

Jameson knew exactly what *he* wanted. Another chance with Ava. He'd be kicking himself for the next week while she filled his every waking thought.

It was too much and not enough. When had he ever asked for something for himself? Never. God had given him more than he deserved, and he'd always counted himself content.

But he wanted Ava. He wanted more of those quiet evenings they'd spent talking and watching the sun set. He wanted more of her bright smile and kindness. He wanted so many things that he couldn't have, and he'd never been this selfish before.

Before Ava. There was an identifiable line separating the times with her and without.

Jameson backed up the few steps to the edge of the porch. If he didn't leave now, he wouldn't be able to get half of tomorrow's to-do list marked off tonight. "I'll see you in the morning."

Ava leaned farther over the porch railing. "Good night."

"Good night, Ava."

This night could go one of two ways: dreams where he got the girl or nightmares where he lost it all—again.

CHAPTER 8

AVA

The soft melody of Ava's alarm pulled her from sleep. The first deep inhale of the day filled her senses with earthy pine and fresh air. She'd left the bedroom window cracked last night hoping for this exact wake up call. Denver never smelled like this, at least not in the city center where she and her mother lived.

Her mother. She'd hoped to put off thoughts of Linda at least until after her first cup of coffee, but it was a lost cause. Linda's disdain for Wolf Creek had painted a dark cloud over Ava's arrival yesterday, and today wasn't looking promising.

She stretched her arms above her head and twisted her shoulders from side to side. The guest bed rivaled the comfort of her own, and she'd slept harder than usual. Either that, or the change in her schedule was throwing things off. Ava was a creature of habit. Schedules were her life. Well, they were her job, and she did it well.

The soothing alarm cut off, and the piercing of her mother's ringtone shattered all hope of a good morning. The sky outside the small picture window was still inky black.

Ava tossed the covers from around her shoulders and reached for the phone. "Hello."

"I hope you're happy. My breakfast isn't here."

There would be absolutely no semblance of a good morning now.

Ava normally woke at four in the morning, got ready for work, and picked up breakfast for the two of them from Linda's favorite French bistro before Linda had to be at the studio for *Good Morning Denver*.

Ava's routine wasn't instinct, it was learned. Linda lived a catered life with every detail planned and executed to her liking by Ava. Despite her efforts to ensure the regular routine was maintained, the train had fallen off the tracks before sunrise.

"Brianna has your breakfast waiting for you at the studio. Kelsey has your outfit ready in your office. I've taken care of everything."

Linda huffed. "I talked to Jordan last night. He's not happy about this either. In fact, he's considering promoting Brianna."

A pang of worry zipped through Ava's middle. She was the top assistant, but Brianna was quickly proving herself. The initial reaction was fleeting, giving way to respect. Ava did her job well, often above and beyond. It shouldn't bother her that Brianna was also a dedicated worker.

Ava slowly exhaled before responding. "I can see why he would want to do that. I told him the reason I requested the time off this week. He was understanding."

"That's not how things work," Linda spat. "You left your post, and now someone else is taking over. Don't say I didn't warn you."

Ava sat up and bunched the warm blanket around her waist. Could she lie back down and get a do-over?

"I'm planning to ask Brianna to move into your room today. You should start looking for a new place to live."

Ava kicked the blanket off and stood. "What?" Linda had made the threat yesterday, but she often wielded words like a sword, jabbing and stabbing to draw blood.

"You heard me. I'm finished with this game, Ava. Get back here or you're out on the street."

Ava gasped for air. Where could she go? Brianna had a roommate, but it was no secret that she wasn't happy with the arrangement. She'd take Linda's offer in a heartbeat.

"Please don't do this. I'll be back in a few days and everything will be back to normal."

"You have a choice to make. I've given you everything. My life has revolved around you since you were born, and I'm tired of your ungratefulness."

Ava's throat was tight and dry. "I've never been ungrateful," she whispered. Her mother had done a lot for her, but she'd also had to work for everything she had. She paid rent to her mother. Granted, it was a minimal amount for the loft they shared, but she pulled her weight. She never wanted her mother to see her as a burden.

Linda's words were shrill now. "Are you kidding me? You go running at the first word from that man, and he hasn't ever been there for you. Am I not enough for you? Did Kenneth not do enough for you while he was alive? Your dad and I gave you everything!"

It hurt. Everything hurt. No one had laid a finger on her, but every inch of Ava's body ached. Whoever said words can't hurt hadn't ever met Linda Collins.

"I'm not here because I want something from him." Ava had never rated her relationships based on what the other person could do for her, but Linda always did. If someone wasn't lifting her up or giving her what she wanted, they weren't worth her time.

Ava pitied her mother, but she would never say so.

"Then why are you there?"

"Grandpa had a stroke. Don't you care?" Ava asked.

Linda's response was quick and emotionless. "No."

Silence hung between them. What had Grandpa done to Linda to make her hate him so vehemently?

Ava swallowed, hoping to soften her next question. "Why?"

Her mother's tone shifted from irate to indifferent. "You'll find out soon enough."

The call ended abruptly. Her mother usually hung up their calls without a good-bye. If she was angry, they often ended with a cryptic threat.

Why did this warning leave Ava's blood running cold?

The sky outside the window had lightened to a midnight blue. She needed to hurry if she was going to meet Jameson at sunrise. Grabbing her clothes, she darted into the en suite bathroom and showered in a rush. The thick, damp air only tightened the panic in her chest. Her mom was kicking her out. How could she do that?

Cool tears mingled with the heated water that pelted her skin. If she knew why her mother hated this place and her own father, maybe Ava would know who to trust. Her mom had always been there for her, but her grandpa claimed he'd wanted to be a part of her life, too. Whatever he'd done, it had to be terrible for her mother to hold such a grudge.

She turned off the water and quickly dried off. Should she have listened to her mother's warnings? Should she get out of here before the same thing happened to her that happened to her mother? What was it?

Should she stay? Or should she forget about all this and go home?

The first signs of the coming morning shone dimly through the window. She didn't have much time to decide.

Here or there?

She'd come here determined to get to know her grandpa. Where had that strong determination gone?

Right out the window when her mother said she'd be homeless. There was no way she could find a new place in Denver. At least not on this short notice and when she was hundreds of miles away. She didn't have the money to rent a hotel room until she found an apartment. She didn't even have the money to splurge on a last-minute plane ticket home to make sure her mother didn't kick her out.

Her grandpa's words from the evening before echoed in her mind. He'd said his home was her home. Had he truly meant it? Could she ask him to let her stay if her mother gave away her room back home? Was that even a good idea? Her mother was right when she kept reminding her that Ava didn't know the people here. They were all strangers.

They didn't feel like strangers to her. Her grandpa seemed genuine and kind. Even his ruse to get her here so Henry could leave without worrying about him was backed by good intentions.

And Jameson. He didn't feel like a stranger at all. He hadn't six years ago, and despite the time and distance between them, he'd swept her back into Wolf Creek Ranch as if those six years were a blink of an eye.

He'd carved out that scarred place in her heart pretty quickly too. She remembered the hurt in his eyes the day she'd left. That look had haunted many dreams in the years since.

She cared about her mother. How could she not? But the tension between them had always been there. Ava imagined it as an unknown resentment her mother had toward her. For not being good enough? For not being just like her mother? She wasn't sure, and her mother had never been forth-coming with details aside from her quick demands.

Now, a foggy image began forming in her mind. What would her life have been like had her mother stayed here and raised Ava where she'd grown up?

When she'd dressed and pulled her hair into a tight bun, she remembered the reason for her rush. She was supposed to meet Jameson.

Ava hefted the blanket up to make the bed, and her phone fell with a thump on the wooden floor.

She stopped and stared at it as she recalled Jameson's whispered words.

Don't bring your phone tomorrow.

Tucking the sheets and blankets around the mattress, she left the phone where it had fallen while she contemplated her options.

Go home. Stay here.

Take her phone. Leave it here.

She laid both palms flat on the made bed and tucked her head. *What should I do? What don't I know? Why am I stuck?* She poured out the questions plaguing her heart, but the answers didn't come.

She stood tall and took a deep breath. Maybe she'd have a clearer direction later. The sky grew a little brighter outside. It was time to meet Jameson or back out.

No, she was meeting Jameson. That decision was clear—made by her heart and protected by an unwavering determination.

CHAPTER 9
AVA

Ava hurriedly typed out a message to the other assistants she worked with at the news station stating she'd be out of touch for a while, but she'd reply to any messages they sent her today as soon as she got back.

With that settled, she tiptoed down the hallway, unsure if her grandpa woke this early, but she got her answer halfway down the stairs. The warm smell of freshly brewed coffee welcomed her to the morning.

Yes, she could still turn things around and have a good day. The distance from her phone was already serving its purpose.

In the kitchen, the coffee sat waiting with no sign of her grandpa. She poured a cup and looked around. The coffee was still too hot to drink, so he couldn't have gone far. After checking the living room and back porch, she decided to look for her grandpa again after meeting Jameson.

Outside, the dew sat heavy over everything, and a thin layer of fog hovered low in the valley. A few ranch hands milled around, despite the early hour, but no one was in a hurry. She definitely wasn't in Denver anymore.

She started toward her car but stopped at the bottom of the steps leading off the porch. Looking up the dirt-and-gravel path, she could see the stables. It wasn't far. She could walk to the stables. Why was the concept so foreign to her? Probably because nothing she did at her job or for her mother allowed enough time to stroll and sip coffee.

The walk to the bench near the stables was peaceful. She passed a few people along the way who waved or wished her a good morning. With two inches of coffee left in her cup, she sat on the cool bench facing the fenced-in pasture. The morning was chillier than she'd expected, so she tucked her arms close and wrapped her hands around the coffee cup. The sun was beginning to brighten the sky as it crested over the Bighorn Mountains.

"Morning."

Ava looked over her shoulder as her grandpa walked up, holding his own steaming cup of coffee.

"Good morning. I didn't see you when I came downstairs."

He pulled at his pants at the top of his leg as he

slowly sat beside her. "I was reading in my office. Didn't think you'd be up so early."

"I'm used to it, but not like this. It's so quiet and calm."

Her grandpa rested back against the bench. "Your grandma loved sitting here in the mornings. She said the sunrise was how God said good morning."

Your grandma. Ava hadn't even met her before she died, but Grandma Lottie still felt like *hers.*

"I was just thinking the sky looks like a water-color painting this morning. I could sit here all day and not get tired of it." She turned to her grandpa and felt a pang of regret. "I'm sorry I missed out on getting to know her. And for not coming back sooner."

"Water under the bridge, sweetheart." He nudged her with his elbow. "I'm glad you're here now."

Ava looked out over the pasture. Why wouldn't her mother want to be here? Was it this place or was it specifically Grandpa that kept Linda from everything at Wolf Creek?

A faint vibration rumbled beneath Ava's feet, and a cloud of dust whirled over the pasture beneath the sun rising over the mountains. "What's that?"

Grandpa lifted his cup. "They're bringing in the horses."

The rumbling grew, and soon she could make out the silhouettes of the first riders and horses. She stood and stepped closer to the fence, entranced by the sight of the herd. There had to be dozens, all galloping together toward the stables.

Soon, the pounding of hooves thundered through the valley, rattling her bones and sending her heart racing along with them.

What a way to wake up. She stood near the fence, stunned at the adrenaline running through her system, despite the calm morning.

When the herd slowed and the wranglers dismounted, Ava spun around to her grandpa. "Do they do that every morning?"

"Yep. Guests can't ride the horses if the wranglers don't bring them in from the east pasture."

She took her seat beside him. "That was amazing. They're so beautiful."

"You know, your mom used to ride."

Ava sucked in a deep breath at the mention of her mother. The sadness was back, weighing heavy on her shoulders. "I didn't know. She won't talk about anything here."

They sat in silence, watching the wranglers leading the horses in. A few guests had congregated near the stables, and the kids shouted in excitement. These families were here together. Parents took time off work. Family vacations weren't something Ava had thought much about, but they'd never done that, not even when her dad had still been alive.

Jameson walked out of the stables and set his sights on her. He adjusted the black, wide-brimmed cowboy hat on his head, and when he looked up, happiness sparkled in his eyes.

Jameson Ford, a man who had been a long-gone memory only yesterday. She'd thought about what it might be like to see him again, but those imaginings hadn't been anything like this.

So much was the same, and so much was different. He was stronger and steadier than before, but he carried himself with the same purpose and responsibility she'd admired all those years ago. She'd always remembered him as if he were the epitome of independence.

Even the bench she'd sat on today was the same. It hadn't been lost on her that she'd sat in that very spot with him six years ago. He'd held her while she cried, not only for her lost grandma, but because she hadn't known her grandma to begin with. How could she lose someone she never had?

"Good morning. You like the show?" he asked.

The playful lilt in his voice sent a thrill rippling up her spine.

"It was amazing!"

His smile grew wider, and his gaze didn't leave hers. That was the look she remembered. No one had undone her as easily and completely as Jameson

Ford when he looked at her as if she were the source of his happiness.

Her grandpa stood, stretching his back. "Welp, that's my cue. Time to get to work."

"What are you up to this morning?" Jameson asked. "I thought you were coming with us."

"In a little while. I have an appointment this morning."

"Is something wrong? Do you want me to go with you?" Ava asked. It hadn't occurred to her that he might still be following up with his doctor after the stroke.

"No, no. It's nothing. I'll catch up with you two later." He reached out to Ava. "I'll take that cup."

"Thanks. I don't have my phone with me, but will you please call Jameson and let me know when you get back?"

Grandpa chuckled. "You're just like Henry."

Ava grinned. "I can't say that's a bad thing."

Grandpa sighed. "I'll keep you posted. You two have fun."

Ava turned to Jameson, who was grinning like he just stole a cookie from the cookie jar. "What's that look about?"

"He knows," Jameson said.

"He knows what?"

"That I wanted to spend some time with you."

"What? Are you saying he doesn't have an appointment?"

Jameson nodded, keeping his gaze focused on her. "I don't believe you."

"I know everything about his schedule. I keep it on my phone along with every other thing I have to do around here. I need to know when the owner will be around in case I need to set up a meeting or phone call that he'll need to be on. Trust me, there's no appointment today."

"That little sneak," Ava hissed.

"Don't get worked up over it. He's trying to be discreet. Plus, he likes to hang out with the guys at Deano's in the morning."

"Well, I don't want to throw a wrench in any of his plans just because I'm here. It's good that he gets out. Speaking of breakfast, I could use a bite."

Jameson offered her his arm. "Let's go."

Ava looked back at the bench where she'd sat with her grandpa this morning. "We sat there last time I was here. On that bench," she said quietly as they walked back to his truck.

"I remember." He looked down at her walking beside him. "I remember everything."

Oh boy. She did too, and that meant spending time with him and rekindling those old flames that still simmered was probably a bad idea. Did he remember the way he'd kissed her? She certainly hadn't forgotten the way his strong hands had pulled her close and the slow, soothing way he'd pushed everything else from her mind with a brush of his lips against hers.

Still, she couldn't ignore the way she felt about him. She'd thought about him way too much in the years they'd been apart.

"Did you drive?" she asked.

"Yeah. My cabin is about half a mile northwest of the main house, so it's a pretty good walk up the hill. Some mornings I walk, but I got up a few hours before sunrise, and it's not always safe to walk around in the dark here."

"You've been up that long?"

"There's always something that needs doing, so I thought I'd knock out a few things so we could take it a little easier today."

Ava blinked through her shock. He'd gone way out of his way to spend more time with her and make their time together more enjoyable. No one had ever done anything remotely close to that for her. In fact, she was usually the one working to make someone else's life easier.

Why was she working her life away for everyone else? Sure, it was her job, and she got paid to do it, but there wasn't any room left in the day to live her own life. She didn't have breakfast with friends at Deano's. She didn't wake up early to watch the horses come in from the east pasture. She jumped and ran for everyone else. She'd worked at the station for almost four years now without taking a single vacation day.

Where was her life?

"Hey, you okay?" Jameson asked.

"Yeah, I'm fine. Just thinking."

He leaned in and whispered, "Is it your mom?"

Ava sighed. "Yes and no."

"Did you bring your phone?"

"Actually, I didn't. I left it in my room." That was one decision she was happy with at the moment.

"Good." Jameson laid his heavy hand over hers where it rested in the crook of his arm. The rough calluses rested against her soft skin. "I haven't asked. What do you do now?"

"I'm a personal assistant." She cringed as she said the words.

They'd reached Jameson's truck and he opened the passenger door for her. "Really? What kind of personal assistant?"

Shame heated her cheeks. Last time she'd been here, she'd had these perfectly crafted dreams of being a business owner and working for herself. "I'm Linda's assistant."

Jameson halted, and she felt the tension in the air.

She hadn't achieved that freedom she'd wanted. In fact, she'd found herself further trapped in the web her mother wove for her.

"Are you serious?" he asked in a low voice.

"Unfortunately."

Instead of berating her for selling out on those plans, he threaded his fingers with hers and squeezed her hand.

She'd sold out, and they both knew it. How could she have given up on her degree when she'd been so close to finishing?

He released her hand and waited until she was in the seat before he closed the door and walked around to take his place behind the wheel.

"Sorry. It's a diesel. It's a little dirty too, so I'm sorry in advance for any stains you get on that nice sweater."

Ava hugged her arms around her middle. "It's fine. Just a sweater." In truth, she was attached to this one, but not because it was expensive or fancy. She'd picked up the faded gray sweater with a mountain silhouette at the Denver airport yesterday morning. It was the opposite of the fashionable outfits she wore at the station, and she'd grabbed it off the rack the moment she saw it.

The only sound on the way to the dining hall came from the loud engine that rumbled the seat beneath her.

Ava wanted to kick herself. Not for telling Jameson about her job, but for not doing what she wanted instead of dropping out of college and taking the job as her mother's assistant. At the time, it had seemed like a good idea. She could get a job and start making money. That would lead to her freedom, right?

Instead, she was still working for her mom and the news station years later. She'd never made her own way like she'd planned. She still lived with her mother.

Her stomach rolled, threatening to revolt. She'd made that plan to break free of her mother for a reason. Instead of sticking to it, she'd run the other way when it seemed like the easier path.

Jameson parked in front of the dining hall, but instead of getting out, he kept his seat behind the wheel and turned to her. "It's okay. If you like your job, that's all that matters. I'm not asking you right now if you do or don't because I'm scared to know your answer. But you're not at work this week, and I'm glad you're here."

Good grief. Did he know what he was saying? It was as plain as day that she wasn't happy with her job, but she did it with a painted-on smile every day because she was too afraid to take that first step and make her own way, away from her mother.

"I'm glad I'm here too."

"Let's get some breakfast."

They got out of the truck, and she fell into step beside him at the porch steps. "Is it too early?"

"Nah. Vera will have something ready. I like to get in and get out early for meals or else I get stuck in the dining hall for hours."

"Mr. Popular," Ava teased.

"Something like that. The wranglers are supposed to mingle with the guests during meal times, but I can get behind in a hurry if I stick around to chat. I love catching up with the families who come every year, but I try to catch them between activities."

"You really are popular."

"I've been working here half my life. These people are like family now."

What would it be like to have relationships with people that lasted years and grew with time? Better yet, friendships that were more like family?

What *was* family anyway? Her dad and grandma were gone, and her mother was kicking her out. She was just getting to know the grandpa who'd been a stranger to her all her life.

Jameson squinted as he looked past her. An old truck was parked at the end of the lot and a man leaned against it. She couldn't tell much about him since he was facing the truck and had his face buried in the crook of his arm.

"Sorry, I need to check on him. I'll make it quick."

"No rush. You think he's okay?"

"I think he's fine. I'll be right back."

CHAPTER 10
AVA

Ava waited on the porch near the check-in office. Curiosity had her sneaking glances at Jameson and the man at the truck. After a few seconds, the guy lowered his arm. It was Dane, the man she'd run into at supper yesterday.

She tucked her chin and waited until Jameson joined her a minute later. "Is he sick?" she asked.

Jameson's gaze didn't meet hers. "No, just hung over."

"Hung over?" Ava didn't fight the urge to peek at Dane this time. She didn't know much about alcohol, since her dad had been adamantly against it her whole life. "Will he be okay?"

"I guess that depends on whether or not I fire him," Jameson said.

Ava fell into step beside him. "Will you?"

"I don't know. He's a lot of trouble."

"I ran into him yesterday. Literally ran into him."

"Was he nice to you?" Jameson asked.

"I don't know. It was my fault. I wasn't paying attention to where I was going."

"Dane is pretty new around here, so I'm trying to give a little grace. He definitely hasn't made it easy."

Jameson held the door to the dining hall open, and she stepped inside.

"Wow. It's so quiet," Ava whispered.

Jameson chuckled. "You don't have to keep your voice down. We just beat the breakfast crowd."

One couple sat at a table off to the far side and four men sat at another table near the serving bar. They wore casual clothes and weren't smartly dressed like the other guests she'd seen around.

A few foods were already out on the serving bar but nothing like the assortment offered yesterday evening. A woman stepped out of the kitchen carrying a silver tray of biscuits. Her smile widened and the shallow lines around her eyes deepened when she saw Jameson.

"Morning, sunshine. Bacon is coming."

"You need a hand?" Jameson asked.

The woman spoke slowly and softly. "No, no. I got this. Thanks for the offer." She rested the tray in the warming station and wiped her hands on her apron. The slate-gray apron was already covered in white dust. "Who's your friend?"

"Vera, this is Ava. She's Mr. Chambers' grand-daughter."

Vera's eyes widened. "Oh! Really? What a surprise. It's so nice to meet you."

"It's nice to meet you too." It was true. Almost every person she'd met at Wolf Creek Ranch had been overly kind to her. If she hadn't made a fool of herself and run into Dane, the percentage would be one hundred.

"Vera is the head chef. We're really lucky to have her. Everything she cooks is delicious."

Vera tried to contain her grin. "Stop it. You're too nice."

"It's only the truth," Jameson promised.

"He's right," Ava said. "Everything at supper last night was fantastic. It's been a while since I had such good food."

Vera's cheeks were a soft pink, and she averted her gaze when she couldn't hide her growing smile. "Thank you. I'm always happy to know someone is enjoying it."

"I'm about to enjoy all of this," Jameson said as he piled two biscuits on his plate.

"How long are you staying?" Vera asked.

"Just a week. I came to help Grandpa so Henry could go on a trip with his wife."

Vera swiped her hand in the air. "Your grandpa doesn't need help."

Jameson chuckled. "Everyone except Henry

knows that."

Vera snapped her fingers. "Let me get you that bacon."

While Vera hurried off to the kitchen, Jameson heaped white gravy on top of his biscuits. "The gravy is amazing. She won't tell anyone the secret."

"Don't the other kitchen workers know?" Ava asked.

"No. Vera isn't secretive about much, but she doesn't let anyone else touch the gravy."

A man stepped up to the end of the serving bar and took a plate from the stack. A thick beard covered most of his face, but it was cut short enough that it wasn't unruly.

Vera hurried out of the kitchen carrying a tray of bacon, but she stopped short when she saw the man. Her timid grin bloomed into a full ear-to-ear smile. "Good morning."

"Morning, Vera," the man said.

Vera carefully placed the bacon on the serving counter. "I didn't think you'd be in this morning."

"Thane rushed me through our run. I had some extra time before the pack ride."

"Well, it's always good to see you," Vera said before turning on her heel and quickly disappearing back into the kitchen.

Ava could have sworn Vera was happy to see the man. Why was she rushing off?

Jameson reached an arm around Ava and patted

the man on the shoulder. "I'm surprised you can still keep up with Thane."

The man huffed. "I'm fifty, not decrepit."

Ava's attention darted back and forth between the men on either side of her. She was half a second away from asking about Thane when Jameson pointed at the man.

"Ava, this is Paul. He's the leader of the pack rides. Paul, this is Ava, Mr. Chambers' granddaughter."

How many times had Jameson introduced her as Mr. Chambers' granddaughter? Probably dozens now. Still, hearing her name in connection to her grandpa and seeing the delighted reactions hadn't gotten old.

"I heard you were coming." Paul moved the plate to his left hand and offered the right to Ava. "It's good to meet you."

She took his hand, and the rough skin scraped against her palm. "It's nice to meet you too. It's nice to finally be here."

Paul turned his attention back to the food. "I can't believe your mom didn't bring you sooner."

Ava's breath halted in her chest at the mention of her mother. "I beg your pardon?"

"I just meant that I haven't seen you around here before."

"You weren't here the last time Ava visited,"

Jameson said. "It was when Lottie died. I think you were in Amarillo."

Paul nodded, more interested in the food than Ava's shock at hearing this man talk about her mother.

Ava realized she'd been holding the gravy ladle longer than necessary. Could she stomach gravy right now? "Um, my mother doesn't come here," Ava said once she'd decided against the gravy—Vera's special gravy that would no doubt feel like a brick in her stomach now that thoughts of Linda had cast a cloud over breakfast.

"I assumed as much. I haven't seen her in over two decades," Paul said.

Ava lowered her plate to the serving counter. "You know Linda?"

"Knew. It was a lifetime ago. I've been working here most of my life, so I remember her before she moved away."

"Denver. I mean, she moved to Denver, where we live." It was surreal talking about her mother with a stranger. Most everyone in Denver knew Linda Collins from *Good Morning Denver* and the five o'clock news, but here, no one but Ava's grandpa and Jameson had mentioned her mother.

"I think I heard that once." Paul's tone now sounded uninterested, or was it sad?

He scooped a heaping of gravy over his biscuits and stepped around Ava toward the end of the serving counter. "I've got to get going. It was nice to meet you."

Ava's reply was a weak mumble as Paul grabbed a roll of silverware and headed out the back of the dining hall. What just happened? The talk of her mother left her neck sweating. What did Paul know about Linda?

"Hey, you okay?" Jameson said, placing a steadying hand on her elbow.

Jameson's concern snapped her out of her daze. "I'm fine. I just didn't expect—"

"Let's not talk about her. Unless you want to. Paul is a great guy, and I doubt he realized talking about your mom might be a sore spot right now."

Ava's breaths were jagged and strained. The conversation she'd had with her mother this morning came back to her in a rush. The heartache, the confusion, the rejection. It was all front-and-center.

All of the blood drained from her face as she whispered, "She's kicking me out."

Jameson leaned in, and his eyes widened. "She what?"

The power behind his words struck her in the chest. His jaw tensed, and his grip on the bar had his knuckles turning white.

Her chest grew tighter as the panic rose. "She said she was going to ask a woman at work to move in with her if I didn't come home today."

"That's crazy. She wouldn't really do that, would she?"

"Maybe. I don't know. My flight leaves in five days, but changing it now would be expensive. I don't even know what I'm doing here. Grandpa doesn't really need me. Should I leave now? Should I—"

Jameson took the plate from her hands and set them both on the bar before wrapping her in his arms. "Stop. We'll figure this out. You won't be out on the street. I'll make sure of it."

She buried her face in Jameson's chest. The warm flannel and the spice that filled her lungs evened her breaths. It felt good to have his arms around her. It felt good to hear his assurances. She'd always worried over the issues with Linda on her own.

The door to the dining hall opened, and the chatter of the group walking in broke up the private moment she'd been having with Jameson. He released her and picked up their plates.

"Come on. Let's eat in my office."

CHAPTER 11
AVA

Ava inhaled a deep breath and followed Jameson out the back door. The back of the dining hall mirrored the front with a long porch stretching the length of the building. Jameson led her to a door on the end that connected to the check-in office and gift shop where she'd met Everly and Stella yesterday, but this entrance led to a back hallway. Around the first corner, he chose the door on the left and stepped aside for her to enter first.

Jameson's office wasn't anything like she'd expected. Two walls had large windows looking out over the ranch: one wall was full of filing cabinets and shelves, and the other was covered in a floor-to-ceiling map of the ranch.

When Jameson closed the door behind them, she felt the pressures of the real world fade away as if her mother's threats didn't exist in this safe space with Jameson. She felt that way about most things when Jameson was around. When someone needed help on the ranch, he helped. When she'd been grieving her grandmother, he listened. When her mother was kicking her out, he made her believe she wouldn't actually be homeless by the end of the day.

Jameson set the plates on the wooden desk and hugged her again. "Are you okay? I promise we'll figure this out. Don't worry."

"I'm okay. Really. I'd done a good job of pushing all of those worries out of my mind this morning, and they all came rushing back when he mentioned my mother."

"I didn't know Paul knew Linda, but it makes sense. He's been working here most of his life."

"I wonder if he knows why she left."

"It didn't sound like it. He acted like he expected her to show up around here."

Ava looked out the window at the bright morning. Guests were everywhere now, and she could tell even from this distance that everyone was smiling.

"I wish I knew why she doesn't like this place."

"She's never said anything about why?" he asked.

"Never." Ava looked at the map on the wall. Wolf Creek Ranch covered thousands of acres in the foothills of the Bighorn Mountains. There were a million things to see at Wolf Creek—a million things she wanted to see and explore for the rest of her life—but she'd never been far from the main house.

Jameson brushed a hand down her arm and linked his fingers with hers. "I can't imagine what she wouldn't like here. Maybe it's too far away from the convenience of a city. That's a dealbreaker for some people."

Ava squeezed his hands and looked up at him. The confusion in his eyes probably mirrored her own. "Maybe that's it, but that's no reason to hate it the way she does."

"This place is like home to me. I love it here. In my book, it doesn't get any better," Jameson said.

"I'm starting to think that way too, but I haven't seen much of it." From what she had seen, Wolf Creek was like a dream, and she didn't want to wake up.

"You want to go on the pack ride tomorrow? Paul is leading. I think I can sneak away for a day too."

Ava exhaled a slow breath. "I don't know. What about—Never mind. I'd like that." She'd stop worrying about her mother. Maybe she could talk to Linda later and smooth things out. It was far-fetched, but maybe her mother would calm down.

"We can play it by ear. If you decide in the morning that you don't want to go, you don't have to."

"That sounds great." She eyed the plates of food sitting on his desk. "Sorry I've derailed breakfast."

"No problem. I just wanted to make sure you were okay." He pulled two bottles of water out of a mini fridge in the corner and moved an extra chair from the corner to the side of the desk.

"Thanks. No more talk about my back-home drama."

Jameson flashed that heart-stopping grin she adored. "Your wish is my command. Take this chair." He offered her the chair behind the desk.

"This one's fine." She pulled up the more rigid chair and moved her plate closer to the edge of the desk.

"Are you sure? I don't mind you sitting there."

"It's really fine. Your office is nice." There were a few framed landscapes on the wall and a quote painted on a rough piece of wood above the window.

Jameson sat and pulled his plate closer. "Stella decorated. It's a shame I don't spend more time in here. No one else gets to see it." He laid a hand on the desk between them with his palm up. "I'd like to say grace."

She wasn't sure what grace was, but it was probably something like the prayer before a meal she'd seen a few times in Hallmark movies. "Um, sure." She placed her hand in his and bowed her head the way he did.

"Father, thank You for this food. Thank You for the blessings all around us. Thank You for the guests who are visiting here, and I pray You'd bless their time here. Help us to be servants for You in all that we do. In Jesus's name I pray. Amen."

They ate in silence for a moment before Ava pointed to the quote above the window and read, "May the favor of the Lord our God rest on us; establish the work of our hands for us. Psalm 90:17." She pointed at the reference at the bottom. "What does that mean?"

"It's a Bible verse."

Ava looked back at the quote. "I remember Grandpa talking about the Bible last time I was here, but I don't know much about it."

Jameson covered his mouth and coughed. Was it a coincidence, or was he surprised she didn't know much about the Bible?

He cleared his throat. "I didn't realize. I just assumed you were a believer."

Ava's cheeks warmed. Did he mean a believer in God? She supposed she did. She assumed someone or something made everything, but she'd been kept so distanced from the topic.

"My mother despises anything to do with the Bible or God. I don't know why, but it's something she feels very strongly about."

Jameson moved his fork around his plate, but he didn't eat. "Mr. Chambers is a deacon at church."

She must have looked confused because Jameson continued.

"That's someone who helps the church and the congregation but also ministers in the community. They truly live a life for Christ." Jameson rubbed the back of his neck. "How did this not come up last time you were here?"

Ava shrugged, disappointed in herself for not knowing more about her grandpa's faith. "I talked to Grandpa about it a little, but there was so much going on that we didn't get to have a full conversation about it. So I left without really knowing much." She tilted her head. "Do you read the Bible?"

"Yeah. I read the Bible, but that's not what makes me a Christian. I believe in Jesus Christ, and I've dedicated my life to Him." He pushed more food around his plate, clearly unsure about eating the rest. "I guess this means you don't go to church."

"No. My grandmother's funeral was in a church, and my dad's. But that's about all."

He rested his fork on the side of his plate. "I'm sorry about your dad and Lottie."

"Thanks for being there for me when she died." She looked at her own plate. She'd barely touched the food. "It was hard to grieve. I wanted so badly to have known her first."

"She was a good woman."

"That's what everyone says. Most of the people I met at the funeral said they'd gone to church with her their whole lives, and they had such sweet things to say about her."

Jameson grinned and picked up his fork again. "The church ladies are the best."

They ate in silence for a moment before Jameson spoke. "I didn't know my grandmother either."

Ava looked up at him. "You didn't?"

Jameson shook his head. "Or my dad."

There was a sadness in his eyes that tugged at the confused and wounded part of her heart. "I had no idea. What happened?"

He hesitated, and for a moment, she wondered if he would answer.

"Nothing happened. My mom never talked about her folks, and my dad was never in the picture. I didn't feel like I was missing out. I had people who looked out for me."

Ava looked down. "Like my grandparents?"

"Yeah. They were always there for me." He laid his hand on top of hers. "I know what it's like growing up with a toxic mom too. I remember Linda from your last visit, and it's hard to believe she's so different from her parents."

Ava shook her head. "I've wanted to come back so many times, but I didn't. What does that say about me? I didn't even call my grandpa because I was afraid of how my mother would react."

He squeezed her hand. "It means you're human. It's normal to want your mom to love you, but it's not healthy for her to control your life and lash out at you when you get out of the box she put you in."

"You know, no one back at home tells me that. I know you're right, but when lots of people see us together every day and don't mention that it's weird that she's so controlling, it makes me think it's normal."

Jameson huffed, his nostrils flaring with the harsh exhale. "It isn't. I remember a lot about Linda, and nothing about the way she treated anyone is normal."

"I don't want to miss out on getting to know Grandpa, but there's this ultimatum hanging over my head."

"You and your grandpa are both fighting for a relationship with each other. That's rare."

Ava sighed. She was still unsure about so many things, but talking to Jameson took away most of her fear. He was always encouraging and assuring. She'd never had someone in her corner like that before.

"I forgot how easy it is to talk to you. You're a good listener."

Jameson released her hand and picked up his fork. "So, what do you want to see today?"

Ava wanted to see the world through Jameson's eyes. She wanted to view things as "the blessings all around us," and she wanted more of that humble appreciation that Jameson exuded in every action and word.

"Anything."

Jameson's cell phone rang before he could take a second bite of his food.

"Sorry. This is one of the wranglers."

Ava held up a hand. "Go ahead. Don't mind me."

"Hey." He chewed another bite as he listened. "Yeah. Make sure you order the same brand as last time. We don't want it to poison Mr. Lawrence's bees."

As soon as the call ended, Jameson's phone rang again. And again. He kept looking at her and whispering his apologies. She didn't mind. Once she finished her breakfast, she studied the map of Wolf Creek Ranch. The namesake was colored a light blue and wound through the valley and around the main house and stables. Hiking trails and pack trails were marked with red lines, and elevations ranged from mountaintops to gorges. It was thrilling and comforting at the same time knowing she'd never see all that her grandpa's ranch had to offer.

By the time he'd finished his breakfast in stolen bites between conversations, he'd placed an order for horse feed, scheduled a visit from a farrier— whatever that was—and approved a work order on a furnace.

He completed task after task efficiently. He just knew what to do. How many years had it taken him to learn everything he needed to know about the ranch?

Jameson ended the fifth call of the morning and looked up at her with a strained expression. "Sorry. I didn't expect the morning to be so busy."

She sat back in the chair beside his desk. "Don't apologize. I like seeing you work. You're good at what you do."

"I hope so. I still can't believe your grandpa promoted me."

"Why? You seem like the perfect man for the job."

Jameson chuckled. "Thanks, but there are a handful of men out there who have a decade more time under their belts."

"Why do you think he chose you then?"

Jameson shrugged. "I'm not sure yet, but I don't want him to regret his decision."

Ava smiled. "That's why he chose you. Because you'd probably proven yourself as a good leader and you wouldn't let him down."

"When he hired me, he told me that if a man is willing to work, he'll never be without a job. I always remembered that and made sure he knew I wanted to work."

With only one job on her resume, Ava couldn't judge the truth of the statement, but something in the words filled her with hope.

Jameson's phone rang again, and he answered it

quickly. "What's up?" His brow furrowed, and he was on his feet. "Get the skidgine out there. Take Blake with you. He's certified to drive it. I'll meet you with the water tanker."

Ava was on her feet when he gestured for her to follow him out of the office. They almost ran into her grandpa at the end of the hallway near the check-in office.

"Whoa, where you going in such a hurry?"

Jameson ended the call. "Fire on the ridge. The fire department is on the way, and Lincoln and Blake are getting the skidgine."

Her grandpa waved him off. "Go. Keep me posted."

Jameson turned to her, and she held up her hands.

"Don't worry about me. Go."

"I'll keep you posted, and I'll be back as soon as I can."

She shoved his shoulder. "Go!"

He didn't hesitate before running out the door.

Ava covered her mouth with her hand and looked at her grandpa. Her heart beat wildly in her chest. A fire sounded like a big emergency.

Her grandpa rested a hand on her shoulder. "Don't worry. Jameson can handle it."

CHAPTER 12
AVA

Ava stared at the words on the page in front of her. The book her grandpa had given her this afternoon was interesting, but keeping her thoughts from anything except Jameson and the fire was an ongoing battle.

He'd been gone for hours. She'd enjoyed the time with her grandpa, who thankfully kept reminding her that Jameson would come straight over with a report when things were under control.

But she'd caved to the temptation to look at her phone after lunch, and the anxiety had been heavy ever since.

Three missed calls from Linda, five hateful texts, and a voicemail that almost brought tears to Ava's eyes.

There were also five work emails and a text from Brianna.

Brianna: Hey, I know you're on vacation, and I'm sorry to bother you, but Linda pulled me aside this morning and asked if I'd like to move in with her. I thought you two lived together, and I wanted to make sure everything was okay. Are you moving?

Though it didn't change what Linda had done, Brianna's text had softened the blow a little. Ava thought of Brianna as a friend, even if they never had time to hang out or get to know each other outside of work hours.

It had taken Ava thirty minutes to put together a choppy response to Brianna that didn't sound uncertain or cryptic. Well, she hoped it hadn't sounded that way. But she really didn't know where she was going from here. If Linda was kicking her out, then she *would* be moving—to an apartment in Denver or somewhere else.

The walk to the archery range and lunch on the back porch with her grandpa hadn't eased her worries about her mother or Jameson. Chatting with Everly and Stella hadn't done the trick either.

Ava closed the book and rested it in her lap. The stories about the women of the Bible were fascinating. They sounded like heroines or fairy tales, and they were different from anything she'd read before. Esther was brave. Ruth was loyal. Deborah was bold. Why couldn't Ava be any of those things? She'd always been scared to speak up and afraid to make waves. That's how she ended up trapped under her mother's thumb.

But how could she change things now? Was she stuck forever?

For starters, reading the book at all was a little freeing. Her mother would have a lot to say if she saw Ava reading a book related to the Bible. She had a feeling Linda's disdain for this place and her aversion to any and all religion were probably linked.

Ava had just read about a woman who was healed because she touched Jesus's cloak. The book claimed it was because of the strength of her faith. What would it be like to have that kind of unshakeable faith? To know that the Lord was always there, guiding and blessing. Her grandpa and Jameson seemed to have that kind of faith, and from what she'd learned so far, she wanted that too.

Ava had excused herself from supper, claiming she wanted to read the new book. That was partially true. She'd read over half of it already, but she also knew she wouldn't be able to stomach anything while her worries for Jameson mounted. She'd seen the smoke from the archery range earlier. He'd missed two meetings that her grandpa had attended in his absence.

Ava still wasn't ready to eat, but she needed to do something to get her mind off the worry. She tucked the book under her arm and wandered around until she spotted a pot of coffee in the kitchen. The last thing she needed was caffeine to amp up her adrenaline, but she remembered her grandpa mentioning he drank decaf after lunch. A cup would at least keep her hands full.

If the coffee was still warm, her grandpa should be close by. She peeked onto the back porch and found him sitting in his usual rocking chair with a steaming mug in his left hand.

It was comforting to know even the little things about her grandpa, like the way he took his coffee and the places he could be found at different times of the day. She was getting to know him by fitting the pieces of everyday life into an ongoing puzzle. But there were so many missing pieces. She wanted to know how he met her grandma and where they'd been married. She wanted to know where Wolf Creek Ranch came from and how long it had been in her family.

Her family. She'd grown up in a three-person family, and then she'd mourned the loss of that complete family when her dad died. The years she'd spent with only her mom at her side were the toughest.

Now, she was learning to think of her family with the addition of her grandpa and the loss of her grandma. Bittersweet and confusing as it may be.

Ava slipped out the door, and her grandpa looked up.

"Well, hey. You ready for food?" he asked.

"Not yet. I just thought I'd sit with you."

He pulled a rocking chair closer to his. "Be my guest."

Ava looked for smoke to the east. "Did they stop the fire?"

"Looks like it. Those men know what they're doing. Jameson used to be a firefighter."

Ava's eyes widened. "Really? I remember him telling me he was training to be a firefighter, but I thought he'd always worked here."

"He has off and on since I've known him. He and his sister went to church with Lottie and me. But he worked for another ranch and the fire department too. He's had his hands full."

"I'll say." Ava stared into the dark coffee. There were so many things she didn't know about Wolf Creek and the people here. "Why did you hire Jameson for the foreman position when Henry retired? You don't have to tell me. It might be none of my business. I was just thinking about a man I met today, Paul. Jameson said he'd been here for decades. If Paul had worked here longer, why didn't he get the job?"

"Paul and Jameson are different. Paul is one of my best employees. Jameson is too. But Jameson is a fighter. He had something to prove from the beginning. Paul? He's a simple man. I don't mean he's not smart enough to run the ranch. I mean he wouldn't have wanted the job. He likes what he does, and he's told me so. He gets up early, runs with his dog, takes guests on pack rides, helps out when he's needed, and never makes a fuss."

Ava grinned. "Sounds like you know what you're doing."

"Yeah, that's one decision I'm pretty sure about. Also, Paul isn't looking to settle down with a wife one day."

Ava's head jerked up. Was her grandpa saying Jameson was looking for a wife?

Her grandpa stretched his arms above his head. "I know which cowboys are wanderers. I know which ones are looking to settle down. And I know which ones will stick around even after they find a wife and start a family."

"Which one is Jameson?" she asked.

"The latter. I noticed you two seem to get along."

Ava chuckled. "Are you matchmaking?"

"Call it what you want. Jameson is a good one, but he leads with his heart." Her grandpa looked up with a serious expression, making sure he had her attention. "He won't be the same when you leave."

"It's not like that," Ava whispered.

Truthfully, she wanted it to be like that between them. Not heartache and longing, but she wanted the connection she felt with Jameson to be as real as it felt when she was with him.

"I might have been born at night, but it wasn't last night. I guess I see that he doesn't look at you the same way he looks at other people. There's a little hope there. That boy thinks he hasn't been enough for anybody his whole life."

"Why?" Ava quickly asked.

"He's got a long story, just like all of us."

If Jameson had a long story, she wanted to know all of it. A pang of hurt slashed through her chest when she thought of how little time she had left here. "But he *is* enough. He's a great guy."

Her grandpa held up his hands. "You don't have to convince me."

Ava looked to the east. The sky was too dark to see if the smoke still lingered.

Her grandfather cleared his throat. "I'm really not trying to matchmake. If you two like each other, I'm happy for you. But be mindful of what you intend to do when you go back to Denver."

Denver. Her grandpa hadn't called it her home, and she was thankful. When she thought of going back and facing her mother, her blood ran cold. Did that make her a coward?

"I don't want to overstep my bounds," her grandfather said as he averted his gaze.

Ava spoke softly. "You don't have to worry about what you say to me. I know we're both figuring this out."

He sighed. "I'm getting old. I've worked my whole life, and having Henry and Jameson around has allowed me to slowly slip into my old age without much of a fuss. But I won't live forever."

Ava rested her hand on his. The weathered skin was covered in age spots and the signs of a life long lived. "Are you okay? Did the doctor say anything?"

"Oh, I didn't have an appointment this morning."

She chuckled. "Jameson told me."

"That boy needs to learn to keep his mouth shut."

Ava bit her lips to hide her smile.

"What I'm saying is your mother doesn't want anything to do with me or the ranch. I don't know if she'll ever come back here. I don't know if she cares about what happens to this place when I die or not."

Ava squeezed her grandpa's hand a little tighter. "I'm sorry."

"Me too. I always hoped Wolf Creek Ranch would continue to be family owned and operated. I guess that's where you come in."

Ava's grip on her mug tightened, and she let her hand slip from her grandpa's. She and everyone else could clearly see what this place meant to him. She couldn't help but love it herself, but she hadn't thought about what came after her grandpa.

"I don't want to pressure you, but I don't know how many opportunities we'll get to talk about this. Would you ever want to be a part of this place? Not temporarily. I'm asking if you'd want to carry on here when I'm gone."

Her throat tightened, and she felt the pricking behind her eyes that signaled the coming tears. This place had felt like a temporary dream escape since she found out about its existence, but her grandpa was talking about it as if she could have a home here, a hand in everything, and a future in a place she loved.

"Something tells me I'd be happy here," she whispered.

Her grandpa continued, "That's another reason I promoted Jameson. He's still learning, but between Henry and myself, Jameson is shaping up to be just the person I want to trust with this place. I know you don't know anything about ranching and running a dude ranch, but you're smart enough to learn. Jameson can handle most everything out on the ranch, and he has a good head on his shoulders for making decisions."

"I don't know what to say. Like you said, I really don't know anything about ranching." She'd been walking around for two days feeling useless. Everyone else knew what to do, but she didn't. Could she ever learn how things work enough here that she could be in charge?

"You'd need to learn a thing or two, but your job wouldn't be in the saddle. Owning a business is more of a paper job. Well, more computers now, which I despise."

Ava's heart pounded. What should she say? "I don't know. I was working on getting a degree in business management, but I didn't finish."

"The paper doesn't matter so much as the fact that you've proven you can be taught. Between Jameson and myself, you could learn how to keep this place running. Everyone else will help too. Most everybody who works here can do their jobs in their sleep, and they can tell you what they need to keep doing what they do."

Ava blew out a shaky breath. "This is a big offer. I'm so grateful, and my initial thought is that I would love to say yes. But—"

Her grandpa interrupted. "You don't have to say anything today. Think about it."

"I only have a few days before I go back."

"And you can still do that. You don't have to decide this week or this month. But whenever you're ready to start, the position is open to you. You could live here with me in the room you're staying in now. I'll get you on the payroll and start training you. It all starts when you say when."

And there it was. Her mom had taken away her home, and her grandpa had offered her a new one. The timing was too perfect. She hadn't even worried about where she would live for a whole day.

It felt a whole lot like some of the miracles and

blessings she had read in the book her grandpa had given her today. So much so that she couldn't ignore the voice in her head telling her to be grateful.

She wiped a single tear from her eye before it fell over her cheek. "Thank you. I'll definitely let you know soon."

"Have I told you how glad I am to have you here?" he asked.

"I'm glad I'm here, even if you don't really need my help."

"I didn't say I don't need your help. If you decide to stay, I think I *will be* needing your help."

Could she be a help to anyone here? She felt comfortable in her job in Denver. She'd been doing it effortlessly for years now, but she hadn't known anything when she started. She could learn a new job, especially one as important as this.

The news reports were shocking and fleeting. One headline slipped seamlessly into the next, over and over. It was a constant barrage of blows, mostly upsetting.

Here, she could be a part of something just as big and important. These people cared about this place. The visitors came back year after year. And the workers woke up before the sun and worked till the sun had set—all with smiles on their faces. She could be a part of that, and it would be rewarding.

Ava shook her head. "Why doesn't she like this place?"

"It's hard for me to understand too, but I've always loved it here. I really don't know why she wanted to leave."

"It doesn't make sense," Ava whispered.

"We loved her. Maybe we loved her too much. Lottie wanted a house full of kids. She came from a big family, and I did too. But the Lord only gave us one, and we had to go through a lot of waiting and asking why before your mother came along."

"I didn't know that." Ava was an only child, and her mother would tell anyone who would listen that she didn't want more children. The comments always stung when Ava overheard them. Had she been a bad kid? Was it her fault?

"Your mom did. Lottie loved your mom to a fault. I think Linda always wanted to make her own way, and Lottie was kind of smothering."

Ava huffed. "Linda smothers, but not in the same way."

"We raised her in church, but she was always strong-willed. The faithful path was always too constricting for her. She wanted to do her own thing. I guess she did a good job of it. She left home and never needed us again."

But Ava had needed her grandparents, whether she realized it or not. It would have been good to have someone to balance out Linda's heavy hand. It might have been easier to understand why her mother was the way she was if there'd been someone around who knew her.

"She gave us a run for our money in her teens. We made it clear we loved her no matter what. At least, I hope we did. Looking back now, I know I should have done better for her. I was harsh, but I wanted the best for her, and I hated seeing her heading down the wrong path."

Ava couldn't look away from her grandpa, not even when he brushed a hand down his face, wiping the moisture from his eyes.

"I was too hard on her. Lottie never said as much, but I think we both knew Linda left because of me."

Ava rested her hand over her grandpa's again. She'd been so caught up in her own problems that she hadn't realized what her grandpa might have been going through.

"Now I know I didn't do anyone any favors by being so hard on her. I loved her through everything. That will never change, and I don't think she understood that. I've only been a parent once, and I messed it all up."

"I don't think anyone is perfect at it," Ava said. At least she hadn't seen a perfect parent yet.

"I ruined my chance to be a grandpa too. I've missed so much, and Lottie missed everything. It broke her heart when we found out Linda had a child and wouldn't let us visit."

The sadness that clogged Ava's throat shifted and morphed into anger. How could her mother have made a decision like that? Linda might not have wanted to see her parents, but that didn't mean she had the right to keep Ava's grandparents away from her.

"I'm sorry. I hate that she kept me away from you when I was younger. If she hadn't come back for Grandma's funeral, I'm not sure I'd even know about you now."

Her grandpa took a deep breath and sat straighter in his rocking chair. "I've learned a lot in the years she's been gone, and I hope to make better choices this time around."

"You already are. I'm happy to be here, and I'm honored you want me to be a part of this place."

"You enjoying yourself yet?" he asked, seeming to shift the conversation in a lighter direction.

"I am. Everyone has been so welcoming."

"You think you could work with Jameson if you decide to stay?" he asked.

The hope in his question had her own heart lifting. "I think so."

"You two seem to get along. I remember you spent a lot of time with him the last time you were here."

Ava smiled at the memories. Not all of them were happy. She'd been grieving for her grandmother when she met Jameson.

She'd never forget the day she met him. She'd been crying alone in the pack shed after backing out of the day's ride. Sitting alone on a horse all day with nothing but her thoughts and the stomping of horses' hooves sounded like a bad idea when she couldn't decide if she wanted to scream or cry her eyes out.

She'd given into the tears just before Jameson walked in and found her alone.

She hadn't even known his name then, and he hadn't asked for hers. He'd walked over and offered her his hand.

She'd taken it and stood, looking up at him and grasping onto the distraction from the sadness that she didn't understand. She hadn't known her grandma. Why was she so saddened to know she'd died?

But Jameson hadn't asked questions. He'd opened his arms, and she'd fallen into them. He held her while she cried all over his shirt. He didn't rush her or tell her to stop. He didn't even tell her it was going to be okay. He just held her. Somehow he'd known that was what she needed.

When she'd exhausted her tears, he'd led her to the river. He'd kept his hold on her hand until he asked, "Are you okay?"

It had meant everything to her that those were his first words. Now, she knew why. Jameson was a selfless man at his core, and he'd put her first time and time again ever since.

Finally, Ava turned to her grandpa. "Linda has a lot of bad things to say about cowboys."

"Do you believe it?" he asked.

Ava shook her head. "No."

Jameson rounded the corner of the house, and her relief was all-consuming.

No, she didn't trust her mother's judgment when it came to cowboys. At least not this one.

CHAPTER 13

JAMESON

Jameson kept his steps even as he walked around the main house. Mr. Chambers would be outside, but would Ava be with him? He couldn't decide if he hoped she was or hoped she wasn't.

One glance at the rocking chairs on the porch made up his mind. Ava stood and stepped to the railing. She was beautiful.

And he was filthy. He smelled like smoke and sweat, and he was covered in ash dust. What a contrast they made.

The soft, relieved expression on her face sealed his fate. He'd spent all day trying to push thoughts of her out of his head, but it was a lost cause. Everything about the look on her face said she was happy to see him, and he was too stupid to care that he'd get his heart smashed when she left in a few days.

"Are you okay?" she asked.

He stopped at the bottom of the porch steps and propped both hands on the railing. "I'm fine, and the fire's out."

"Good news," Mr. Chambers said.

"Hunter offered to keep an eye on things tonight."

Mr. Chambers nodded. "I appreciate that."

"I told him I'd bring him something to eat in a little while."

"I saved you a plate from supper," Ava said.

Food wasn't the way to his heart, but her consideration paved its own highway straight to the middle. He'd never wanted to kiss a woman as much as he wanted to right now.

Except her grandpa might not like the show.

And she was leaving in a few days. Probably for good. He'd been struggling with the sense of keeping his distance and the eagerness to soak up as much of their time left together as possible.

"Thanks. I'm starving."

"I'll be right back." Ava turned and darted inside.

Seconds later, Henry stepped out onto the back porch and eyed Mr. Chambers. "I should have known I'd find you here."

"I'm doing my job," Mr. Chambers growled.

"You do a good imitation of a knot on a log."

Mr. Chambers humphed and stood. "Don't you have some packing or something to do?"

"All done," Henry said. "I heard about the fire and came to check on things."

"We can handle things around here without you. Why don't you get going?" Mr. Chambers barked.

"You mean the young ones can handle it?" Henry asked.

Jameson rubbed his temples. "Will you two stop bickering? I have a headache."

"The smoke'll do that to you," Henry said without the cranky tone he'd used on his best friend.

Jameson had worn a respirator all day, but the smoke clung to his clothes and hair.

Mr. Chambers held up his empty mug to Henry. "Let's go have a cup."

"Is that—"

"It's decaf, you old coot!" Mr. Chambers shouted.

Henry shrugged. "I'll take a cup. And did I see pie in the kitchen?"

"Stella brought that by earlier. Jameson, you want some?"

Ava stepped out onto the porch holding two plates with two bottles of water tucked under one arm.

Jameson tried to smile, but he was tired down to the bone. "Nah. I think I'm good. I'll catch up with you tomorrow about the meetings."

When Jameson and Ava were alone on the porch,

she handed one of the plates to him. "Do you want to eat inside?"

"I smell pretty bad. I'd rather not stink up the house."

He'd thought she'd smile at his comment, but her expression stayed slack.

"Hey, you okay? Did something happen today?" He glanced at the second plate she held. "Did you not eat supper?"

"No. Everything was fine. I was just worried about you."

Jameson sat on the top step and rested his hat on the porch railing. "Nobody got hurt. We all know how to handle things like this, and we got to it early."

Ava sat beside him. "I'm not used to emergencies like that."

Jameson stared at his plate, remembering Ava's questions about the Bible verse in his office earlier. He said a prayer of thanks before every meal, and he hadn't expected Ava to tell him she didn't pray or know God.

Mr. Chambers poured his faith into everything at Wolf Creek. It had never occurred to Jameson that Ava might not be a Christian. "I'd like to say grace."

"Go ahead." She tucked her chin and closed her eyes.

Did she know why he prayed? She'd said she didn't

know much about her grandpa's faith, but how little did she know? Her reverence when he prayed told him she was tolerant, but would she seek the Lord?

He had so many questions, but his exhaustion jumbled them in his thoughts. He'd think more about it tomorrow. Maybe she'd go to church with him on Sunday.

When he finished the prayer, he nudged her knee with his. "I wish I could have called you, but I don't think I have your number."

She frowned. "I thought you did. We texted for a few weeks after I left."

"You stopped replying, so I assumed you got a new number or something."

Ava's eyes widened. "I replied to all your messages."

Jameson chewed the big bite he'd just put in his mouth. What was she getting at? He took a big gulp of water before responding. "I sent about five messages that you didn't respond to before I stopped trying."

Ava shook her head. "I didn't get them."

He held out his hand, realizing too late that it was almost black. He probably should have washed his hands before eating. "Let me see your phone. I'll add my number."

She handed over the sleek phone, and he pulled up the contacts. Sure enough, she had his number, but the status listed it as blocked. He held up the phone to show her the screen.

She gasped. "It's blocked? How? I didn't do that."

He handed the phone back to her. "You get one guess."

Ava's eyes narrowed. "Linda."

Jameson turned his attention back to the plate of food. "She was serious about keeping us apart."

"I knew that, but I had no idea she'd blocked your number from my phone." Ava's pitch rose. "She crossed so many lines."

He hated seeing Ava upset. It ripped and clawed at his insides, making the little bit of food he'd eaten unsettled in his stomach. "Is she still talking about kicking you out?" he asked, his voice low as if someone might overhear. She probably didn't want to announce it to the world that her mom was giving her room away to someone else.

"She asked Brianna to move in."

Jameson's jaw ached as his teeth ground against each other. He wasn't supposed to hate anyone, but he hadn't heard a single good word about Linda Collins.

"Did she take Linda up on the offer?"

"I don't know. Brianna probably wouldn't if she knew why my mother offered it to her, but Brianna doesn't like her roommate. She's probably jumping for joy right now."

"Let's not worry until we're sure," he said.

Ava rested her head on his shoulder. "Thanks for keeping me grounded. It would be easy to let the worry gnaw at me all the time."

Jameson wrapped his arm around her shoulder. "What did you do today?"

"Hung out with Grandpa mostly. We talked to Everly and Stella for a while. I like them."

Jameson lifted his arm from her shoulders. "Yeah, they're good to have in your corner."

"I started reading a book Grandpa gave me." She stood, cradling her plate in one hand and reached for the book. The green hardcover was worn, and the gilded title was faded.

"Women of the Bible," he read. "What do you think about it so far?"

"It's good. Grandpa said he had some more about the Bible if I was interested."

Jameson took the book from her and turned it on its side. He pointed to the old bookmark that was closer to the end than the beginning. "Is this where you got to today?"

"Yeah, I couldn't put it down. It kept my mind off worrying about you."

"If it makes you feel any better, I was thinking about you too."

Ava leaned back and looked at him. "Even while you were fighting a fire and saving the ranch?" she asked.

"Even then."

Ava looked down at her plate and grinned.

He put the book down beside him. "Are you planning to read more?" he asked.

She set her plate to the side and propped her elbows on her knees. "I'd like to. I told Grandpa how Linda feels about religion and that I wanted to learn. He was upset. Really upset. But I think he was happy that I wanted to know more."

Jameson scratched at the scruff on his face where the dirt and ash made his skin itch. He hated to be sitting here having an important conversation with Ava while covered in ash. "I'm glad you're reading. Actually, I bet most people around here would be happy to answer questions if you had any, myself included."

"Thanks. I have a feeling I'll have a lot."

He sucked in a deep breath, but the smoke tickled his lungs, making him cough.

Ava rested a hand on his back. "Are you okay?"

"Yeah. I usually wear more gear when there's a fire. And I change my clothes as soon as I can."

"Do you need to go?" she asked.

"Not right this second. I wanted to see you first."

She smiled. "I'll be here after you get cleaned up."

"I have to get back to work. I missed a whole day, which might set me off for the next few days." He rubbed the back of his neck, feeling the dirt scrape his skin. "I can't go on the pack ride tomorrow."

"I figured you'd say that. It's okay."

He'd been rearranging his schedule in his head for the last hour. He could make time to see Ava this week. He *would* make time. He worked long hours, but he would find a way to be with her while they still had time.

"You could still go if you want. Paul will be there, and I think you'd have fun. The scenery is beautiful."

Ava tucked her hands between her knees. She was smiling, and he held onto the hope that he hadn't run her off yet.

"I'll probably hang around here. I have some things I need to talk to Grandpa about."

"Right. I'm sure you two have tons of catching up to do." He looked up and thought about his schedule. "The rodeo is tomorrow evening. Want to go?"

"Of course. Stella said it's always fun."

He cleared his throat, deciding it was time to bite the bullet. "Sunday morning is church. Would you like to go?"

He didn't want to pressure her, but he had a few good reasons why he wanted her to say yes. Some were selfish, like how he wanted to spend time with her. Others were genuine, like how he prayed she'd open her heart to the Lord.

That last one was important. He'd always imagined his future role as a husband to be alongside a God-fearing woman, and that wasn't something he planned to compromise.

Not that she'd agreed to even be his girlfriend. Marriage was so far from the casual line they were toeing this week.

"I'd love to."

He felt the tension in his shoulders relax with her words. Then the exhaustion gripped him harder, demanding the rest his body and mind needed.

"I don't want to pressure you. That's what Linda did. She forced her beliefs on you, or actually, her lack of beliefs. But I'm here if you ever want to talk about it."

"I appreciate that. I appreciate a lot that you've already done for me, and I'm glad Grandpa has had you to help take care of things here while he's recovering."

Jameson lifted her hand from where it rested on her knee and laid her palm against his. They were night and day, just like his dirt-covered hand against her smooth, delicate skin. There were a million reasons it shouldn't work between them, but he couldn't shake that instinct to do everything he could for her. If her mother would turn her away, Jameson intended to be there to help her.

"Listen, I've been thinking about what Linda did today. I'm staying in one of the wranglers' cabins, and I'm the only one who isn't paired up with a roommate. Ridge and Blake, some of the other men who work here, have a house not too far from here. I'm sure they'd let me move in if you wanted my place."

He'd also thought about the room she was staying in right now at the main house, but that wasn't his place to offer her. Neither was the larger foreman's cabin that Stella and Vera shared. He hadn't needed that much space, and the two friends made better use of it.

Jameson looked up from their hands to find Ava smiling at him, and it made him want to freeze time. He wanted to capture that happiness and keep it forever.

"It's not much, and I don't know if you'd be okay leaving your job. I can ask my sister and some friends around town about any job openings. Between your grandpa and me, we'll make sure you have everything you need. I promise."

Ava laughed. It was a mixture of a nervous chuckle and a happy, bubbling laugh. The more she laughed, the more his own smile grew. She laughed until tears formed at the corners of her eyes, and she wiped them away.

She didn't speak at first, and Jameson hung on every second, every heartbeat.

Was she going to say yes? What did that mean?

She stood, and Jameson got to his feet beside her.

She wiped the tears again. "Jameson Ford, that sounded a lot like a proposal. You're not obligated to take care of me."

He grabbed her hand, and his grin didn't waver. "I know that. It wasn't a proposal, but I do mean it."

She rested a hand on his shoulder and slid it up his neck. The heat in her touch rivaled the wildfire he'd fought to contain all day.

"You're so good to me." She tugged on his shoulder, pulling him down so she could wrap her arms around his neck.

"I want to be," he whispered.

She looked up at him, and there wasn't a hint of worry in her expression. "I don't think you need to move out just yet."

He tried to control his reaction, but he had no idea what to make of her comment. Was he moving too fast? Was there anything he could say to make her stay? Did she think he was manipulating her into staying the way her mother would?

"Okay, but the offer stands," he said as he stepped out of their embrace.

"Trust me. It'll work out."

The confidence in her voice was new, and he wasn't sure if the things that were going to work out were going to be in his favor or not.

All he could do was pray and hope. The rest was up to Ava.

CHAPTER 14

JAMESON

"Jameson!" the barista yelled.

Jameson nudged his way past the other customers waiting for their orders at Sticky Sweets. He loved the food and drinks—everyone did. That meant fighting the crowd during the busy morning hours.

Tracy handed over the tray with his and Felicity's orders on it. "Here you go. Tell Felicity I'll come chat when things slow down."

Jameson chuckled. "Yes, ma'am." They both knew the crowd wasn't going to die down.

He held the tray high as he moved back through the crowd. Business was booming for Sticky Sweets, and rightfully so. It was the best bakery in Blackwater.

Jameson doled out his and his sister's orders on

the small table near the far wall. "You really like the pumpkin spice thing?" he asked.

"It's really good." She held up a silencing finger. "One joke about how basic I am will get you the silent treatment for the rest of the morning."

Jameson chuckled. "I don't think anyone has ever made the mistake of thinking you're basic."

His sister straightened her shoulders. "Don't forget it."

He wouldn't.

She bowed her head. "Pray."

Jameson asked a blessing for their food, then grabbed the greasy Texas bacon, egg, and cheese sandwich on his plate. "Did Hunter make it back this morning?"

Felicity swallowed the bite she'd been chewing. "He got in around five this morning and crashed."

"I really appreciate him watching the fire."

Felicity waved a hand. "He didn't mind. How's Mr. Chambers doing?"

Jameson huffed. "Nothing slows him down. He's still into everything. Henry leaves tomorrow."

Felicity's eyes widened. "You're kidding. He's really leaving. I thought you were going to have to beat him off with a stick."

"I thought so too, but Mr. Chambers' grand-daughter came to visit so Henry would feel like Mr. Chambers had someone around in case he needed anything."

Felicity leaned to the side and frowned at something behind him. "That woman is looking at us. Do you know her?"

Jameson turned and saw Ava standing at the counter. Her gaze darted to him and back to Tracy standing behind the register.

"That's her," Jameson said as he swiped a napkin over his face and stood. He almost knocked the chair over as it scraped across the tile floor.

"Who?" Felicity asked.

Jameson was already halfway across the bakery when he heard the question. He'd explain after he talked to Ava.

Her whole face was a deep red by the time he reached her, and she didn't look up at him. She'd seen him coming. He knew it.

"Hey, what are you doing here?" he asked.

"Um, just picking up some apple fritters for Grandpa. Stella said he likes them."

"Loves them."

Ava rubbed her thumb up and down the leather strap of her purse, and she didn't raise her chin as she said, "I didn't know you'd be here."

Jameson jerked a thumb over his shoulder to the table where Felicity waited. "I talked to my sister yesterday after the fire. Her husband volunteered to be the night watch, and she wanted to have breakfast."

Ava cut her eyes toward Felicity. "Oh, your sister."

Jameson frowned. "You thought I was here with a date?" Great. The last thing he needed was for Ava to think he was a two-timer.

Ava slowly raised one shoulder. "I don't know. I just didn't expect to see you here. I didn't know she was your sister."

Jameson brushed a finger against the side of her hand. "I'm not dating anyone." He couldn't even entertain the thought when Ava was here, even if he couldn't have her. A small spark of hope was enough to keep that dream alive.

Ava sucked in a deep breath. "Me either."

Jameson grinned and leaned closer to whisper in her ear. The noise of the people around them made it difficult to have a serious conversation in public. "I know."

He hadn't questioned whether or not Ava had a boyfriend. She was loyal to the core—something he'd learned during her last visit to the ranch. She wouldn't have flirted with him and let him have that impossible hope these last few days if she'd been seeing someone.

Tracy yelled, "Ava!"

Ava reached for the bag. "Thank you."

Jameson jerked his chin toward the back of the bakery. "Do you have time to meet my sister?"

Ava cast a glance that way. "I don't know. She doesn't look too happy about you talking to me."

"It's not you. She's mad because I jumped up so fast."

"Oh, well. All right."

Jameson took Ava's hand as they weaved around the tables. It felt good to have her hand in his. That simple link turned that spark of hope into a kindling, despite his better judgment.

"Felicity, this is Ava. Ava, this is my sister."

Felicity stood and held out a hand. "It's nice to meet you. How do you know Jameson?"

"My grandpa is the owner of Wolf Creek Ranch."

Felicity's eyes widened. "Mr. Chambers? I didn't know he had a—. Wait. Have you been here before?"

"A few years ago," Ava said.

"I remember Jameson mentioning you." Felicity slapped a hand against her forehead. "And he just mentioned Mr. Chambers' granddaughter was in town. I should have put two and two together." Felicity's eyes sparkled. "I remember now."

Jameson was afraid to know what his sister remembered him saying about Ava. He'd been head over heels for Ava the last time she'd visited, so he'd probably spilled all those beans to his sister. The look of mischief in Felicity's eyes said she remembered something juicy.

Felicity pointed to a chair. "Sit with us."

"I wish I could." Ava held up the bag. "I'm

meeting my grandpa back at the ranch to talk about some things."

To talk about some things? That made it sound more like a meeting than casual quality time with her grandpa.

"I bet that old man has some stories to tell," Felicity said.

Ava nodded. "He sure does. He's teaching me so much about the ranch."

All the tension Ava had carried a moment ago was gone now that she knew he wasn't out with some other woman and his sister was easy to talk to. Jameson started to relax too. It was nice seeing Ava and Felicity together. His sister was a strong woman who didn't let anyone push her around. He'd noticed a fire in Ava's eyes last night when they talked about her mother. Maybe she was getting close to standing up for herself.

"You should come out to Blackwater Ranch sometime. Jameson used to work there. It's as beautiful as Wolf Creek."

"I wish I could, but I'm leaving in a few days."

There was that familiar spike of heartache. Jameson hated that looming date.

"Oh, where are you from?" Felicity asked.

"Denver. That's where I live with my mother."

Ava's face lost its color the moment she realized what she'd said. She didn't live with her mother anymore, since Linda spitefully evicted her.

"That's not too far," Felicity said. "Get with me next time you visit, and we can hang out."

"I'd love to." Ava gestured toward the door. "I need to get going, but it was nice to meet you."

"I'll walk you out," Jameson said.

"Bye." Felicity waved. "Hope to see you again soon."

When they were outside on the sidewalk, the street noise didn't seem as stifling as the people noise inside.

Jameson leaned against the brick wall outside the bakery. "I'm glad you got to meet Felicity."

Ava smiled, clearly relieved that the meeting had gone well. "Me too. She seems nice."

"She is. I wish you had time to see Blackwater Ranch. There are some women there you'd get along great with."

Her smile grew. "Maybe I will one day."

One day. He wished so bad that those words were a promise.

"Are we still on for the rodeo tonight?" he asked.

"I wouldn't miss it." She was clearly happy now, and he hoped that same eager smile greeted him after work this evening.

He stepped forward and leaned in. "Maybe we could leave early and go to the creek?"

Ava raised her chin and scooted an inch closer. "I'd love to."

Jameson's heart rate spiked and his breaths grew

deeper. She smelled like vanilla, and he gave in to the urge to reach for her. When his fingertips brushed her hair behind her ear, she leaned into his hand.

They both wanted this. Why couldn't it work?

"I'll see you soon," he whispered.

"See you soon," she said smiling.

Jameson took a step back, sure that if he didn't leave now, he would stand here with her all day. "Have fun."

"You too." Ava backed away too, but they were both reluctant to leave.

What was he doing? This was as crazy as going back and forth on a phone call over who would hang up first, but he couldn't make himself turn around and walk away from her.

That idea seemed to apply to all matters of his life that included Ava Collins.

When he walked back inside, Felicity was giving him a look that said he had a lot of explaining to do. He sat down and hoped to avoid the interrogation.

"So, is that really her?" Felicity asked.

He wouldn't be spared the questions, it seemed. "That's her."

"Like, that's *the* Ava you talked about years ago?"

"That's the one," Jameson said as he picked up the last of his sandwich.

"She's back, but only for a few days? That sucks."

Jameson huffed. "You don't have to tell me."

"Sorry. That stinks. She isn't interested in moving here to be a rancher's wife?"

Jameson swallowed the last bite of his sandwich and regretted eating it at all. His stomach was unsettled just thinking about Ava leaving. "Very funny."

Felicity reached across the table to shove Jameson's shoulder. "You okay? I was just joking. Is it that serious?"

Jameson pressed his lips into a line and nodded.

"Oh, I really am sorry. What are you going to do?"

"Not much I can do. She's here to see her grandpa, not settle down with a cowboy."

Felicity hung her head. "No chance of her staying?"

Ava was leaving just like last time. Ticking time was a broken record where Ava was concerned.

"I don't think so. I don't blame her, I guess. This life isn't for everyone."

It hadn't been Ava's mother's cup of tea, but Ava seemed to love it here. Was that enough to make her stay?

"Don't start," Felicity said.

"Start what?"

"Thinking it's because you're not good enough. That's dumb."

"That's not what I'm doing."

"Isn't it? I know you."

Jameson gathered up their trash and stood. "Thanks for the psych evaluation, but I can handle it."

Felicity stood and laid a halting hand on his shoulder. "You'll find someone one day. Everything changes when you're part of a whole with someone else. I want that for you."

His sister was happy in her marriage. She'd found someone who matched her perfectly. The two were made for each other, and Jameson was happy for them. It also triggered the urge to seek out that happiness for himself, and he was beginning to wonder if family life was meant for him.

CHAPTER 15

AVA

Ava stretched her arms above her head and yawned. She'd sat with her grandpa in his office and talked about everything from maintenance to damage waivers to income reports. When the lunch bell rang, her grandpa opted to eat leftovers while she ate in the dining hall with Everly.

When she found her grandpa's note in the kitchen saying he was taking a nap after lunch, she picked up the book Stella had given her and curled up on the couch until she'd finished it. Now Ava wanted to talk to her friend about it before the rodeo.

Ava stood, but the first step landed her on the floor with a thud. The hard wood jarred every bone in her arms as she caught herself.

"Oww."

Stella burst into the living room and gasped.

"Ava!"

"I'm fine," Ava said quickly. "My foot fell asleep while I was reading."

Stella crouched to help Ava to her feet. "Don't scare me like that. Your grandpa has been a fall risk for years now, and I'm always worried I'll come in one day to find him collapsed on the floor."

Ava pushed up onto her knees, then her feet. "Should someone be living with him? Is it bad?"

"No," Stella said. "I just worry. He'd never allow a live-in caretaker."

Ava limped to the couch and sat to rub her tingling foot. "I'm glad he has you to look after him."

"That man's been good to me."

"You take good care of him. I know he appreciates the food you bring."

Stella waved her hand. "Vera makes most of it. I just deliver."

Ava picked up the book. "I was actually coming to find you."

"You finished?" Stella asked.

"I did. It was..." Ava looked at the ceiling, searching for the right words. "It was inspiring."

"I'm glad you enjoyed it. My quilting circle read it together last year, and when you said you wanted to learn more about being a Christian, I knew this was the one. It's educational, but it's also interesting and easy to understand."

"It was perfect. It answered a lot of my questions." Ava handed the book to Stella. "Did you say quilting circle?"

"I did. Do you sew?"

Ava chuckled. "I don't. I also don't think I've ever known someone who sews or makes quilts."

Stella patted Ava's knee. "Now you do. Your Grandma Lottie got me started quilting about eight years ago."

Ava perked up at the mention of her grandmother. "Really?"

"She loved sewing anything she could get her hands on." Stella pointed to the quilt rumpled beside Ava on the couch. "She hand stitched that one not long after I met her."

Ava pulled the quilt close. It was still warm from when she'd been wrapped in it while she read. The muted gray and hunter green was contrasted with a deep red in the octagonal sections. "It's beautiful."

"I always loved that one. It reminds me of Christmas." Stella looked around. "Where's your grandpa?"

"I think he's still napping."

Stella checked her watch. "We have time. I want to show you something."

Ava stood and followed Stella up the stairs. Ava had been searching for every little thing in the house that might have a touch of her grandmother. The photos were her favorite. They were everywhere. Now that she knew the quilt was made by her grandmother, she'd be sneaking it up to her bedroom tonight.

Stella stopped at the top of the stairs. "Are you still in the Frontier Room?"

"Yes," Ava said.

Stella walked into the room and straight to the cedar chest at the foot of the bed.

"This was one of Lottie's chests. She kept the unfinished quilt tops in this one and the finished ones in the chest in the other room."

Stella opened the lid, revealing the pile of stitched fabric layered inside. Every color pieced together, touching and contrasting as they fought for her attention.

"There are so many," Ava said in awe.

"That's not the half of it. I have another chest at my house. Before she died, she told me I could have them to work on and teach the others."

"The others?" Ava asked.

"It's a group of ladies from the church. They come over on Tuesday evenings."

"Tuesday." The day Ava would be leaving for Denver.

"You're welcome to join us. I think Lottie would have loved that."

Ava stared down at the quilt tops. "I can't this trip, but maybe when I come back."

Stella knelt in front of the chest and didn't question whether Ava truly meant to come back or not.

She would have told the truth that she was planning to take her grandpa up on his offer to stay here for good. No one had asked yet, and her excitement over the decision threatened to bubble over more each hour.

Stella rummaged in the chest until she found one and held it up. "This one." She handed it to Ava. It was mostly dark red and purple, but patches of beige broke up the deeper hues.

"Lottie told me she started this one with your mother."

Ava's eyes widened. "My mother? Are you sure?" It was so unexpected. She studied the stitching. It looked just as good as the others.

Stella nodded. "Lottie asked me not to finish it."

Ava laid the fabric in her lap. "Why?"

"She was waiting for your mom to come back."

All the air left Ava's lungs in a rush. "My mom isn't coming back. Ever." She rubbed the fabric between her fingers. "Grandma never got her daughter back," Ava whispered.

Stella wrapped an arm around Ava's shoulders, and she leaned into the hug. Pulling the quilt top closer, Ava felt a cold tear slide down her cheek.

"Hush now," Stella said. "Lottie missed her daughter dearly, but she knew how to appreciate what she still had. She died a happy woman."

A chuckle bubbled up in Ava's chest. "How can someone die happy?" she asked.

"I know it sounds silly, but she was. She loved every day of her life. She followed the Lord. She gave the best of herself to anyone and everyone who needed her. She was a good woman to her bones. Genes are a powerful thing. I see so much of her in you."

"How?" Ava whispered. It was a rhetorical question. There wasn't an answer, but she'd been wanting so much of her grandma for years now, and to know she carried a piece of Lottie with her everywhere was comforting and confusing at the same time.

"You'll do just fine here," Stella said as she released the hug and stood.

Ava wiped her cheek and rose to her feet. "How do you know?"

"You have a look of determination that reminds me of Lottie. It wasn't always easy being a rancher's wife. She told me stories. But I knew one thing: She made up her mind that she'd do it, and she did."

Ava's insides warmed, and she smiled. She could run this ranch. She could learn from Grandpa and build a life here. It would take years, but right now, she wanted every second of that time to be spent here.

"Ava?" Jameson's muffled voice came from downstairs.

Stella wrapped Ava in a quick, tight hug. "That's your date. It's rodeo time."

CHAPTER 16
JAMESON

The screams of the small crowd filled the night as Jameson threw his hands in the air. He could rope a calf in his sleep, but these folks acted like he'd just scored the winning goal.

The dust settled, and he waved at the kids lining the gates. They jumped and squealed as he walked back to the chute. Jameson reached through the barrier and high fived a dozen of them.

Brett slapped Jameson's shoulder as he walked out of the cages. "Dude, they love you."

Jameson shook his head. "They don't know what they're missing tonight." Brett was usually the grand finale, but his ankle was still giving him fits. Jameson had agreed to fill in at the last minute only because Ava seemed excited to see him out there. She'd practically pushed him off the bleachers.

"Get on back to your date," Brett said. "Colt can take care of the rest."

Jameson handed over the lasso. "See you in the morning. Don't call me tonight."

"Wouldn't dream of it. Give her a kiss for me," Brett said.

Jameson walked away while his friend made kissy noises.

The night was pitch black outside the circle of lights directed at the arena, and Jameson squinted as he searched for Ava. Her dark hair would blend in, but she'd been wearing a cream sweater.

He spotted her by the announcer's booth talking to Everly. Ava turned to him before he'd had a second to appreciate her carefree smile as she chatted with her friend, but her eyes grew brighter when she saw him coming. He'd never get used to seeing her like this.

She said good-bye to Everly and jogged to meet him halfway. He picked up his own pace and opened his arms. Ava crashed into him, wrapping her arms around his neck as he lifted her feet off the ground and twirled.

When he set her feet on the ground, he kept his face buried in her hair. She didn't let go, and he didn't want to either.

"You ready to go?" he asked.

"Let's go."

When Jameson released her, he threaded his

fingers with hers. There weren't any lights between the arena and Wolf Creek, so he headed for the truck. He focused on the feel of her palm against his as they walked. He wanted to memorize this feeling. It might be gone too soon.

In the truck, the noise of the rodeo silenced, leaving room to breathe in their moment alone.

"Did you like the rodeo?" he asked.

"So much fun." Ava giggled. "I've never been to a rodeo before."

"This is small, but it's always hilarious."

Ava laid her hand on his arm. "Those kids riding the sheep!"

Oh, he wouldn't be forgetting that anytime soon. Ava had laughed until tears streamed from the edges of her eyes.

Ava leaned over the console and whispered, "I had the best time."

"I did too. We do this every Friday night, as long as it doesn't snow or get too cold."

She laid her head on his shoulder. "I guess that'll be happening soon."

"Yeah, things really slow down around here in the winter."

Ava let out a deep breath. "I talked to Everly tonight. About church."

Jameson tried not to react. "What about it?"

"I didn't bring any nice clothes, but she said she

thinks I could borrow something of Remi's. We're probably the same size."

Jameson laid a hand on Ava's knee and squeezed. "You're really planning on going?"

She nodded. "I've been doing a lot of reading."

"That's good. You've got a herd of people here if you ever want to talk, but church is the best place to learn."

"I'm nervous. But it's like an excited kind of nervous."

"Don't worry. You'll know half the people there. On a serious note, you might want to check the pockets on anything Remi gives you. She spends all day with kids, and I've seen her pull some strange things out of her pockets." There was a reason Remi was the children's activities coordinator at the ranch. She was full of surprises, and the kids loved it.

Ava laughed. "Noted."

He parked at the picnic area by the creek and killed the diesel engine. They were far enough away from the arena that the rodeo noise couldn't reach them, and the half moon only gave off a dim light that reflected off the creek.

Ava reached for the door, and light filled the cab.

"Ava."

She looked back at him, her hand still on the door handle.

What had he been about to say? All he wanted

was to pause and enjoy more of this with her, but their time was running out. He wanted more. He wanted all of her.

When she looked at him the way she was now, he couldn't just let her walk away again. Everything clicked into place. Ava saw him, even if his own parents hadn't. She recognized him and the scars on his heart that matched hers. She acknowledged him for who he was as a man in ways no one else ever had in his life.

He didn't know how they were going to sort anything out, but he would do everything in his power to be with her.

"Let me get your door."

It wasn't what he'd wanted to say, but the words were still tumbling around in his brain. He opened her door and she held his hand as she stepped out of the truck and the darkness closed in around them.

She wrapped her coat tighter around her as they reached the creek bank. "I forgot how bright the stars are here."

As far as Jameson knew, the last time she'd been out here was the night before her mother had dragged her away crying. The memory had every muscle in his body tensing.

Ava squeezed his hand. "Hey, you okay?"

Jameson halted, and Ava stopped with him. "I don't think I can be okay right now. I've known from the moment you got here that you'd be leaving, but that didn't change how I feel about you." He scrubbed a hand over his face. "This is harder than I ever expected."

Ava stepped into his arms, and he held her tight. The thought of not seeing her every day ripped him in half. He'd known it then, and he knew it now. She was the one for him.

Jameson leaned back and cupped Ava's face in his hands. "I feel like I got a second chance. I'm grateful for every second of time we've had together."

He leaned closer and rested his forehead against hers. Closing his eyes, he wished everything was different. He could be with Ava, and she would be happy to choose him. He'd never been anyone's first choice, but now he wanted that when he couldn't have it.

"This might be the last chance I get to kiss you, and I'd like to take it."

Ava's nod was small, but it was there. He pressed his lips to hers, and the contact instantly took his breath away. He inhaled, hungrily filling his lungs with the air between them. Her soft lips brushed against his in tantalizing movements until his fingers and toes tingled. He threaded his hands in her thick hair as she pulled him closer.

Why couldn't this be their beginning? A real beginning without an expiration date?

Why couldn't he keep her?

When they broke the kiss, Jameson wasn't sure which way was up. His world was turning upside down, but he could right it—if she would stay.

Ava gasped for short breaths as she stared up at him. Her face was in shadow, and he'd never wanted a shred of light more in his life than right now.

Jameson forced each muscle in his body to relax. One by one, they released their tension so he could say what he needed to say. "I let you go before, but this time, I can't let you go without a fight. I would do anything to have you here with me."

Why hadn't he planned this big talk for a time when he could read her expressions? "Ava, I need to know. Is this what you want? Or is it that?" He pointed off into the distance, not caring that Denver might be in the other direction. "Because I want you."

Ava pushed up onto her toes and pressed her lips to his again. Their second kiss was as amazing as the first, but it was slow and sure in a way that drove him crazy. What was she doing to him?

When she pulled away, her chin tilted up so high that moonlight cast a dim glow over her face. Her smile was full of joy and relief.

"I'm staying," she whispered.

"You are?" There was no sweet whisper in Jameson's reaction. Nothing could contain his excitement. "Really?" he asked.

"I am. Well, I have to go back to Denver to work

out my two-week notice and pack up my things, but I'm coming back."

"For good?" he asked.

"For good."

He crushed her body to his and buried his nose in her hair. She was staying.

After holding each other for what seemed like an hour, she pulled away and wiped her face. "I have so much to tell you."

He placed a hand on the small of her back and led her to a large bench facing the water. "We've got time. Tell me everything."

"Grandpa told me a few days ago he'd like to start training me to run the ranch. He said he wanted things to stay the same around here, and he knew I could do it."

"You can. I know it," Jameson quickly added.

Ava chuckled. "Thanks for your confidence in me. I think I can do it too, but I have a lot to learn."

"I'll help."

She smiled and threaded her hand with his. "That's part of the plan too. You know I never got my degree. I was so close to finishing. I looked into it, and I can do it online. From here."

"That's great." Jameson took a deep breath, still trying to process everything. "Why didn't you tell me you were planning all this?"

"I wanted to make sure I knew enough to make the right decision. I want to get away from my mother, but I didn't want to make this decision because of her. I wanted to make it because it was right for me." She squeezed his hand. "You're right for me. This place is right for me."

"That's the truth if I ever heard it," he whispered.

Ava rested her head on his shoulder. "I'm still worried about how she'll react."

"Don't worry about her. We can handle whatever she throws at us."

Ava hummed. "Us?"

"Us," Jameson said.

"My grandpa said something about you the other day."

"Uh oh."

Ava chuckled low, and the vibration radiated through him. "He said you needed to prove something. That's why he trusted you to run the ranch." She lifted her head. "What do you have to prove?"

Jameson sighed. He didn't like talking about his mom any more than Ava liked talking about hers. "I told you I didn't know my dad and grandparents, but I didn't tell you about my mom."

"You don't have to tell me," Ava whispered.

"It's okay. It doesn't bother me now." It truly didn't, but it had taken years to get to that point.

"I lived with my mom for years, and she never paid any attention to me. Some days, she looked right through me."

He hadn't had a great childhood, to say the least. His flesh and blood hadn't cared about him. He'd been forced to work harder and grow up fast to help his sister.

Ava had the same childhood in a way. She'd been forced into everything and every path she'd taken in life.

Ava scooted closer. "I'm sorry. You didn't deserve that. No kid does."

"I know. That's why I know you don't deserve what Linda does to you." He cleared his throat. "My sister was nine when I was born, and my mom wasn't a good mom. Felicity was too young to be taking care of an infant, so the church ladies stepped in."

Ava sighed. "I had no idea about your mom. That was nice of them to help when you were little."

He shrugged. "Mom liked drugs and alcohol more than anything, but those women didn't hold that against me or Felicity. They even helped pay for the burial costs when Mom died. They prayed for me. They prayed *with* me. They've always been there for me. I guess what I'm trying to say is that I don't know where I'd be without them and the Lord. I can't imagine going through any of that without faith."

Ava kept her head down. "Sounds like I've been missing out on more than I thought."

He hated the sadness in her voice. Hated that

she'd faced her mother's meanness on her own her whole life.

Jameson lifted her chin with a finger, and those dark eyes looked back at him, reflecting all the hope he had inside him. "You have me now, and she can't tear you down here. You can make a life here. With me."

Ava tilted her chin higher and sealed her lips with his. They made a promise without words. They were in this together.

CHAPTER 17

JAMESON

Jameson fisted and flexed his hands as he stood in front of the back door of the main house. Ava was leaving today, and they only had a few hours before she had to head to the airport. His throat had been tight all morning, and he'd been too worked up to sleep much last night.

Everything was fine. She was leaving today, but she'd come back. It was only two weeks. They could make it through two weeks. Those thoughts had been a broken record lately.

He truly believed they could, but the fact that they hadn't made it through one week together yet was a sneaky little cloud casting a shadow over his optimism. What if her mother talked her into staying when she got back to Denver? What if her boss offered her a raise to stay?

What if he lost her and there was nothing he could do to get her back?

He pulled his phone from his pocket and texted Ava, letting her know he was waiting outside. The sun wasn't up yet, but he knew she was awake. She'd sent him a good morning text before sunrise every day for the last five days.

Sticking his phone back in his pocket, he settled on the top step of the porch to wait. He rested his arms on his knees and bowed his head. As soon as his head lowered, he was reminded of the prayers he should be saying for Ava.

Please, Lord, keep her safe as she travels today.

Please, Lord, give her strength to face the troubles waiting for her.

Please, Lord, give her confidence to guide her through this move.

And, finally, *Lord, help me to be patient. Help me to be strong and focused so I can help her when she needs me.*

He hoped she wouldn't need him, at least not in any drastic way. Her confidence was growing every day, and he knew she could face her mother on her own.

The question was, did *Ava* know that?

The door behind him creaked, and he stood in a rush. Ava stepped out with a cup of steaming coffee in each hand.

He reached for one of the cups and closed the

door behind her. "That was fast. I thought I'd be waiting longer."

Ava rose up onto her toes and pressed a lingering kiss on his lips. Her vanilla scent mixed with the cold air, tingling in his nose.

When she broke the kiss, her eyes remained closed for a few seconds. "I wouldn't make you wait out here in the cold alone."

His smile faded on that last word. Alone. They'd both be alone in just a few short hours.

Ava cupped her hand around his chin. "No, no. None of that."

"What?"

She stared up at him with a look of determination. "I'm going to need you to stop thinking about being apart and start remembering that we're together. We're together now, and we'll still be together tomorrow. And the next day. And the next day. Until I get back."

He wrapped an arm around her and kissed the top of her head. "I know. Thanks for the reminder though. I'm just nervous."

"Don't be nervous," she whispered against his chest.

"Easier said than done. I'm going to miss you. A lot."

She lifted her head and smiled up at him. "And then we'll be together again like this in just a few weeks. I'm just kind of thinking past the time in Denver and looking forward to more of this."

His smile returned, and he pressed her closer against him, basking in her warmth and optimism. "You're right. I promise not to waste the time we have left today being a stick in the mud."

She grabbed his hand and stepped toward the edge of the porch. "Good. Now, let's go watch the horses come home."

J ameson stepped into the check-in office and narrowed his eyes at Everly. "What are you still doing here?"

"Ridge is my ride, and he's running late. He got caught up at the rodeo. I thought I'd hang around here and wait for him."

Jameson rapped his knuckles against the desk as he walked past toward his office. "Let me know if you need anything."

"Hey, wait," Everly said.

"Yeah."

"How's Ava?"

Jameson shrugged. "She seems to be doing okay." She really did. They talked a few times a day, and she always seemed happy.

"Good. I've been getting texts from her, but it's

hard to read beyond the words when I can't hear her voice."

"I know what you mean. Being away from her has been tough."

Everly tilted her head and crooned, "Aww. You two are the cutest."

Jameson pressed his lips together. "Don't tell anyone I said this, but I hope that never changes."

Everly waved a hand in the air. "It won't. I know a good match when I see it. The two of you are made for each other."

Shaking his head, Jameson turned back toward his office. "Night, Everly."

"Night, boss."

He settled into the dozens of emails and got lost in his inbox. An hour later, he still had seven unread messages to respond to.

He pressed the heels of his hands into his eyes. The pang of a headache was throbbing just out of reach, and he needed something to help him push through the last bit of work he had for the evening.

Picking up his flannel coat, he stalked down the hallway and out of the dark check-in office. Mr. Chambers would have coffee, and he hoped the old man had cheated and skipped the decaf.

Jameson jogged to the main house, and as soon as Jameson closed the front door, Mr. Chambers yelled.

"In the kitchen!"

Jameson kept his coat on and headed toward the voice. "How'd you know it was me?"

Mr. Chambers sat at the small kitchen table with the newspaper spread out in front of him. "Henry is gone, and Stella and Vera are sewing something. Plus, you're the only one wandering around like a lost puppy these days."

Jameson reached for a mug from the cabinet. "Am not."

"Are too," Mr. Chambers mocked. "Have you talked to her today?"

"Twice. She said everything is packed up except the things she needs to get ready to go to work the next few days."

"Good. Sit," Mr. Chambers ordered as he lifted his mug to his lips.

Jameson filled his cup and fell into the chair beside his boss. "Any good news?"

Picking up the paper, Mr. Chambers read, "It's festival season, local lawyer was disbarred, a new bookstore is opening downtown. The usual."

"How you feeling?" Jameson always asked the question because his boss wouldn't tell him anything if he didn't.

"Doc said I'm a free man."

"Really? Like, no follow-ups?"

"Yep. It feels good."

"Ava will be happy to hear that."

Mr. Chambers stood and took his empty cup to the sink. "She's coming back, son."

"I know. I just miss her."

"I do too." Mr. Chambers looked down and nodded. "I know what that feels like. To be fair, I didn't have to miss my Lottie until the end. I don't think we spent a night apart in all the years we were together."

"Okay, you win. I'm thankful I don't have to miss Ava forever."

Mr. Chambers rested a hand on Jameson's shoulder. "If Ava is anything like her grandma, she'll find her place and plant her roots. Lottie was the most steadfast and loyal person I ever met, and it made loving her a high honor."

Jameson rapped his knuckles on the wooden table. "Thanks, old man."

Mr. Chambers cleared his throat. "Now, since Ava's father is gone, I believe the intentions talk falls to me."

Jameson looked up and laughed. "You're kidding."

"Nope. I've been waiting my whole life to do this. Don't take it from me."

"Got it. Carry on."

Crossing his arms over his chest, Mr. Chambers steeled his features into a stern expression. "What are your intentions with my Ava?"

Jameson lifted his cup. "To eventually make her my Ava."

Mr. Chambers' scowl didn't waver.

"I know she's the one," Jameson said.

"It's been two and a half weeks."

"I don't care. Ava is the only one for me."

Mr. Chambers pursed his lips, but a grin was fighting to break free. "I asked my Lottie to marry me when we were fourteen."

Jameson choked on his coffee and coughed hard. "You old rascal."

"She didn't marry me until we were sixteen."

Jameson slapped his hand on the table. "Sixteen? That's insane."

"Insane or smart. I got sixty years with her."

Resting his back against the chair, Jameson breathed, "Wow. That's a long time."

"Wouldn't trade a second of it," Mr. Chambers said.

Jameson had been counting down the hours until Ava came back, but he was looking forward to counting the days they had ahead of them. Sixty years sounded like a good record to beat.

CHAPTER 18
AVA

A long shadow fell over the valley as Ava drove toward the main house. The sky was a dark purple in the last minutes of daylight, but the thin clouds promised snow soon. She'd opened the car window an inch when she hit Blackwater, and the icy air was fresh and welcoming.

This was her new home, and she wanted to soak up everything about it.

A few of the main house windows glowed, but the dining hall shined as bright as daylight. Everyone would be finishing up the last meal of the day and getting ready to either crowd into the dance hall or around the fire.

The silhouette of a man stood on the front porch, and she slowed to park near him. She'd know Jameson by his stance any day. He leaned on the railing, ready and waiting for her return.

Linda had made sure Ava's last weeks in Denver were as miserable as possible, but she'd been able to endure it with the knowledge she'd be rid of the drama soon. She'd been brave enough to tell her mother to back off, and even if Linda didn't, Ava felt the satisfaction of standing up for herself.

She parked in front of the main house and jumped out of the car. Jameson was already jogging down the porch steps, and she ran straight into his arms.

Ava breathed a sigh of relief as she relaxed in his embrace. This was where she was meant to be—her new home.

"I missed you," Jameson said.

"I missed you too. You have no idea."

Jameson chuckled. "I think I do."

She lifted her head. "Where's Grandpa?"

"Inside. I'll get your bags while you catch up with him."

She pecked a kiss on his cheek. "I'll be right back to help."

The main house was warm inside, but she didn't stop to take her coat off. "Grandpa?"

He stepped around the corner from the living room with his arms open. "Welcome home."

Her heart did a funny pitter-patter at his words. "I'm glad to be home. You doing okay?"

"Good as gold. You have a safe trip?"

"I did. I've only flown here, but the drive was gorgeous."

"Good. Let me get my shoes on and I'll help you bring your stuff in."

Ava opened her mouth to protest, but she remembered what Stella had said about Grandpa's independence. "Thanks. Jameson is helping too."

Ava and her grandpa passed Jameson on their way out. His arms were loaded with boxes.

"All of it upstairs?" Jameson asked.

"Yes, please."

Could grandpa walk up the stairs, much less carry boxes? She worried for nothing because he managed fine.

"You seem to be doing great. What does your doctor say?" Ava asked.

"Fit as a fiddle," Grandpa said. "Or something like that. He says I'm fine."

Over the next quarter of an hour, the three hauled boxes up the stairs and piled them near the southern window.

"Is that everything?" Jameson asked.

Ava held her arms out. "That's all. I did some downsizing."

She'd done more than a little. She'd gotten rid of almost everything she owned in the last two weeks. She sold most of her wardrobe to Brianna, and she hadn't needed any of the furniture. This was a new beginning as well as a cleansing. She wanted everything to be new and untarnished by her old life.

Jameson looked at his watch. "Have you eaten?"

"No. You?" Ava asked.

"Nah. I was waiting for you."

Her grandpa waved. "Well, you two head on over to the dining hall."

"Are you coming?" Jameson asked.

"I already had my supper. It's coffee time."

Ava wrapped her arms around her grandpa. "How could I forget?"

Her grandpa patted her back and headed for the door. "See you two later. Don't stay out too late."

"We won't," Ava and Jameson said in unison.

When her grandpa was out of sight, Ava turned to Jameson and bounced on her toes. "I can't believe it!"

His smile was a country mile wide as he watched her jump for joy. "Me either."

She slid her arms around his waist, and he held her close. "I don't think I've ever been this happy. Thank you."

Jameson's gaze dipped to her lips. "Me either."

She tilted her chin up and didn't have to wait for his welcoming kiss. The warmth in her chest burned hot and uncontrollable until her whole body was consumed with the heat. Jameson held her strong and steady as he kissed her hungrily and adoringly.

It was overwhelming, but she didn't want to pull away.

When he finally broke their kiss, they were both breathless.

Jameson looked around the room. "As much as I'd love to keep kissing in your bedroom, I think your grandpa will meet me downstairs for the intentions talk if we don't go soon."

Ava laughed and covered her mouth. "We're not being scandalous are we?" she asked playfully.

"I'm afraid we are. There will be talk all over town tomorrow."

Ava swatted his chest and grabbed his hand. "They'll have us married off on grounds of compromise."

Jameson lifted her hand and kissed her knuckles. "I wouldn't fight it."

Ava rolled her eyes and grinned as he pulled her into the hallway. "You didn't have to wait on me to eat."

"Yes, I did. Most of the crowd will be cleared out. We can go dancing after if you want."

"It just so happens dancing is on my bucket list."

Jameson stopped at the top of the stairs. "You mean you haven't been dancing before?"

Ava shook her head.

"Never been line dancing?" he asked.

"No. No dancing at all."

Jameson winked and gestured for her to lead the

way down the stairs. "We can fix that."

When Jameson was called away to help with a foaling, Remi quickly stepped in and offered to teach Ava some basic dance moves. The children's activities coordinator had a knack for teaching with patience, and Ava's feet were moving in no time.

The rhythm pulsed in Ava's veins as she nailed every step Remi had taught her. Turns out, line dancing wasn't hard. It was choreographed and freeing at the same time.

"Get it, girl!" Remi shouted above the music. Her friendly smile and auburn hair radiated in the dance hall lights.

Ava laughed as she missed a step. "Thanks for teaching me."

Remi waved a hand. "I teach the kids every Tuesday night. Anyone can do it."

Two of the wranglers, Colt and Brett, played song after song as the crowd kept dancing. Ava couldn't wait to show Jameson what she'd learned. She hadn't stopped smiling since Remi dragged her to the dance floor.

Everyone was panting by the time the music stopped, but no one seemed ready to leave.

Ava huffed a tired breath. "My cheeks hurt from

smiling so much."

Remi threw her head back and laughed. "You gotta get those muscles in shape. I'll be your trainer."

"I bet you will," Ava said.

Remi locked her arm with Ava's and headed toward the drink stand. They propped their elbows on the cold wooden bar to wait their turn. Stella and Everly dodged each other behind the counter as they filled cups with soda and water left and right.

"I'm glad we met later in life," Ava said as she fanned her face.

Remi pulled her long hair into a high ponytail. "Why's that?"

"I don't think my parents would have let me play with you."

"Ha! A few years ago, you'd have been right. I'm safe now." Remi winked and rapped her knuckles on the bar.

Ava caught sight of Jameson and waved him over.

"Did I miss all the fun?" he asked before pressing a kiss to her cheek.

Ava rubbed her hands together. "Remi taught me how to line dance."

Jameson laughed. "I should have known she'd wrangle you in. That woman has more energy in a day than I've ever had in my life."

Remi playfully punched his shoulder, and

Jameson turned around. "Oh, hey. I didn't see you there."

"I know. You only have eyes for Ava."

Ava felt her cheeks warm at the comment. "Did everything go okay?" she asked Jameson.

"All taken care of."

Stella slapped a hand on the counter beside them. "What can I get for you?"

"Water for me," Remi said.

"I'll have the same," Ava added.

Jameson held up a hand. "Nothing for me. Thanks."

Stella returned with their drinks, and Remi chugged the glass of water. "I need to get some things set up for tomorrow before Colt's next set starts." She waved at the musician, who promptly made his way across the dance hall toward her.

"Thanks for the lessons," Ava said.

"Anytime!" Remi shouted as she followed Colt out the back door of the dance hall.

Brett sat on a stool in the corner of the big room and began singing a slow country song.

Jameson tilted his head toward the dance floor. "May I have this dance?"

Ava placed her hand in his as he offered it to her. "I'd love that."

Under the dim lights and surrounded by the slow croon of a country song, Ava rested her head on Jameson's chest. "I've had fun tonight."

"Sorry I couldn't be here for it, but I'm glad Remi kept you entertained."

"What's it like having a job that's demanding and also fun like this?" Ava asked.

"It's more than I could have asked for. I saw my mom struggle to keep every job she had, and I thought it would always be an uphill battle. Somehow, I fell in with some good people around here, and I've never had a job I didn't like or had to fight to keep."

"I'm glad," Ava whispered, so low he shouldn't have heard her.

"Having you here is more than I could have asked for, too." He tightened his hold around her waist. "I never thought I'd be happy like this."

Ava lifted her head from his shoulder and smiled up at him. "Me either."

Jameson groaned and reached for the phone in his pocket. "Sorry. Let me see if this is important."

He didn't let go of Ava as he talked to the person on the phone. He said "Okay" and "Yes," but not much else. When he ended the call, he kissed the top of her head. "I have to run to the stables, but I'll be right back. This shouldn't take ten minutes."

"I'll go with you," Ava said.

"Or you could stay with me," Remi said as she popped up behind Ava. "I can teach you some more dances."

Jameson tilted his head toward Remi. "Stay and have fun if you want. I'll hurry."

Ava shrugged. "If you say so."

"Be right back," Jameson promised. He kissed Ava's forehead and headed toward the door.

"Whew. He's got it bad," Remi said when Jameson was out of sight.

Ava laughed. "Is that a bad thing?"

"Not at all. He needs a good woman beside him. I'm happy for the two of you."

"Thanks," Ava said, thankful to have made another friend here.

Remi clapped her hands together. "Let's start with the 'Boot Scootin' Boogie.'"

Ava laughed. "You just made that up!"

"I did not. It's a classic," Remi said as she tugged Ava to a corner where they could practice.

Apparently, Remi had been telling the truth about the 'Boot Scootin' Boogie' because there were real steps to learn. After a few run-throughs, Ava had the heel-touches down pat.

"Lookin' good," Remi said. "I'm going to run to the restroom. Be right back."

"Take your time," Ava said as she plopped down in one of the chairs lining the walls. She checked her watch. Jameson had only been gone a few minutes, but she was starting to wish she'd just gone with him to the stables.

"Hey."

Ava looked up and recognized the wrangler she'd bumped into on her first day at the ranch. "Hey. Dane, right?"

"Yeah. We met a few weeks ago. I heard you're back for good." He sat down in the chair beside her.

She'd been unsure about Dane before, but he seemed friendly tonight. His sandy-blonde hair was cut shorter and cleaner, giving him less of a ragged look. "That's right."

"Where are you from?" he asked.

"Denver."

"Oh, I'd pick this place over Denver any day. Good choice."

"I thought so too. How long have you been here?" she asked.

"I came from Houston about a year ago."

"Wow. Far from home," Ava said. It was nice talking to someone who'd moved here. Everyone else seemed to have been here for ages.

"Nah. That's not home. I guess nowhere is home. I like a change every few years."

That was something to keep in mind. Did her grandpa know they'd need to replace Dane soon? "Oh, what brought you here?"

Dane tilted his head as if trying to decide how to answer. "Some old family ties."

Ava rested her elbows on her knees, relaxing a little. "Same."

"Yeah. I didn't know Mr. Chambers had a granddaughter until you showed up. I heard someone's trying to buy the place. You know anything about that?"

Ava straightened, sure she'd misheard. "What?"

"I heard Old Man Chambers got an offer on the ranch. A big one. I like it here, but changing bosses sounds like something I'd rather miss. It may be time to move on sooner than later. Just wondering if you could shed some light on the rumor."

Ava's pulse pounded in her ears, muffling the music and chattering mixed in. "That's the first I've heard of it."

She'd just gotten here. Her grandpa wouldn't invite her here just to sell the place, right? Surely there was more to the story. Maybe it was just a rumor. The ranch wasn't up for sale, was it?

"That's good news, I guess. He'd have told you," Dane said.

No, no, no. There couldn't be a real offer on the ranch. At least not one her grandpa would entertain. He loved this place.

But everyone had a price, right? What was this place worth?

Ava barely noticed when Jameson returned.

"Hey, everything okay?" he asked.

Dane stood, completely unruffled by the revelation he'd just dropped on Ava. "Oh, yeah. I just hadn't had a chance to welcome Ava to the ranch yet."

He hadn't actually welcomed her. He'd made small talk and potentially turned her world upside down.

She looked up at Jameson, and he quirked a brow. "Ava?"

Jameson was picking up on her reaction. It wasn't too hard to do. She felt sick to her stomach, and her face was probably as white as a ghost.

"Yeah." She swallowed before turning to Dane. "Nice talking to you."

Great. She couldn't even use complete sentences, and she was starting to sweat.

Thankfully, Dane lifted a finger in a half-wave and said, "See you later."

Jameson stepped closer to her and asked, "Are you okay?"

"I am, but can we go?" She wanted to talk to her grandpa. He would put her worries to rest.

"Sure. Come on." Jameson grabbed her hand and started toward the door.

Ava tugged on his arm. "I need to tell Remi I'm leaving."

"You can text her when we get outside."

Deciding that was a good plan, Ava followed Jameson around the room and out the front door of the dance hall. When the doors closed behind them, the sound of the music muffled, but the laughter at the fire pit nearby reminded her that they still weren't alone.

"Let's get you back to the house."

Ava didn't argue. She sent a quick text to Remi and didn't speak as they walked through the dark. This part of the ranch was bustling at night. Guests crowded to the fire pit and dance hall when the sun went down, and everyone was having a good time.

She'd been having a good time too, just minutes ago. Her worries were ridiculous. Dane didn't know what he was talking about, and she'd let a rumor ruin the rest of her night with Jameson.

When they stepped up onto the back porch at the main house, Jameson whispered, "Want to tell me what spooked you back there?"

"Just something Dane said. Have you heard about Grandpa getting an offer on the ranch? Is it silly to worry about something like that?"

Jameson's frown was even darker in the shadows. "No. I hadn't heard that. I wouldn't worry over it though. I don't think he'd sell."

"It's not even on the market, right?" she asked, desperate for some validation.

"It's not." Jameson wrapped his arms around her. "It's not."

"Okay. I panicked for nothing."

"You could just ask him. He's always been upfront with me. I think he would tell you, especially if he's training you to take over."

"Right. I think he'd tell me. Maybe he didn't because there's nothing to tell. He wouldn't sell

Wolf Creek." The more she said it, the more she was inclined to believe the words.

Jameson leaned back and wrapped his hands around her upper arms. "Don't worry. Just be upfront if you want to know. But don't hold onto anything Dane says. How would he know about an offer anyway?"

"Right. You're right," Ava repeated.

Jameson wrapped his arms around her again. "Nothing is going to jeopardize what you have here. You'll be happy here, and you don't need to worry."

"Thanks. I should trust that." Ava sighed.

Jameson leaned down, nuzzling against her hair. "Don't be afraid of him. He's an honest man."

Jameson was right. She didn't have to tiptoe around her grandpa like she did with Linda. "I don't know if I could have done any of this without you."

"You did it all yourself. You can do anything."

"But you believed in me," Ava whispered.

Jameson leaned in, sealing their lips in a powerful kiss that defined what she'd been saying. He was a rock standing beside her through everything. His words were blocks, building her higher and higher.

And his kiss? He was adoring her without words and writing his name on her heart with every slow, seeking movement against her lips.

When the kiss ended, she rested her cheek against his chest. She'd been worried about losing her connection to this place, but that fear was unwarranted. As much as she was coming to love the ranch, the possibility of losing the friendships she'd made here frightened her more.

Love wasn't something she claimed to understand, but the spark of recognition was kindling in her heart with each passing moment. Her grandpa openly claimed his love for her, Jameson was her constant support, and the women of the ranch had adopted her as their friend without judgment. They'd quickly led her to the Lord, who claimed her as His daughter should she accept Him.

And she had. There had always been a void within her, and she knew now what had been missing. Or rather, who had been missing. With God in her heart, how could she not know love?

Heat grew within her, despite the cold night air. She loved Jameson, but she hadn't gathered the courage to claim her feelings.

Jameson kissed her forehead. "Good night. I'll see you in the morning."

Ava smiled. "It's my first official day of work."

"You'll do great. I know it. You're a rock star."

Ava chuckled as she stepped back toward the door. She wasn't a rock star, but she felt braver and stronger than she ever had before. "Good night."

CHAPTER 19
JAMESON

Ava pointed to a ravine and gasped. "That is gorgeous!"

Thunder Creek Trail was one of the shortest, but it also had some of the best scenery, which made it perfect for Ava's first trail ride. Well, her first ride since she'd been back at Wolf Creek Ranch for good.

Evergreens clung by their roots to the edges of the cliffs, while the colorful cottonwoods and birch trees dotted the distance. Wolf Creek snaked its way down the mountainside, always near the trail their horses followed toward the peak.

"You've said that about a dozen times," Jameson joked.

Ava turned in her saddle to face him. "And I'll probably say it a dozen more. This is gorgeous!"

Jess laughed from her horse behind Ava's. "Let

her say it. I know I'll never get bored with this view. It's been too long since I've seen it."

Jameson could agree. He didn't go on trail rides much anymore, and it had been a couple of years since he'd been on an overnight pack ride, but the beauty of the range still left him in awe.

"I'm glad you came today," Ava said over her shoulder to Jess.

"Me too. I love the stables, but I needed to get out. I just hope Brett hasn't burned the place to the ground by the time I get back."

"He'll be fine," Jameson said. At least he thought Brett could manage. The guy did seem to attract the worst luck.

"I think this is my favorite trail. Or maybe Lonesome Trail. They're probably tied for first place."

"Which one is Lonesome?" Ava asked.

"The longest trail," Jameson said. "It's a four-day, four-night trip."

Ava's eyes widened. "Wow. That sounds fun and intimidating at the same time."

Jess sighed and rubbed her horse's mane. "But there's nothing better than being out here with your friends."

Jameson, Ava, and Jess were bringing up the rear of the train with only a couple of pack mules behind them, but he watched for Ava's reaction when they entered the clearing where they'd stop for lunch. Frost had killed any remaining grass, and brown leaves made an almost perfect circle around the opening in the trees. Of all the rest stops on all the trails, this one was his favorite.

"This is gorgeous!" Ava shouted.

Even the guests laughed at Ava's innocent delight. It had taken every bit of Jameson's willpower not to pull her horse closer to his so he could kiss that smile she'd been wearing all day.

The group was small since the season was almost over, and that made today's trip perfect for Ava's education. She'd spent the last three weeks in Mr. Chambers' office or visiting the ranch's local vendors, but her grandpa wanted her to know more about what guests got to experience. He'd all but pushed her out the door this morning when she tried to protest.

Ava had been working hard, and Jameson couldn't be prouder. She'd slipped into her new role at the ranch with confidence and determination. He couldn't have done it better himself.

Once everyone had dismounted, Lincoln, Jess, and Paul led the horses to a nearby grazing pasture while Jameson and Ava started preparing the meal. Lincoln and Jess liked to mess around whenever they got together, but Paul would keep them in line.

"Wow. This is a lot of food to bring out here," Ava said as she pulled out the portable grill.

Jameson took it from her and started assembling it. "You work up an appetite on long rides. Plus, this is nothing compared to the amount of food we have to bring for the larger groups."

Ava stood with her hands on her hips. "Tell me what to do."

Jameson chuckled. "I thought you were the boss."

Ava swatted his chest. "Stop it. I can't learn if you don't teach me."

"I know. I know. You don't have to learn this part. You'll be around the main house most of the time."

"No, but I need to know about this stuff too. How can I ever be a good leader if I don't learn everything I can?"

"Have I told you how much I appreciate you taking the time to learn this stuff? Not all people would care."

Ava frowned. "I definitely care, and I want to do my best here."

Her words were strangely familiar. He'd told Mr. Chambers something similar during his job interview. "You're doing great. Now, it's time to relax and have a good meal."

Jameson couldn't keep his eyes off Ava the rest of the afternoon. He rarely got to spend this much time with her during the day, and he intended to soak up every minute they had together. She laughed with Jess and brushed her hand over Thane's thick fur while they talked.

Winter was coming. The guests would leave, but the work wouldn't end. His time with Ava would be cut to early mornings and late evenings.

Not that he minded the idea of cuddling up with Ava by the fire. In fact, he was looking forward to it.

After the meal, Jameson, Ava, and Paul took the dishes to the river to wash off and pack up, while Jess and Lincoln led songs around the small fire for the guests.

Jameson and Ava crouched by the creek and rinsed dishes. When they were fairly clean, they handed them to Paul to dry and pack. Thane lay close to the ground on the bank next to Paul and lapped at the running water. The forest was quiet, except the bubbling of the creek and the wind rustling what few leaves remained on the trees.

Ava passed a plate to Paul and asked, "How long have you been here?"

Paul's brows drew closer together as he thought. "I guess about twenty-seven years or so."

"Where are you from?" she asked.

Jameson knew the answers to many of the questions she asked Paul, but it was nice watching Ava open herself up to someone else at the ranch. She'd been eager to get to know all the workers, and Jameson imagined they appreciated her efforts.

"I guess I'm originally from Amarillo, but I've been here so long I think this might be the last place I call home."

"How did you end up here?"

Paul shrugged. "I don't remember. I moved around a lot for a few years when I was younger, and I guess I came through here, got this job, and decided I liked it."

"That's good, right?" Ava asked, clearly happy with his answer.

"As good as I could've ever hoped for."

"You like it here?" It was a question, but she said it as if it were a statement.

"I do," Paul said as he packed up the last of the dishes.

Ava stepped closer to Paul and wiped her hands on a drying rag. "How did you know my mother?"

Jameson busied himself with the packs, trying to give Ava and Paul a chance to talk, but his own curiosity burned. He'd been wondering the same thing since Paul's comment about Linda when Ava first came to Wolf Creek, and Jameson was glad Ava had mustered the courage to ask.

"I knew of her. We didn't talk much, but she was around here and there back then."

Ava twisted the rag in her hands. "What was she like?"

Paul lifted his hat and scratched his head. "She was young. I don't remember much. It was a long time ago."

"I know. I just thought I'd like to hear something

about her from someone who knew her when she was here."

"How is she doing?" Paul asked.

Jameson halted. Paul was talking about Linda Collins like she wasn't a snake most people wanted to stomp beneath their boots. Had Paul and Linda been together, or was it just a one-sided crush?

"She's okay, I guess. She's a news anchor in Denver."

Paul nodded. "That sounds about right. I recall she liked attention."

Jameson cleared his throat. Liked attention was an understatement. This was Linda's world, and everyone else just lived in it, as far as she was concerned.

"Yeah, she worked at a smaller station when my dad was still alive, but we moved into the city when she got the new job. She likes it, I think."

"I'm sorry to hear about your dad."

Ava didn't talk much about her dad, but when she did, she only had good things to say about him. Jameson wasn't sure how a man that Ava respected could have put up with Linda, but maybe she *had* been different before. Paul didn't seem to think she'd been all that bad when she was young.

"Thanks. I miss him a lot."

Jameson sighed. He could hear the silent ending of that sentence—that Ava didn't miss her mother, and that had to be a disappointing revelation.

Paul grabbed the bags, hefting them over his shoulder. "You settling in okay?"

"I am. It gets better and better every day," Ava said.

"What did you do back in Denver?"

"I worked at the news station with my mother. I was an assistant."

"That had to be interesting. I can't imagine working with my parents."

"Do they live around here?" Ava asked.

"Nah, my folks are long gone."

Jameson walked back to the group a few paces behind Paul and Ava. He'd known Paul was a lone wolf in more ways than one, but he'd never asked about the older man's parents. Maybe that was the reason Thane always stayed so close. They were a tight-knit pair.

"I'm sorry to hear that," Ava said softly.

Paul shrugged. "It's been a long time."

Ava stopped and turned from left to right. "I think I left my water bottle at the creek."

"I'll go back and get it," Jameson said. Everyone at the ranch made a point never to leave trash or anything on the trails.

"I'll walk with you," Ava said. "I could use the exercise."

Jameson handed Paul his pack. "We'll be right back."

When Paul and Thane headed toward the clearing, Jameson took Ava's hand in his and turned back toward the creek. They didn't speak until they reached the bank and Ava found her bottle.

When she lingered, Jameson wrapped his arms around her. "Is it still hard to talk about her?"

"She hasn't called me once since I left," Ava said.

Jameson's blood heated with his anger. Linda continued to hurt Ava, and Jameson hated the pain in her eyes.

Composing his thoughts to something that wasn't hateful took some time. "I hope she has a change of heart."

"Me too. It just doesn't seem likely."

Jameson buried his face in her hair, and his words felt thick in his throat. "You have people who love you here."

Ava backed out of his embrace and looked up at him, but her surprised expression quickly shifted to fear as her foot slipped over a rock, sending her falling backward toward the rushing creek.

CHAPTER 20
AVA

All the air whooshed out of Ava's lungs just before she hit the freezing water. The creek was shallow but still deep enough that her whole body submerged.

Pain shot through her right elbow, radiating up her arm in an instant. She gasped at the shock, filling her empty lungs with water. There wasn't up or down, just weightlessness.

Her body jerked, hard. She was rushing through the water, and then she was bursting into the air in the same second. Her chest burned, and she wanted to vomit.

Jameson yelled as he pulled her from the water. She'd been standing right in front of him, but she'd fallen so fast he hadn't been able to catch her before she hit the water.

"Breathe, Ava!"

She did, but the gulp of air hurt on the way down and then back up again as she retched the cold water. The coughs were punctuated by gasps. Jameson knelt beside her, ready to jump into action if she couldn't get the air she needed.

When the coughs started to dwindle, the tears came. They were hot against her freezing cheeks. A second later, Jameson was holding her against his chest, drying them with his thick flannel shirt.

He didn't hold her for long before he stood, pulling her to her feet. "We have to go. You need to get back to the main house. Now."

She stumbled behind him as he nearly dragged her up the slight incline to the clearing where everyone else waited. After only a few steps, he turned and swung her into his arms.

"I'm okay," she croaked. If he heard the heavy rasp in her voice, he knew as well as she did that she wasn't okay.

"Just hang on," he said, determined and focused on climbing the hill like he was trained to carry injured people to safety.

Then she recalled his firefighter and paramedic training. Of course, he knew what to do. Even if he hadn't been certified in keeping calm and managing traumatic injuries, she felt safe in his arms.

Jameson burst into the clearing and ran faster on the flat ground. Ava lifted her head from his shoulder and saw two men and Thane running toward them. It had to be Paul and Lincoln.

"She fell in. I'm taking her back," Jameson yelled.

"Lincoln, get the horses," Jess said as she scrambled to her feet.

"I'll get the emergency blanket. You need to get the wet clothes off of her," Paul said.

Jameson sat her on a nearby boulder. "Ava, did you hear what he said? We need to get these clothes off."

Every inch of her body shook as his warmth left her, and she hoped he could see she was nodding.

Jameson lifted her arms and removed her sweater. She hadn't realized how heavy it was until the weight lifted. She wore a thin camisole under it, and despite her arms being exposed to the frigid air, she didn't feel any colder.

"I think we can leave that on. I need to get your jeans off," Jameson said.

"I'll help," Jess said.

The others had moved away to give Ava some privacy, and she stood on shaky legs to remove her pants. "I'm wearing leggings," she breathed.

"Whew!" Jess said. "I think you can leave those on."

Ava wanted to sigh in relief, but her breaths were still shallow and shaky. If she wasn't so cold, her face would be burning hot taking her clothes off in the middle of the woods with other people around.

"Hold onto me," Jess said as she pulled Ava's jeans over her feet. "Don't worry. We'll get you warm in a second."

"Get her over there by the fire," Jameson said. "Paul is getting the emergency blanket."

Ava hobbled to the fire just as Paul raced up with a thick blanket in his arms.

Jameson wrapped it tightly around her and lifted her into his arms. "We need to go."

A second later, Lincoln returned with the horses, and Jameson hoisted her onto the saddle before taking his place behind her.

"I'll be right behind you," Paul said.

Ava gripped the horn of the saddle, but she couldn't feel her fingers. Fear mixed with the stinging pain. "Jameson."

"I know. We'll be there in no time," he said with confidence.

She leaned into his warmth, and he wrapped his arm around her. "I've got you."

She was thankful for his strength when her bones started to feel like ice. Soon, her hands slipped from their hold on the horn, and her head fell back against his chest.

He'd been telling the truth when he'd told her they would be back at the main house in no time. In her frozen state, she wasn't sure how time worked anymore, but she felt the jolt when the horse jerked to a halt.

Jameson pulled her from the saddle straight into his arms and bolted up the porch steps. "Mr. Chambers!"

Her grandpa's voice was muffled. "In the living room!"

Jameson's boots thudded loudly on the wooden floor. Ava could feel the last shreds of her energy seeping out of her body.

When he stepped into the living room, Jameson halted. Ava lifted her head from his shoulder and saw her mother standing in the middle of the room beside her grandpa. Was she hallucinating, or was her mother really here?

Linda's short, pretentious laugh twisted Ava's heart. Yes, her mother was really here. In her navy suit coat and pencil skirt, she looked out of place in the rustic ranch house.

"You've got to be kidding me," Linda said.

Jameson took a deep breath and ignored Linda's comment. "Where is Stella?"

"At her place," her grandpa said. "What happened?"

"Ava fell in the creek. Call Stella and ask her to come help."

Grandpa rushed out of the room. "I'll get her here as fast as I can."

Linda crossed her arms over her chest. "Fell in a creek. How ridiculous."

"It won't be ridiculous when she gets hypothermia," Jameson growled. "Do you care at all?"

"I do care!" she shouted. "I'll help her. Put her down, and I'll take it from here."

Jameson took a step back. "Not a chance."

"You'd let her freeze before giving her to the care of her mother?" she asked.

Jameson called to her grandpa over his shoulder. "I'm taking her upstairs." He took the stairs two at a time in a matter of seconds.

Ava pressed her cheek to Jameson's chest and closed her eyes. Maybe if she fell asleep this would all end up being some terrible nightmare.

Linda shouted from behind them, "Who do you think you are?"

"It's okay. I'm not leaving you," he whispered in Ava's ear, ignoring her mother's sharp tone.

He pushed open the bedroom door with his elbow and went straight for the bathroom. Slowly, he sat Ava on the closed toilet and started the water in the bathtub.

Linda stormed into the tiny bathroom with her hands on her hips. "What are you doing?"

Jameson rounded on her. "Saving her life! What are *you* doing besides yelling at everyone?"

Ava wanted to cry, wanted to scream. She wanted to do something, but she couldn't force her body to work. The shaking was uncontrollable now, and each breath was harder to draw than the last.

"What was she even doing by a creek?" Linda snapped.

Jameson crouched in front of Ava, and he must have read the confusion on her face. She couldn't keep up with what was going on. Her thoughts were slow and disoriented.

"You can get in with your clothes on for now. When Stella gets here, I'll get you some dry clothes."

Ava nodded. At least, she thought she did.

"Let's get you in. I'll hold you steady," he said.

The water was scalding, and she cried out at the searing pain.

"It's not hot. Just warm. You're just so cold. It'll get better soon."

The tears came again, but they were silent. A steady stream flowed down her face and fell into the tub.

Jameson looked over his shoulder at Linda. "Can you get some blankets?"

"Where?"

"The hall closet."

Linda left silently, and Jameson whispered assurances in Ava's ear as she lowered her body into the water. She couldn't focus on what he was saying, but she was thankful he was beside her. She didn't have the energy to deal with her mother right now, and she appreciated how he'd stood up for her.

Stella rushed into the bathroom. "I'm here."

Jameson stood and stepped back to make room for Stella to kneel next to the bathtub.

"What is she doing?" Linda spat.

Jameson posted himself between Linda and Ava. "She's helping."

Linda scoffed. "I can help."

"I think you've done enough helping," Stella barked. "Both of you get out of here."

Ava couldn't see her mother's face, but she heard the stomping of her heels as she left the bathroom.

Jameson leaned over Stella. "I'm getting some warm clothes."

"I'll get her out of these. Maybe make a pot of coffee. She'll need something to warm her insides too."

"I'll be right outside," Jameson promised.

Ava mouthed, "Thank you."

He lingered in the doorway, clearly worried. Ava wasn't sure if he was worried about her or having to face Linda again.

"Those two need to learn to shut up," Stella said.

"Yeah," Ava whispered, unsure what to think about her mother's unannounced visit. Well, to her it was unannounced. Her grandpa might have known about it. She didn't want to doubt whether he was being open and honest with her again after she'd made the decision to trust him.

"Hey," Stella said. "Don't fret. You told me about

your mother, and I know you're worried about her being here. Whatever happens, I'll be right here beside you. Jameson and Ronald too."

Stella's use of Ava's grandpa's first name made her smile. The two were close and looked out for each other. "Thanks. I really appreciate your help."

"I can't wait to hear how you ended up in this mess," Stella said.

"It's not a very interesting story. I fell in the creek."

"Save your energy. Let's get these clothes off you."

CHAPTER 21

AVA

An hour later, Ava was dry and dressed in warm layers. "Thanks again."

Stella waved her hand in the air. "No need to thank me. I'll be here whenever you need me. Lickety-split."

"I know." Ava wrapped her friend in a hug. She might never find the words to tell Stella how much she appreciated that unfaltering support, but Ava intended to give back to her friend every chance she got.

A knock sounded at the door before Linda asked, "Will you open this door now?"

Stella snickered. "I think we should leave her out there a little longer."

Ava stifled a laugh. "I'd love to, but I hate to do that to Jameson." She knew if Linda was posted outside the door Stella had locked, Jameson would be right there with her.

No one here trusted Linda enough to let her out of their sight.

"Poor man. I think he's paid more than his dues tonight."

Ava had heard him arguing with Linda every so often through the bedroom door. He was mostly trying to keep her from lashing out at Stella for locking the door, but he'd taken more than one of Linda's slurs directed at himself.

Ava burned with embarrassment and anger. How dare her mother talk to Jameson like that when he'd been nothing but kind since Ava met him?

Her mother didn't know that. She'd never given Jameson a chance.

"I'm ready if you are," Ava said.

"Okay, you grab her arms, and I'll tie her up."

Ava did laugh then, but the sound was hoarse. "I don't think I have the energy to take her down right now."

"You don't even have to go out. You can just go to bed," Stella said.

"I could, but I want that coffee you promised. And I'd like to see Grandpa. He looked worried earlier."

"I bet he's been wearing a hole in the floor pacing down there. Let's go."

Stella opened the door, and Ava prepared to step

out first. Her mother and Jameson were squaring off in the hallway, and they both turned.

Linda's expression was one Ava hadn't seen before. Her jaw was tight, but her eyes weren't as angry as she'd expected. Before anyone had a chance to speak, Linda wrapped Ava in a hug.

The hallway fell silent, and Ava returned the hug. There had been a time when Ava and her mother had been close, and not in the same way as now. Linda had helped Ava through the struggles of high school and encouraged her through the first few months when she dropped out of college and started working at the news station.

Ava caught Jameson's eye over her mother's shoulder, but she couldn't read his expression either. He looked tired and a little confused.

"Are you okay?" Linda asked.

Ava pulled back and nodded. "Just tired now. I'd really like some coffee."

Jameson jerked his head toward the stairs. "It's ready and waiting."

The four of them walked down the stairs in silence. Ava wasn't sure what to make of her mother's change of heart. She and her mother hadn't hugged in a long time, but maybe there was hope for them yet. They might not ever be close again, but maybe Linda was here to patch things up.

"I'll get things ready in the kitchen," Stella said. "Tell Ronald I'm making him a cup too."

Linda stopped and looked around. "None for me. I need to be going."

Stella humphed and turned toward the kitchen.

Ava laid a hand on her mother's arm. "At least say bye to Grandpa."

Linda turned her attention to the door, then looked back at Ava.

Please show me you care. Please don't turn this into another letdown. Ava prayed. She was learning to pray in the moment the way Stella had taught her. So far, she'd done a lot of talking and hoping God was listening. She wasn't sure how He liked to talk back, but maybe that would come later.

"Okay, but I need to get going. I haven't checked into my hotel yet."

Ava gave Jameson a quick look. There weren't many hotels in town. Hopefully, Linda had reserved a room. If she hadn't, maybe she'd come back and stay at the ranch. If she gave this place a chance, she would love it.

Ava led the way to the living room. She could hear Grandpa talking, probably with someone who'd heard about the creek incident.

When Ava stepped into the living room, Paul and her grandpa stood.

Linda halted behind Ava, and the room fell silent.

Her grandpa looked her up and down, looking for any sign of harm.

Paul was looking at her mother like he'd seen a ghost.

Ava turned to Jameson and confirmed he was seeing the same silent reactions. As if having her grandpa and her mother in the same room wasn't weird enough, Paul was thrown into the mix, making the already existing mud murkier.

Her grandpa stepped over to her. "Are you all right?"

"I'm fine. Just tired," Ava said.

"Get some rest," he offered.

"I will. I'd like a cup of coffee first. Stella said she's making one for you too."

"Have all the coffee you want."

Linda took a step back, and her heel clicked against the floor. "I need to be going. I'll stop by tomorrow afternoon."

Ava desperately wanted to know what her mother wanted to talk about, but she also wanted to crawl into bed and sleep for two days straight. She also wanted to hang onto this version of her mother who wasn't frowning and pushing her agenda.

"Come by whenever," Grandpa said.

Linda turned for the door, and Ava glanced at each person left in the room. Jameson looked confused, Paul looked horrified, and her grandpa looked worried.

Ava couldn't make heads or tails of what was going on with anyone, but there hadn't been any closure tonight, and she desperately needed it. "I'll be right back."

Racing to the front of the house, Ava caught up with her mother before she'd opened the door.

"Hey, you don't have to go," Ava said.

"I do. I really have a room in town. I just came straight here. I was hoping to see you."

"I'm glad you came," Ava said, hoping her mother wouldn't make her regret the words later.

Linda frowned, but it wasn't as deep as usual. "I still think you should come back to Denver."

"I don't," Ava said. One thing was clear: She belonged at Wolf Creek Ranch.

"I'm sorry about a lot of things," Linda said. "I didn't know that until tonight. I came here furious with you, but seeing you like that—"

"Stop. I'm fine," Ava interrupted. "I'm okay, but I hate that it took something like this to get you to realize that you'd hurt me."

Linda looked down and tightened her jaw. "I don't want to hurt you. I want what's best for you."

"This is what's best for me," Ava said.

Linda sighed, looking tired and less intimidating without an airbrushed face of makeup. "I'll come back tomorrow. Get some rest."

Ava didn't want to argue. She could see they'd made as much progress as possible in one day, and she was satisfied with the step forward. "Good night."

She watched her mother walk out the door before she made her way into the kitchen. The voices stopped when she walked in.

"Coffee?" Ava asked.

Stella handed over a full mug. "Just the way you like it."

Ava sipped the warmth, aware everyone was waiting to hear her take on the events of the night.

"I have no idea why she's here," she finally said.

Stella crossed her arms over her chest. "Can we send her back? Did anyone get a receipt?"

Jameson chuckled, and the sound made Ava's shoulders relax. Maybe they were all reading too much into Linda's ominous arrival.

"She said she'd come back tomorrow to talk."

"We don't want what she's selling," Stella said.

"I'm with you," Jameson said, lifting his mug in solidarity. "She's not here for anything good."

"What did you say to her in the hallway? Why did she do a one-eighty?" Ava asked.

Jameson shrugged. "I said a lot of things. If one of them stuck, I'm not sure which one it was."

Ava walked over and rested her head against his chest. "Thank you, for whatever you said."

Jameson put his mug down on the counter and wrapped his arms around Ava. "Maybe she was really worried about you and realized she's your mother, and she should actually care."

"Maybe," Ava whispered. "I can't focus hard enough to piece it all together tonight."

She looked around. "Where did Paul go?"

Her grandpa pointed to the back door. "He slipped out. He just came by to see how you were doing."

"Is he okay?" she asked cautiously.

No one answered. Probably because no one knew the answer. The talk she'd had with Paul earlier was unexpected and only served to confuse her more. So Paul had known her mother a long time ago, but she still didn't know how well he knew her. He'd talked about Linda cautiously, as if he were afraid or ashamed. Ava wondered briefly if the two had dated, but it all seemed unlikely. Her mother hadn't ever been impressed with a cowboy.

"I'll go check on him," Stella said. "You get some rest."

Ava held up her mug. "As soon as I finish this. Thanks again."

"Anytime. See you tomorrow."

Ava's grandpa walked Stella to the door. The moment the two were out of the room, Jameson put his hands on either side of Ava's face. Looking up at him, she could see all his worries from the evening rushing out.

"Are you okay?" he asked.

"I'm fine. I will be as soon as I get some sleep."

"Drink more," he coaxed. "Oh, and Everly

brought you something to eat. She got worried when we didn't show up for supper."

Ava's stomach rumbled at the mention of food. "I'm starving. Did you get something?"

"Not yet. But she sent enough for both of us."

"Everly is the sweetest," Ava said just before she let out a yawn.

Jameson pulled a bowl of soup out of the fridge and heated it in the microwave. Ava turned the cup up and took bigger gulps. The warmth was soothing to her insides, relaxing her tense muscles inch by inch.

"You better eat fast. Looks like you're about to hit the hay."

"I will. Will you pray?"

Jameson prayed. Then he looked up at her. "I'm glad you're okay," he whispered.

"All thanks to you," Ava said.

He wrapped her in his arms again. "Please don't scare me like that again."

Ava chuckled against his chest. "I'll try."

"No, really. My heart can't take it. My stomach has been in knots all night."

"Speaking of night. What time is it?"

"Probably close to seven."

Ava gaped. "It's been that long?" They'd been having lunch at the creek when she fell in.

"Time flies when you're surviving."

"That's the truth." She covered her mouth as a huge yawn overtook her.

"You ready to give it up?" he asked.

She handed him the mug. "Yes. I can't keep my eyes open."

"I'm going to get some of my things and sleep here tonight. Mr. Chambers said I could use the other guest room. I want to be able to check on you in the night, if that's okay."

"That's fine, but I don't think it's necessary."

Jameson's expression was stoic. "I do."

She pushed up onto her toes and kissed his jaw. "Then hurry back."

CHAPTER 22
JAMESON

The old wooden door creaked as Jameson entered Ava's bedroom. The whole house was silent, and Ava didn't stir.

His throat tightened as he leaned over her, checking her breathing and color. She looked perfect and peaceful, but the memory of her cold body against his still gripped his chest. He'd experienced a new level of fear last night, and the realization was hard to shake.

Ava slowly rolled onto her back and inhaled a deep breath. Her eyes fluttered open before closing again. "Hey."

He sat on the side of the bed and brushed a hand over her hair. It was another assurance of her status —her skin was warm. "Good morning. How are you feeling?"

"Great. Still tired."

"I didn't mean to wake you up. I just needed to check on you before I get to work. Go back to sleep."

She wrestled her arms out of the tangle of covers and reached for him. He leaned in, letting her arms wrap tightly around his neck as he slid his arms around her. She was warm all over.

"Thank you," she whispered.

The words were on his tongue. *I love you.* He loved her so deeply and surely that his chest ached, but he held the confession in, unsure if telling her when she was half asleep was the best idea.

"I'm glad you're okay. You scared me."

"I'm fine. Thanks to you."

He tightened his hold on her, reluctant to let her go. Her breathing evened, and he knew she was falling asleep. "Call me when you wake up?"

"I promise. Have a good day."

He kissed her temple and tucked her back under the covers. "You too. I'll be back soon."

She turned on her side and tucked the covers under her chin as he tiptoed out of the room. He slipped out of the main house just after dawn.

The frost that covered the valley crunched beneath his boots as he headed toward his first stop of the day—the pack room. He knew he'd find Paul at work. He and Thane ran at the archery range every morning before he packed for the day's ride.

The old metal door creaked when Jameson

entered. Paul turned, and Thane stood from where he'd been lying at Paul's feet.

"Crazy night," Jameson said. He propped his shoulder on the doorframe, trying and failing to look casual.

"Yep," Paul said. He'd already turned back to his work.

"What's there between you and Linda?" Jameson asked. "I'm not trying to pry, but I need to know who to trust in all this. I don't trust Linda as far as I can throw her, and I'm wondering if this means I can't trust you either."

Paul rested the metal lid on the feed can with a clank. "I don't know her."

"But you did. What do you know?"

"Nothing. It's true. I really don't know her."

"Put the pack down and talk to me," Jameson demanded.

The older man dropped the bag and crossed his arms over his chest. "I don't have any problem with you, Jameson."

"Then tell me a story. What's there between you and Linda?"

Paul huffed. "It was stupid. We were young. Nothing..." he trailed off, looking anywhere but at Jameson.

"I think you meant *something*."

Paul stayed silent.

"Was she the one that got away or something?"

Jameson asked. That was how it had been between Ava and himself. He'd be no better off than Paul if she hadn't come back into his life.

But what if Ava had come back and she wasn't anything like the woman he'd known? Had that happened to Paul?

Paul shook his head. "Not really. I'm being honest when I say I didn't really know her. When I was young, I didn't talk much. I kept my head down and worked."

"So, not much has changed?" Jameson asked.

Paul chuckled. "I guess not. Linda always ran around out here. You could tell she was bored. Her parents were busy running the ranch, and she was an only child. She didn't have much to do, so she hung around. All of the wranglers talked about her, and she made a show of teasing. Constantly. She wanted all the attention."

Jameson listened, trying to imagine the young version of Linda that Paul was painting. It wasn't far from the Linda he knew now.

Paul looked at the ground and rubbed his chin. "One day, she set her eyes on me. I let things get out of hand. It was a fling, but there wasn't any substance to it. We never talked." Paul shook his head. "I should have been smarter."

Jameson kept quiet, wishing Paul would rush through this story and get it out in the open.

"This is why I don't want to talk about it, especially with Ava. It was a fling. A meaningless fling, and I'm not proud of it." Paul held his hands out at his sides. He was talking faster now, and saying more words than Jameson had ever heard from the older man. "It's impossible to be with someone like that and not feel like you know them. Your mind plays tricks on you. I made so many mistakes. I confused love and lust, and I thought we were heading somewhere." Paul huffed. "Now that sounds stupid. We never talked. It was all physical. We weren't ever going anywhere. Linda wasn't confused. She didn't want me."

Jameson looked around, unsure what to say. "I think you were better off without her."

Paul huffed. "I've heard enough about her since Ava's been back. I think I dodged a bullet."

"How close was this bullet, exactly? Like, did she stomp on your heart?"

Paul thought for a moment before he answered. "I told her I wanted us to be more than just sex. It was really the first meaningful conversation we'd ever had."

"And she said no," Jameson finished.

"She left two days later."

"Oh," Jameson drawled. "You think some of this is your fault?"

"Probably," Paul said.

"You can rest easy. I'm pretty sure Linda didn't

leave because of you. At least not only because of you. It doesn't seem like she was happy here."

"And to be honest, I wasn't happy with her. After it happened between us, I had a lot of guilt, and I thought I could make things right if I married her."

"Whoa. You proposed?" Jameson asked.

"Not in so many words. I'd started going to church with the Chambers, and I knew what we were doing wasn't right. I think I said something like we should do the honorable thing and make it official."

Jameson covered his mouth with a hand to hide the chuckle. "I'm sorry. You said what? And you wondered why she didn't just say I do?"

Paul scratched the back of his neck, but a smile tugged at the corners of his mouth. "I told you I did a lot of stupid things."

Jameson clapped a hand on Paul's shoulder. "I'm sorry, man. You live, you learn."

"Don't be sorry for me. I did learn my lesson. I just hate that I might have run Linda off, and because of that, Ava didn't get to grow up here knowing her grandparents."

Jameson watched Thane pacing the pack room, clearly picking up on Paul's discomfort. "Speaking of Ava, have you thought about the timeline?" Jameson didn't know when and where, so he'd considered it could be a possibility, but he had no way of confirming it.

Paul sat heavily on a square bale stack. "I don't know how old Ava is, and I've been terrified to ask."

Letting his head thunk back against the wall, Jameson said a prayer of thanks that he wasn't in Paul's position right now.

"Do you want me to tell you?" Jameson knew her birthdate, but he also wasn't ready to know the truth of Ava's parentage. If Paul was her biological father and Linda knew about it, that would be another rift between Ava and her mother.

Paul thought for a moment. "Yes and no. Even if things do line up, it's still not proof."

"You could ask Ava for a paternity test," Jameson said.

"I don't know her very well yet. She doesn't know me either. What does it say if I come in claiming she might be mine, when her mother has told her the man who raised her is her dad?"

"It says you're as confused as the rest of us."

Paul stood and looked around the pack room. "I didn't sleep much, and I don't think I will for a while."

Jameson got to his feet. "Maybe I could talk to Ava and see what she thinks. She could ask her mother about it when she comes by today."

Paul chuckled. "You make it sound so easy."

"I guess it could be. I don't know any other way to go about it. Sure, everything might change for Ava, but it would be in a good way. She lost the man she thought was her dad. I think she'd be happy to know she had someone else in her corner."

"I can't imagine I'd be a very good dad. I missed everything. She's grown. She doesn't need a dad now."

Jameson shoved his hands in his pockets. "I never had a dad, but I could use one, even now."

Paul looked up at Jameson and a look of understanding passed between them. They were both on their own in this world, and the possibility of a family wasn't something either of them would turn away.

"Maybe I should talk to Ava myself," Paul said.

"I'm sure she'd be happy to hear what you have to say."

"Thanks for talking it out with me. I wasn't looking forward to having this conversation with anyone."

"Anytime." Jameson jerked his head toward the door. "I need to get going, but I could go with you when you talk to Ava, if you want."

Paul nodded. "I think I'd like that."

Jameson shook hands with Paul. Just knowing they were united eased both of their worries.

CHAPTER 23
AVA

Ava pulled the needle through the quilt square. "Now I know why Grandma Lottie never finished these."

Stella chuckled. "It takes a lot of time. I like to do the interior stitching by hand and use the machine to put on the backing. We can use the machine if you want."

"No, I'm fine doing it this way. I want to do it the way she did."

Ava had thought about canceling on Stella today, but they'd both been looking forward to their weekly lesson. The one-on-one time was cathartic and peaceful, while the Tuesday night meetings with the other ladies were lively and uplifting.

The moment Ava started feeling like she was a part of something here, her mother showed up. Linda had said she was coming back today, but Ava hadn't heard from her. It wasn't unlike Linda to just show up when she was ready.

"Any word today?" Stella asked.

"Not yet. I'm sure she won't wait too long before she comes out with the reason for her visit."

"Well, you make sure someone is around when she shows up. I don't like the looks of that snake."

Ava rested the square in her lap. "Why can't she just let me be happy here? I didn't ask her to come when I knew she didn't want to, and that should have been enough."

"It should have. From what you've said about her, I could have guessed she wouldn't let you walk out without a fight," Stella said.

"But I didn't mean to walk out on her. I just needed my own life. We could talk on the phone. We could visit each other. We could spend holidays together. It doesn't have to be all or nothing."

Ava stopped pulling the thread and huffed. "I messed up again."

"If you're not feeling it today, we can try this again some other time," Stella offered.

Ava let the fabric fall to her lap. "I want to enjoy this today, but I'm having a hard time."

Stella stood, taking the square Ava had been working on and setting it on the end table. "Let's walk back to the main house. Walking always helps me clear my head."

"Yeah, that sounds good. Grandpa should be up

in a little bit, and we'll need to get back to work. Sorry I don't have my head in the game today."

"No problem. I'll grab us something hot and we'll head out."

Five minutes later, they stepped out into the cold, October sunshine with coffee cups in hand.

Ava looked back at Stella's place as they started on the trail toward the main house. "How did you end up in the foreman's cabin? Well, I guess it's not the foreman's cabin anymore."

"When I came here, Henry was the foreman. He had a house in Blackwater with his wife, and they liked it there. They'd raised their kids there, and they were getting grandbabies too. I was having trouble finding a place for myself after I decided to move here when Chuck died. Ronald offered to let me live here. The next year, Vera came along, and we ended up rooming together. I can't imagine things any other way now."

Ava had a hard time imagining the cabin without picturing Stella and Vera. The two didn't spend much time together during the day, but they were always together after hours. "You two are such good friends. I'm glad you have that."

Stella bumped Ava's arm. "You have that now too. And you have Jameson. Don't think I haven't considered what it means that the two of you are together."

"What do you mean?" Ava asked.

"If you and Jameson decide to make a life together, you'll want to live somewhere better than his old cabin."

Jameson's cabin wasn't in bad shape. He'd remodeled a few parts of it, like the bathroom and kitchen, but it was tiny. Jameson didn't mind living in a small space and Ava didn't either.

Ava pulled her coat tighter around her neck. "I haven't thought about that. Why are *you* thinking about it?"

"Because I'll need to find a new place. It's fine. Vera and I will find something, and you two will love the cabin."

Ava halted. "We don't want to kick you out." She hadn't talked to Jameson about it, but she knew he wouldn't even consider taking Stella and Vera's home from them.

"You'll need a place on the ranch," Stella said. There were a few laugh lines and crow's feet around her eyes, but she didn't look old by any means. Stella and Vera could live happily in that cabin for decades to come.

Ava wouldn't take that away from them. No matter what.

"We will, but it won't be your place," Ava said. "You can rest easy. Good grief, I can't believe you thought we were going to take the foreman's cabin away from you."

Stella held up her hands and started walking

again. "I wouldn't blame you! You'll need a place to raise kids."

Ava bit her lips to contain her smile. "We haven't talked about kids yet. You're getting ahead of yourself."

"Stop acting like that isn't what both of you are thinking. I mean, that boy has texted you twenty times since you got to my place."

Ava pulled out her phone. "He has texted more than usual today. I think he's worried about Linda showing up last night."

"As he should be. She's up to no good."

Ava looked up at the gray sky. Snow would be coming soon, and the ominous weather had her looking for potential trouble everywhere. "Have you heard anything about Grandpa getting an offer on the ranch?"

"I haven't, and if he didn't mention it to me, then it isn't important," Stella said. The revelation didn't seem to bother her in the least.

Ava exhaled a warm breath that clouded in front of her face. "Good. I heard a rumor, and I didn't know what to believe."

"Your grandpa wouldn't be deceiving. If he asked you to come here, he wouldn't just sell the place. You've had a lot of things changing in your life. You've met new people, left the life you knew, and I can see how it's all a lot to take in."

"I don't know who to trust. Everyone tells me

different things, and I don't know what's the truth and what isn't," Ava said, her words soft enough to carry away with the wind.

Stella wrapped an arm around Ava's shoulder. "You'll figure it out. You're a smart woman. You have to listen very carefully to hear the truth. Sometimes it's only a whisper, and everything else is just noise drowning it out."

Ava leaned into Stella's embrace. "That's exactly what it feels like right now. I'm trying to find my place here, and I keep questioning things I shouldn't, like Grandpa. He's been nothing but good to me. I shouldn't be sitting around wondering what it means that he might have gotten an offer on the ranch and didn't tell me."

"Like I said, if it was important, he'd have told one or both of us," Stella said.

They rounded the corner, and the main house came into view. Stella huffed. "Looks like Mommy Dearest hasn't shown up yet."

"I wish she'd get it over with," Ava said with a sigh. "Waiting around feels a lot like she's the one in control."

"She's not. Not around here, and not with you anymore."

"I know," Ava said. "I'm really not as afraid of her as I used to be."

"Good. Keep growing like that, and you'll be just fine. You want me to stay?"

"No, I can handle it. I *need* to handle it on my own."

Stella patted Ava's back. "That's my girl. Show her who's boss."

"Thanks for the pep talk."

"Anytime!" Stella waved over her shoulder as she made her way to the gift shop next door.

CHAPTER 24

AVA

Ava walked inside and smelled coffee. Grandpa was up early from his nap.

She made a cup for herself and found him in the office. He'd added a desk and computer to the small space so she could work independently but also be close enough to ask questions or slide her chair over to see his screen if needed.

"You're up early," Ava said.

Grandpa peeked over the monitor. "Yeah, I forgot Louise asked me to send her an email about the payroll last week, and I couldn't rest well until I got up and marked it off my list."

She'd been expecting to see his usual solitaire game on the screen when she leaned in to give him a one-armed hug. Instead, a few lines were typed in an email draft. "You were serious. I thought Louise did the payroll."

Ava had met Louise last week when her grandpa had taken her around town introducing her to their various business partners. Louise was a sweet older lady who worked for a small accounting firm.

"She does, but Dane had told me last week that he wanted to count some of his overtime hours as regular hours instead of using vacation for half a day he took off during the week, and I forgot to tell her."

"I see," Ava said, taking a seat behind her desk.

"I hated payroll back when I used to do it. Everything got so complicated with taxes and withholdings. It was all computer stuff that I hated."

Ava tried not to grin at her grandpa's disdain for electronics. "Then letting Louise take care of it seems like the best thing for you. How long has she been doing it?"

Her grandpa narrowed his eyes as he thought. "Maybe a year? Before that, the old accountant did it. He's really the one who convinced me to hand it over."

"Who was the old accountant?" Ava asked.

Her grandpa huffed. "Some young buck who tried to strong-arm me into doing a bunch of stuff I didn't want to do. Handing over the payroll was the only idea of his that I liked."

"How did you end up with him as your accountant if you didn't like him?" Ava couldn't imagine anyone bullying her grandpa into doing anything he didn't want to do. No wonder their partnership hadn't worked out.

"Randy was my accountant, but he retired a few years ago. The firm he was with stuck me with Mr. Bright Idea. I gave him a chance, but I knew things weren't going to work out."

Ava thought about all the partnerships her grandpa had forged and cultivated. Would she ever be able to measure up to his reputation in Blackwater? "Well, I'm glad you found Louise."

"Me too, and I was relieved when she suggested I continue outsourcing payroll because I was getting too old for that headache every week."

Ava studied her grandpa, noting the strength of his hands despite the bruising skin that told his age. He still had a full head of hair, but it was as white as fresh snow. She'd been looking for any physical similarities between them, but she hadn't found any except the dark-brown eyes they shared. She'd noticed from the photos on the staircase that his hair had once been as dark as hers.

She watched him any chance she could. What kind of knowledge could a man who had lived over seventy years contain? How many secrets and stories made up a life like that?

Secrets. Not everyone had secrets, and she often forgot that fact when she started questioning everything.

The question that had been eating her alive

bubbled up in her throat until she was sick to her stomach.

"Ava, you okay?" her grandpa asked.

"I'm fine. I've been thinking about something I heard."

"Heard where?"

Ava looked around the office, desperate to change the subject or blurt it out and get it over with. The words flooded out in a mad rush, tumbling over each other. "Did you get an offer on the ranch?"

Her grandpa humphed. "I did, but it's not for sale. Pretty bold to try to buy a man's land out from under him."

Ava's shoulders relaxed. "So, you're not thinking of selling?"

"No. I've had offers like this before, but it doesn't mean anything. I'd have to want to give it up, and I don't."

Twisting her fingers, she asked, "Was the offer too low? What I mean is, if someone offered you enough, would you ever sell it?"

Her grandpa looked at her closely, studying her face as if he could read something there. "Do you want me to sell it?"

"No! I definitely don't. I just wonder if everyone has a price."

He sat back in his chair and crossed his arms over his chest. "I can't be bought."

Ava grinned. "I was hoping you'd say that."

"As for the price, this offer was a fair one. Almost too fair. From what I can put together in my head, it's almost exactly what I would say this place is worth." He leaned forward and put a hand over Ava's. "But I won't be bought out. I wanted you to come here because I think you could care about this place as much as I do one day. I don't want to sell it to some bigwig with more money than he knows what to do with."

A knock sounded on the door, and Stella stepped in. "I found a stray hanging around the front door." She hooked a thumb over her shoulder as Ava's mother stepped into the doorway.

"I knocked," Linda said in defense.

Stella rolled her eyes like a teenager. "Usually, when no one comes to the door, people get the hint."

Ava stood and walked around the desk. "Sorry. We were back here and didn't hear the knock."

Stella waved a hand over her head as she turned to leave. "See you later."

Ava had said she needed to do this on her own, but when Stella walked out, Ava wished she'd turn around and come back.

No one spoke for a moment, and Linda took another step into the office. "Did I hear you got an offer on the ranch?"

Ava didn't want to wish her mom away, but as

soon as Linda started talking about the ranch—
Ava's ranch—she wanted to close the door and lock
her mother out the way Stella had last night. Ava
was just beginning to build a home here, and she
didn't want her mother's hand anywhere near it.

Was it selfish to want to keep this place for
herself? Her mother had just as much right to it, but
that thought made her stomach turn.

"I did," her grandpa said. "It's just a bunch of
smoke in the wind."

"Why wouldn't you want to sell it? You're
getting old, and running this place must be tiring."

Her grandpa sat up straighter in his chair, as if
trying to rally the strength of his youth. "Jameson
manages the ranch now, and Ava is training to take
over the business side that I've been handling."

Linda glanced at Ava before turning quickly back
to her grandpa. "I didn't realize Ava was actually
taking a part in things here."

"She's more than qualified," her grandpa said.
"She's taking the last few classes to get her degree,
but I told her that's not necessary. She's already
proven she can be taught and she wants to learn."

Hearing her grandpa's affirming compliments
made Ava's eyes flood with moisture. Her mother
hadn't ever believed in her like that.

Linda looked around, studying the office as if
noting the changes since she left. It was odd for
Linda to be so guarded. She was the type to enter a

room and declare herself the alpha, not shuffle her feet and avoid eye contact.

"I was hoping we could talk," she said to Ava.

Ava looked to her grandpa for approval. She was on the clock, and she'd taken a long lunch break to go to Stella's.

"Go ahead. I have things covered here," her grandpa said, adjusting his glasses and turning his attention to the computer screen.

Leaning over her grandpa's desk, she whispered, "Thanks."

Ava walked behind her mom into the living room. The house was quiet, and neither wanted to break the silence.

Linda tugged at her pencil skirt, smoothing out the wrinkles as she crossed her legs at the ankles. Her outfit wasn't practical for the ranch, but Ava knew her mother had walked over the loose gravel in the parking lot like a pro.

Ava sighed and resigned herself to the conversation. "It's good to see you."

Her mother was slow to reply. "It's good to see you too."

A sadness hung in her mother's eyes that Ava hadn't seen before. "Is everything okay?"

Linda looked up, and her slack expression remained. "I don't know. I came here prepared to talk some sense into you. I was angry and hurt that you'd left."

Ava interrupted. "You kicked me out."

"I didn't want to. I shouldn't have." Linda covered her mouth, and her next words were muffled. "I can't believe I did that."

Instinct told Ava to comfort her mother. Someone was hurting, and she should try her best to help, even if that person had hurt her in the recent past. But there was frustration behind that urge to soothe, and it kept her still.

"What brought on this change?" Ava asked.

Linda swallowed hard. "Last night was a lot to take in. I was angry and frustrated that you'd left, but when I saw you..." Her words trailed off and softened. "You were almost lifeless."

Last night had been a haze for Ava. The freezing water had been painful on her muscles and lungs. She'd slept until almost nine this morning. She hadn't slept past six since before high school.

Time had meshed together in the pain and discomfort, and she'd barely been aware of what was going on around her. Had she looked bad enough to worry her mother?

"I'm sorry I scared you like that. My muscles are sore today, but Jameson assured me that's normal."

"That boy who brought you in?" Linda asked.

Ava didn't want to be looking for a reason to argue, but it bothered her that her mother didn't know his name and had called him a boy when he wasn't a child. "Jameson brought me home. He was a firefighter and a paramedic, until he took the foreman job here. So he knew what to do to help me."

Linda sighed, looking defeated. "He told me that."

"He's also my boyfriend. I would appreciate it if you treated him with respect."

Linda pinched the bridge of her nose. "This visit isn't going anything like I'd planned."

Ava crossed her arms. "So you came to tell me I'd made a mistake in moving here? A phone call would have been better."

"I got tired of calling. It felt like I was yelling at a brick wall."

"Because you were," Ava said quickly. "You can't boss me into doing what you want anymore."

Linda narrowed her eyes, but there was confusion instead of irritation in the expression. "I don't want to boss you. I just want—"

"You just want me to do what you think I should do. I know. And that part of our relationship is over. I will welcome your calls if you'd like to catch up, but I'm not chained to you anymore. I've moved on. Maybe we can fix things one day, but it takes two."

Silence fell around them, and the ticking of the old grandfather clock in the corner marked the seconds as Linda considered Ava's proposal.

"I want that. I do." Linda fidgeted, looking almost nervous as her breaths quickened. "I hated everything about last night. You were hurt, and some other woman was taking care of you. That should have been me."

Ava couldn't argue with that statement, but Linda hadn't proven herself to be a nurturer in over a decade.

"Then Jameson was there." Linda paused on his name as if waiting to make sure she'd gotten it correct. "He said all those things I was thinking about how it should be me in there with you, and I knew everything had gotten mixed up between us. You were my baby, and now you don't need me."

Understanding seeped into Ava's heart. "Caring about someone doesn't have anything to do with how much you need them. I don't want to put a value on someone based on what they can do for me or how much I need them. I don't want love to be fragile or conditional. It should be constant and unbreakable."

Linda's eyes glistened as tears welled in them. "I haven't loved in a long time, and I'm sorry for that."

Ava froze and stared at her mother. Linda Collins had never uttered the word sorry, and Ava wanted to soak it up and let it patch the wounded parts of their relationship—the ones that were born in anger.

What did it mean that Ava had to be injured before her mother saw the brokenness between them? What if Stella hadn't been there to step into the motherly healing role? What if Jameson hadn't been there to defend and champion her to her mother?

Would this conversation be happening if there hadn't been some traumatic reunion between them?

Ava looked to the bookshelf behind the couch. It was lined with countless books she'd read these last few months. They were filled with the biblical wisdom she'd been starved of all her life. So many of them taught the importance of forgiveness.

She knew this was one of those times when she should forgive, but it was easier said than done. She wasn't going to wrap her head around it right now. She needed time.

The phone in her pocket buzzed, and she pulled it out. Jameson's name lit up on the screen.

Jameson: Are you busy? Paul wants to come by and talk to you in a little bit.

She typed a quick reply.

Ava: Sure. Tell him I'll be in the office.

Ava slipped the phone back into her pocket. She still hadn't responded to her mother's apology, and her time was running out. "I'm sorry to cut this short, but one of the workers is coming by to meet with me. I'm technically at work."

Linda brushed her hands over her hair, smoothing the already tamed style. "Okay. I'll be here for a couple of days. Can I come back and see you?"

Her hands seemed to almost tremble where they rested in her lap. What had Linda so shaken up?

Whatever it was, seeing her mother so out of sorts softened Ava's heart. "I'd like that." It seemed like a great start to building new trust and understanding between them.

But a couple of days wasn't much time, and things might fizzle out if Linda went back to Denver. It was hard to believe Linda had taken time off work at all.

Resolved to take the first step toward mending things between them, Ava took her mother's shaky hand in hers. "Listen, I'd love it if you'd come back and spend some time here. In fact, I'd like it if you came to stay here while you're in town. I know Grandpa would be thrilled to have you, and it would give us more time to talk."

Linda nodded rapidly, but Ava wasn't sure if she was shaking or agreeing. "Okay. I'll think about it."

"You could hang around the ranch if you want. Supper will be served in a few hours, and we could take a walk to the stables and talk."

Linda bit the inside of her cheek as she considered.

Desperate for a link that might draw her mother back here, Ava pulled from the first thing on her mind. "Paul will be here in a little bit. He's the man who was here last night before you left. He said he remembers you from before you moved to Denver."

Standing in a rush, Linda swiped at her hair again. "I think I'll come back later. I have some things to do in town."

Ava stood slowly. What could Linda possibly have to do in Blackwater? "Okay. Do you remember Paul? He's a nice man."

"I don't. There were a lot of cowboys here, and they were all the same."

A hint of the old condescending tone lingered in her mother's words. "They're not all the same. They're people, and they don't deserve to be painted with your broad brush."

"I wasn't being malicious, Ava. I was just saying that they don't ever do anything different. If they start out as cowboys, they die the same way."

Ava narrowed her eyes and took a deep breath. The fiery defense was on the tip of her tongue. "Have you ever considered that they might like it here? Jameson isn't spinning his wheels. He's doing what he loves and making people happy too. He's good and responsible, and I don't know why you can't see that."

Linda's gaze darted around the room as if looking for a way out.

"Paul is good too, but he's his own person. He's not just a cowboy. These people are all worth a chance, and your preconceived notion about them isn't fair."

Linda hung her head. "I'll call you tonight."

The talk didn't feel like a complete loss, and time would do them both good. "Okay. Thanks for coming."

Ava walked her mother to the front of the house and said good-bye. Back in the office she shared with her grandpa, she sat down to get caught up on the work she'd missed.

Her grandpa asked, "Everything go okay?"

"As good as I could have hoped, I guess."

He stood and grabbed his empty mug. "I think it's time for another cup. You want one?"

She handed him the empty mug on her desk. "Please and thank you."

CHAPTER 25
JAMESON

Jameson parked in the space between the main house and the check-in office. Today had been one fire to put out after another, and he hadn't seen Ava since he left her this morning. She'd assured him she was feeling fine multiple times, but he was ready to see for himself.

A day's worth of thinking about his conversation with Paul that morning hadn't produced any bright ideas about how to break the news to Ava. Paul would be heading this way soon to talk to her about it, but Jameson felt like he needed to soften the blow ahead of time. Was that even possible? Did it matter what he said or when he said it? The news would be overwhelming either way.

Why hadn't Linda told Ava the truth? Maybe she had and Paul wasn't Ava's dad, but it seemed too close to rule out the possibility.

Jameson still had no idea if Linda had stopped by today, or if she'd be showing up later. The unprompted visit had been hanging over his thoughts all day, and he knew Ava would be nervous.

He stepped out of the old work truck and dusted off his flannel shirt. He didn't get his hands dirty as much these days, but a late hay shipment came in, and he'd had to rush out to unload it.

He'd just rounded the corner of the house when he spotted Linda walking out the front door. Backpedaling, he waited and hoped she hadn't seen him. He wasn't afraid of Linda Collins, but running into her was just asking for trouble. She didn't have anything nice to say to him.

Jameson peeked around the corner to see if the coast was clear when he saw Dane jog up to Linda as she was about to get in her car.

"How'd it go? Did you get him to agree?" Dane asked.

Hold up. How did Dane even know Linda? And what were they pushing here?

"We didn't talk much about the offer," Linda said.

She nervously shifted her weight from one side to the other. It was a completely different demeanor from the bold stance she'd held last night and every other time Jameson had seen her.

"Come on," Dane spat. "Just tell the old man it's time to give it up."

Jameson's hands tightened into fists at his sides. That *old man* had given Dane a job, and now the guy was trying to rip Mr. Chambers' home out from under him. Jameson hadn't had a problem with Dane that he could put his finger on before, but now he had a good one.

Linda straightened her shoulders and faced Dane. "I came by last night, but Ava had fallen in a creek, and she was freezing. I couldn't just ignore the fact that she was in trouble and talk about selling the ranch."

"I'm sure she was fine," Dane said, sounding more exasperated by the second.

"You don't have kids. You don't know what it's like to see them in trouble."

"She's fine!" he repeated.

Linda looked left and right, checking to see who was around to hear. "There have already been two mentions of Paul since I've been here. I have to tell Ava soon. Now that she's back for good, she's bound to find out, and I need to be the one to tell her. I should have told her before. Now I'm afraid she'll hate me."

Jameson looked at the ground and shook his head. How had Linda lied to Ava for so long? How could she have possibly thought that was okay? The fact that Dane knew and Ava didn't had Jameson's blood boiling. Who else knew?

What would that mean for Ava? She might not have a good relationship with her mother, but she could have a chance with her real father. He wanted to look on the bright side for her sake.

Linda *should* be afraid to tell Ava. Jameson couldn't think of any excuse for keeping a secret like that.

"Who cares?" Dane asked.

"I care," Linda said, pointing to her chest. "I wanted my daughter back in Denver. I didn't want her to hate me." She pinched the bridge of her nose as if explaining mother-daughter relationships to Dane was a lost cause. "Seeing Ava last night changed some things."

"Like that?" Dane spat. "You're afraid people will find out about Paul, but no one else knows. So what? It doesn't matter if Paul or Ava know. He doesn't have any claim to this place. We want the old man to sell, and that's what's important. Not some baby daddy drama."

Linda huffed and reached for the door of her rental car. "Things have changed. I'm not sure about this anymore."

Dane grabbed Linda by the arm and whirled her around to face him. "Listen—"

Jameson's feet were moving before he'd fully thought through the consequences of beating an employee to a pulp, but he wouldn't stand by and let a man jerk a woman around. Adrenaline pumped through his veins as he ran toward Dane and Linda.

"Hey! Get your hands off her!" Jameson said.

Dane and Linda both jerked their attention to him, but they all three turned toward the house when a door slammed.

Jameson's run slowed to a stop as they all watched Mr. Chambers stomp out onto the porch. The old man had a commanding demeanor at times, but Jameson had never seen his boss angry before now. With narrowed eyes, a furrowed brow, and a tense jaw, Mr. Chambers looked ready to spit fire.

Holding still, Jameson was grateful the fiery stare wasn't directed at him.

Mr. Chambers walked slowly to the edge of the porch. "Dane, get to work."

Dane stepped away from Linda, looking relieved to be let off the hook.

Jameson waited for Mr. Chambers to tell him to leave too, but he didn't. Instead, he kept his attention on his daughter.

"I overheard," the older man said. His tone was level, but the words carried a silent reprimand. "Why did you keep this from us?"

Us. Jameson had been worried about Ava, but Mr. and Mrs. Chambers had been kept in the dark about their granddaughter's parentage and almost everything else about her life for over twenty years.

They'd been wronged just as much as Ava. So much time had been stolen from them, and Mrs. Chambers had missed out on getting to know Ava at all.

Linda's shoulders lifted and fell with her deep breaths, and her usually polished features were covered in fear. "You'd have disowned me. You'd never have approved."

"I would never disown you," Mr. Chambers said sternly.

Linda's words shook. "I wasn't a good Christian girl like you expected me to be. I wasn't ever going to be that, and you were ashamed of me."

"It's best you don't tell me what I would've done," he said sharply. "I never claimed to be a perfect father, but I would never turn you away."

Jameson stood paralyzed as Mr. Chambers confronted his daughter. Should he leave?

"Ava was born out of wedlock. You wouldn't have approved," Linda said shakily.

"You are my daughter, and Ava is my granddaughter, no matter who her father is. I wouldn't have approved, but I would have loved you both through everything."

Linda squeezed her eyes closed and hung her head. "How could you?"

"It wasn't under the best circumstances, but a child is always a blessing. It broke your mother's heart not to get to be a part of yours and Ava's lives."

Linda shook her head and whispered, "I don't believe you."

Mr. Chambers lifted his chin. "That's my fault. I should have done a better job of making sure you knew we loved you unconditionally. I'm sorry for that."

Jameson's stomach rolled as Linda's chin began quivering. He harbored a lot of dislike that bordered on hatred where Ava's mother was concerned, but he didn't enjoy seeing her upset.

Then he remembered how upset Ava would be, and his sympathy for Linda died.

"Does Paul know?" Mr. Chambers asked.

Linda bit her lips between her teeth and slowly shook her head.

"Why doesn't he?"

Linda glanced at Jameson for only a second before turning her attention back to her father. "I didn't want this life—for her or myself."

"What about this life didn't you like?"

She looked around as if the answer would jump out from behind a building or from under a nearby shrub. When she finally spoke, her words were tired and whiny, as if she were a reprimanded child. "Paul wasn't going anywhere. He wasn't going to make anything of himself."

"And I suppose you've done those things? You've gone somewhere and made something of yourself?"

Linda's expression fell in defeat. "You don't care?"

Mr. Chambers didn't look impressed. "I care if you're happy, but I also care about Paul. He's been wronged in this too. He's been a great employee and a long-time friend, and I do not envy the road ahead of you as you explain your actions."

A trail of tears slid down Linda's cheeks. "I-I—"

"As for where Paul is headed, that isn't the most important thing when it comes to being a good parent. Ava would be proud to call him her father."

Linda covered her chin with her manicured hand. "Are you going to tell her?"

"No. You are."

The door behind Mr. Chambers creaked as Ava stepped out onto the porch.

A wrecking ball made of every emotion Jameson felt for Ava slammed into his chest. He wanted to step in front of her and shield her from the mess that was coming for her. He wanted to wrap her in his arms and protect her from her mother's betrayal.

But as she took her place beside her grandpa, she didn't look like she needed protecting. She stood tall with her shoulders back and chin high.

When she spoke, her words were even and strong. "Is Paul my father?"

Linda took a step forward, but Ava held up her hand. "No. I need an answer."

Linda hesitated, staring at Ava as if begging her to understand.

"I heard your conversation, but I need to hear you say it to me," Ava said.

"Ava, I don't know—"

"You don't know?" Ava asked.

"No, I do know," Linda said, tripping over her words. "I just don't know what to say."

"You could start with the truth."

Linda shook her head as if Ava had asked her to do the impossible.

Ava held up a hand. "You know what? Let me know when you're ready to be honest with me." She turned and walked quickly back into the house, closing the door forcefully behind her.

Linda lunged as if ready to chase her daughter, but her father held up a hand—the same gesture Ava had used twice in the conversation.

Turns out, Ava was a lot like her grandpa when it came down to the things that mattered.

"She'll need some time before she's ready to talk to you," Mr. Chambers said. He turned to Jameson and jerked his head toward the door.

Jameson didn't hesitate. He ran for Ava and hoped he could ease the hurt of her mother's betrayal.

CHAPTER 26

AVA

Ava ran straight through the house to the back door stopping only to jerk it open and keep running. The freezing air filled her lungs as she pumped her arms faster, but she didn't want to be anywhere near her mother—the catalyst of this pain in her chest.

She hadn't been sure where she was headed until the stables came into view.

Jess. Jess was the one person she could trust to be blunt with her, and she needed an honest friend right now.

The guests were out on rides, and the stables were nearly deserted. Good. She wanted to talk to Jess and maybe scream a little bit without an audience.

The run from the main house had Ava gasping, and the tears in the edges of her eyes were frigid.

She slowed to a jog, looking for the stable manager in every stall.

Jess stepped out of the feed room at the far end of the stables. "Hey, you look winded."

Ava didn't care that Jess spoke the first thing that came to her mind. That's exactly what Ava was looking for right now. "Did you know Paul is my father?" she asked through panting breaths.

One of Jess's brows lifted. "No, but wow. Really?"

Ava nodded and bent at the waist, propping her hands on her knees.

Her mother knew, of course. Now her grandpa and Jameson knew. They'd been standing outside talking about it as if the news wasn't a shock. She hadn't heard the whole conversation, so maybe they'd both just found out and had been talking for longer than she thought.

"I knew," Dane said behind her.

Ava turned quickly and eyed the wrangler. "How did you know?"

He lifted his shoulder. "Jameson knew too."

No. No, no, no. Jameson hadn't known. He would have told her.

Paul was her dad, and her whole life felt like a carefully constructed lie. She'd loved her dad, or the man she'd always assumed was her dad. Had he known, or had her mother kept it from him too?

Ava covered her mouth and sucked air through

her nose. If she couldn't trust her mother, her grandpa, or Jameson, who *could* she trust?

"Does Paul know?" Ava asked.

Dane shrugged. "Probably. If I know and Jameson knows, it's probably common knowledge."

Jess frowned. "I didn't know, and you don't know if Paul knows or not."

Ava still hadn't caught her breath, and the panting was growing quicker now.

"Did you really not know? Wow, that's a big secret," Dane said.

Jess rested a hand on Ava's shoulder and pointed toward a chair against the outer wall of the office. "Sit down. I'll get you some water."

Just then, Jameson pushed past Dane and skidded to his knees in front of Ava.

A mixture of relief and uncertainty swirled within her. Was he a part of this, or was he here to help her wrap her head around the secret her mother had kept?

"Ava, are you okay? Talk to me."

Dane huffed. "Jess went to get her some water. She looks like she's hyperventilating."

Jameson jerked his attention to Dane. "Get out of here. Now."

Dane straightened, looking irritated. "What's wrong with you?"

"I just watched you grab a woman. You're fired."

Ava gasped. "He what?"

"You can't do that!" Dane shouted.

"I just did. Get out of here before I call Ridge and Linc to escort you out."

Dane stormed off, and Jameson turned his attention back to her just as Jess jogged over with a cup of water.

"Sorry. The water tank in the office is out. I had to run to the store room."

Ava accepted the cup and chugged the water before handing it back to Jess.

Jameson's worried look had her hopes falling. Was he worried because he'd kept the secret from her too, or was he worried about how she would react to the news?

"Let's go to the office," he said, rising to his feet.

She let him lead her into the nearby room and close the door. She sat in the chair in front of the desk and rested her head in her hands.

"Ava, are you okay?"

He'd asked that before, but she hadn't answered yet. She was physically fine, but she hadn't come to terms with the revelation yet.

"Did you know?" she asked.

"About Paul?"

That response didn't sound promising.

"Yes."

Jameson sighed, and she knew she wasn't going to like his answer. She'd given him her whole heart, and now he had the power to break it in two.

"I didn't know for sure until Linda said it a little bit ago, but I suspected it last night."

Last night? That wasn't long ago, but she still felt like the last to know.

"Does Paul know?"

Jameson shook his head. "He doesn't know for sure, but he thought it was a possibility."

"Why didn't you tell me?" she asked.

"I was going to. As soon as I saw you, I was going to tell you. Paul was coming to talk to you too, even though he wasn't sure."

She remembered Jameson's text from earlier asking if Paul could come by and talk to her. She'd assumed it was about vacation time or his schedule, but it made sense now that he was planning to talk to her about this.

Jameson knelt in front of her and slid his fingers into her hair, turning her to face him. His warm brown eyes and the firm line of his jaw assured her he was serious. He'd been nothing but responsible and steadfast since they'd met, and she knew now that his worry was that he would lose her.

He adjusted his stance on his knee and looked her in the eye. "I will always tell you the truth. I would never keep that from you. My place is beside you through everything because I love you. I want you in my life, and I'm so far gone that I *need* you in my life. Every day. Every night. I love you, and I don't want this to be something that breaks us because I would rather break my heart than yours."

Tears spilled over Ava's cheeks, but they weren't born of the hurt and betrayal from her mother.

No, they were tears of relief and acceptance because she would never have to face the struggles and heartbreaks of life alone again. Jameson had given her that and more, and she had just as much love to give back to him.

"I love you too." The words were hoarse and shaky, but she meant them with her whole heart.

Jameson stood, wrapping his arms around her on the way up and clutching her tightly to his chest. The power in his embrace overwhelmed her. He was washing out the doubt and hurt that had crept in and flooded her soul with love and acceptance like she'd never known.

It didn't matter that Paul was her real father or that her mother had lied to her about it. She didn't have to heal from that injustice alone.

Jameson cradled her face in his hands and tilted it up so she could see the sincerity in his eyes. "I want you to know my heart is honest, and it's you and me. Forever. I don't care about anything but you."

He didn't need to scream or beg or give her an ultimatum. Jameson's word was true, and that's all she needed.

She leaned in, resting her forehead against his.

She hadn't known the extent of love before she came here, but her heart had been opened to a new home, family, and friends she never expected.

But Jameson had transformed her heart. He'd intertwined his life and future with hers, bonding their souls until they couldn't be separated.

When she lifted her head to look up at him, the adoration in his eyes was enough to warm her through the Wyoming winter.

"I love you so much," he whispered on a relieved breath before he pressed his lips to hers. Every move they made held a promise, and every breath was a vow.

This man would be kissing her for the rest of her life. She'd never been more certain of anything, and knowing he would always be beside her was enough to chase away any hurt.

When they broke the kiss, he held her until she slowly lifted her head from his shoulder.

"You want me to put in a delivery order for supper? I bet Jess would bring us something," he offered.

Ava chuckled, and the sound freed what was left of her sorrow. "I know she would, but I'm ready to face the world." She wiped her eyes and ran her fingers through her tangled hair. "Just let me put myself back together."

"Leave the tangles. You're beautiful," Jameson said. "We can eat on the back porch."

"I like that idea." If they hurried, they could catch the sunset.

Jameson rested his hand on the knob. "You ready?"

Ava took a deep breath. "Ready as I'll ever be."

He took her hand in his before pulling the door open. The stables were teeming with people and horses now as the afternoon rides came back before supper.

The news had rocked her for a little bit, but the world was the same. Guests laughed and interacted with the horses as Jess and Brett herded them into stalls or into the pasture.

The colder air wrapped around them as they stepped out of the stable, but that wasn't what took Ava's breath away. Paul was walking toward them with Thane at his side, and from the look on his face, he still meant to have that conversation with her he'd mentioned earlier.

Jameson gripped her hand tighter and whispered, "You ready?"

She looked up at him with more courage than she'd ever felt in her life. "I'm ready."

CHAPTER 27

AVA

Ava held tight to Jameson's hand as they stopped in front of Paul and Thane. She was feeling a lot braver these days, but breaking the news to him wasn't something she wanted to do alone.

As if he knew what was coming, Paul faced her head on and gave her a simple and assuring grin. "I've been looking for you."

If only he knew what those words did to her. She had no idea how this new relationship would play out between them, but she'd come here looking for family. It was hard to say for sure, but she wanted to believe God had a hand in this. Even with the lingering hurt of her mother's secret, it was still an answer to her prayers.

"You already know?" Ava asked, grateful this was going much easier than she'd expected.

Paul glanced at Jameson, who gave an assuring nod. "Looks like I do."

"Linda confirmed it today," Jameson said.

Paul inhaled a deep breath. "Wish she'd have let me know."

Ava shuffled her feet a little. Jameson knew Paul much better than she did, and she didn't want to be nervous, but she was. "What does this mean?"

Paul chuckled. "I was planning to ask you the same thing."

They all shared a laugh, and any tension disappeared with the sound.

Sticking his hands in his pockets, Paul looked at Ava with kindness and she saw many of the same features in his face as hers. "I don't know what all this means, but I know it isn't a bad thing."

Ava nodded and bit her lips between her teeth.

Paul rubbed a hand over his jaw, contemplating what to say. "I hate that I missed out on so much of your life, but it sounds like you had a good man to raise you."

She nodded again, sure of her love for her dad—the man she'd always known as her dad.

"I don't ever want to change that. I'm frustrated with Linda for not telling me. Well, I'm more than frustrated. She stole my chance to be a dad."

Ava hung her head. She'd been thinking of herself since she found out, but Paul might have it worse. She wanted kids one day, and the thought of her child growing up without her ripped her heart to pieces.

"Hey, none of that anger is directed at you," Paul said, placing a hand on her shoulder. "I'm glad you had a man in your life who was there for you when I didn't know I needed to be."

Her dad had been the best, but she'd still longed for something more—something here. She thought it was her grandpa drawing her back, but now she knew it was a father too.

Paul lifted her chin with a finger until she was staring into his eyes. "I would have moved heaven and earth to be there. Even back then. I don't have much, but I would have given up everything to be there. And if you ever need me, I'll be here now."

Her floodgates shattered, and tears flowed down her cheeks, leaving cold tracks. The sobs were quick to follow, and Paul's arms were around her.

Jameson released her hand, but she could feel him close beside her. He was another man at Wolf Creek she hadn't known she'd been searching for until the pieces of her puzzle fell into place.

"I know," she whispered. She didn't know everything about Paul, but she knew he was honorable and respectable.

And from the way he held her right now, she knew he would have loved her—would love her soon enough now that they knew the truth.

She pressed her eyes closed and pushed away the thoughts of how close she could have been to growing up here at Wolf Creek. She didn't have a bad childhood, but things would have been so different here.

"I don't know whether I'm happy or angry," she gritted through her teeth.

Paul released her and leveled his gaze at her. "Don't let the anger take your happiness."

Ava wiped her eyes. "You're right. I really don't want her to get the most of my emotions today." It was freeing and relieving to accept the news as good instead of bad.

Jameson slid his hand into hers, and she looked up at him with a grin. How many times could she swing from nervous to happy to angry to happy again in one day?

Paul rested a heavy hand on her shoulder and squeezed. "I may have missed the first twenty-five years, but I don't intend to miss the rest."

Ava laid her hand on his. "Thanks. This has been weird, but I'm feeling good about it now."

Paul took a deep breath. "Now I have to confront Linda."

Jameson huffed. "Good luck."

Ava chuckled, knowing she wasn't ready to talk to her mother yet. She was grateful she didn't have that daunting task ahead of her today and also sad that Paul had to endure it.

"I guess I'll head that way," Paul said, looking at the main house.

Jameson nudged Paul with his elbow. "We'll walk with you, but you're on your own from the door onward."

"I appreciate it. I'm not looking forward to any of it."

"We'll be around after if you want to talk," Ava said.

"I think I'm about talked out already for today," Paul admitted.

Jameson chuckled. "You've said more in the last ten minutes than I've heard from you in the last three months."

"I'll get back to my usual self tomorrow," Paul promised.

Ava couldn't help but feel an inkling of hope at the mention of tomorrow.

———

Jameson knelt at the small fireplace in his cabin and added another log. Ava let her head rest against the back of the couch and closed her eyes. After a late supper, they snuck away to the cabin, and the exhaustion of the day hit her hard.

Jameson stood and brushed his palms on his jeans. "You think we should worry about Paul?"

Ava didn't open her eyes. "He said he'd come by after they finished talking."

"But he's been gone for over an hour. I'm kind of worried."

Ava chuckled. "Her bark is worse than her bite. Plus, it's not like she's the one angry this time. She kept the secret and brought this on herself."

Ava would normally be concerned that Paul and Linda's talk was dragging on so long, but she didn't have the energy right now. She hadn't fully recovered from her body temperature dropping so low the night before.

Jameson sat close beside her on the couch, and she leaned into his warmth, resting her head on his shoulder and tucking her feet beneath her. He kissed the top of her head, and she grinned even in her half-asleep state.

"I'm proud of you," Jameson said close to her ear.

The rumble in his deep voice sent a waking tingle up her spine. "Hm?"

"The way you stood up to her today. Linda has a way of intimidating people with just a look, but you stood your ground and made sure she acknowledged what she did and how it affected you."

"I love you," Ava whispered.

"I love you too. I have for years." Jameson rested his cheek against her head.

Ava lifted her head to look at him, knowing what

she would see—honesty, remorse, and a little sadness. "I've loved you for years too. I didn't know what love was then, and maybe I didn't love you in the few weeks we spent together, but after, I knew that you were different, and that I'd missed something amazing."

Jameson swallowed hard. "I'm sorry."

Ava shook her head slowly. "Don't be. Not now. Don't think about what we missed. We're where we're meant to be now." She twisted the edge of a blanket between her fingers, thinking about how they'd come full circle. "I was afraid to admit it or think it back then because I was scared of what that meant: that I'd given my heart to someone I couldn't be with."

A shallow crease formed between Jameson's brows, and she brushed her thumb gently over the worried place. A frown didn't belong here tonight.

Her hand slid to his cheek, and her fingertips brushed along his jaw. "Once I came back, I realized I'd been right all along. You were different, and you were worth fighting for. Then I was scared I wouldn't get another chance because I'd been too afraid to stand up for us last time. I did love you back then. Even as quick as our time together was, I knew what we had between us was special. You're the only one who has been honest with me from the start. All those times you told me I was enough and that I could be strong, you were right. I didn't know then that I could trust you, that I could believe the impossible things you said."

His face was inches from hers, and her words were as soft as the crackling of the fire. With every word, he moved immeasurably closer.

"Now I know you were always right, and I was right when I thought I loved you. I did, and I do. I know what love is now. You showed me."

Jameson leaned in, slowly brushing his nose along hers before dipping his chin to slide his lips against hers. His warm hand slid around her waist and pulled her closer.

He kissed her slowly at first. Then his tempered brushes morphed into something stronger. She slid her hand around the back of his neck and sighed when a low rumble sounded in his chest.

Three quick knocks at the door had them jerking apart, and even the intrusion didn't dampen her urge to fall back into the kiss.

Jameson grunted. "Must be Paul."

Oh, she'd forgotten about Paul when Jameson started kissing her. She touched her lips and grinned as she stood and went to the kitchen while Jameson answered the door.

"Hey, come on in."

Paul stopped just inside the door, only letting in a little of the snowy chill. "She's gone."

Ava reached for a mug in the cabinet, appreciating Paul's signal that it was safe for her to return to the main house. "You want coffee?"

"No thanks. I'm going to be on my way. Just wanted you to know how it went."

Ava turned and rested her backside against the counter. "And?"

Paul rubbed the stubble on his jaw. "It was awkward and a little unexpected. She got in a few jabs about my lowly station, but otherwise she was apologetic."

"I'm really sorry, man. I can't believe she did this to you and Ava," Jameson said.

Paul shook his head. "Can't change it now. I reined in a lot of the yelling I wanted to do, so I think I'm going to have a run with Thane in the indoor arena to let off some steam." He looked back to Ava. "You okay?"

She grinned, appreciative of his concern for her. "I'm fine. I hate to say it, but I'm glad she's gone for now."

Paul jerked his head toward the door. "I'm going to the stables. Let me know if you need anything."

"I will. Thanks for being so understanding today." It was enough that he'd had the news dropped on him, but he'd been concerned for her too.

Paul left with a farewell nod. Jameson closed the door behind him and blew out a relieved breath.

"Glad that's over," Jameson said as he joined her in the kitchen.

He wrapped his arms around her, and she melted into the safety he brought.

"I still can't believe he's my dad," she whispered. It had come as such a shock.

"Me either. I suspected this morning, but then I overheard Linda talking to Dane about it at the main house. It was still hard to believe."

Ava lifted her head. "Wait, why was she talking to Dane about it? He told me today that he'd known for a long time and you had too."

Jameson frowned. "When did he say that? That's not true."

"In the stables, before you got there. Why was he talking to my mother anyway?"

"They were trying to get Mr. Chambers to take the offer on the ranch. I don't know why they'd want him to do that. I can't see how Dane would get anything out of it."

Ava tilted her head, remembering something she'd dismissed earlier. "Why did you fire him?"

His arms tensed around her. "He was rough with Linda earlier. She told him she wasn't sure about getting Mr. Chambers to sell the ranch anymore, and he grabbed her. I was stepping in to put a stop to it when your grandpa walked outside."

Ava's eyes widened. "Really? That's crazy. Did he hurt her?"

"No, but it was rough enough that I wasn't about to let it play out any longer."

"I never thought he'd do something like that." She scoffed, knowing now that people were sometimes capable of greater betrayals than she could imagine.

Jameson rubbed his hands over her back in soothing circles as they talked. "He's fairly new. Mr. Chambers said his old accountant called him up and asked if he'd give Dane a chance. Dane was his nephew or something. I guess your grandpa wanted to give him a fair shake."

Ava straightened. "Wait. Which old accountant? The one we had for years or the one he fired before he hired Louise?"

"Not Randy. He retired and moved to Bloomington to be closer to his grandkids. He's not kin to Dane."

Ava turned and paced in the few feet of kitchen space. "I wonder if this has something to do with the accountant that Grandpa fired. He said the offer he got was almost exactly what the ranch was worth."

Jameson rubbed his jaw. "If he was the accountant, he would know all about the finances around this place. I bet he saw that it was profitable and wants in on the cash cow."

She drummed her fingers on the counter as she

considered the possibility. "You think Grandpa suspects?"

"I don't know, but it would be worth mentioning to him. It sounds plausible to me."

"I just don't have any way to prove it."

"Yeah you do. Ask Linda."

Ava rolled over the idea in her head, not liking the idea of talking to her mother. It was too soon, and the hurt was still too raw. "Like a test?"

"I think it'd be a good one. It could be a way to prove whether or not she has really changed or if she still plans on pulling the rug out from under you and Mr. Chambers."

Ava stepped back into Jameson's arms and smiled up at him. "You're amazing. Have I told you that lately?"

Instead of answering, he tightened his hold around her and kissed her. They could figure everything out later together.

CHAPTER 28
JAMESON

Ava tugged on Jameson's hand, walking briskly along the sidewalk in Blackwater. Her excitement was contagious as she gasped and awed over the local vendor booths and decorations.

"Hot chocolate!" she shouted, pointing toward a tented booth on the other side of the street.

The bags he carried in one hand jostled as he tried to maneuver through the crowd, though Ava was doing a great job dragging him through a cleared path she made. "Looks like they have cookies too."

Ava gasped. "They're from Sticky Sweets!"

Jameson's smile grew wider. He'd never been to the Blackwater Christmas Festival before, and being here with Ava was more exciting than he'd ever expected.

With two weeks left until Christmas, Ava wasn't

holding anything back. She'd found gifts made by local artists for almost everyone at the ranch. Seeing how elated she was to give the gifts did something crazy to his chest.

A thin layer of slushy snow lined the streets on both sides, and the first new snow began to fall as Ava stepped up to the booth to place her order.

"I'd like a large hot chocolate and two snicker-doodle cookies." She turned to look at Jameson over her shoulder, whipping her dark ponytail behind her. "What do you want?"

He hesitated, hypnotized by the pink tinge on her cheeks and nose and the way her dark eyes sparkled with her smile. "Um, I'll have the same."

Ava turned back to Tracy, the owner of Sticky Sweets. "Double it."

"You two finishing up your Christmas shopping tonight?" Tracy asked as she bagged up the cookies.

"I think we're finished." Ava cast a tentative glance at Jameson.

He kept quiet. He really didn't have anyone to buy for at Christmas except his sister, and she usually told him what she wanted him to get her a few months before the Christmas rush began.

A young woman handed them their cups of hot chocolate, while Tracy handed over the bag of cookies. "It's so nice to see the two of you."

"It's great to see you too," Ava said with a smile.

"I need to come by the bakery this week and catch up if you're not too busy."

"I always have time," Tracy said. "Bring that old man with you too."

Jameson frowned and adopted an accusing tone. "Did you just call me old?"

Tracy chuckled, low and heartily. "Not you. You're still young."

Ava reached over the table to give Tracy a one-armed hug. "I'll bring Grandpa with me. He's been staying inside a little more because of the cold."

"A cup of coffee will take care of that. Bring him with you."

"Yes, ma'am," Ava agreed.

Jameson scanned the crowded street as they walked away from the booth. "Have you heard from Felicity?"

Ava pulled her phone out of her pocket. "No, but she said they'd be here about this time. I'm sure we'll run into them."

Felicity said she had talked her husband, Hunter, into coming to the festival, and Jameson wouldn't believe it until he saw it. Christmas festivals weren't really Hunter's scene.

Just as Ava moved to put her phone back into her coat pocket, the screen lit up. Her mother's name was shining bright and imposing.

They stopped walking, and Ava looked at the screen for long seconds. "Should I answer?"

It had been two months since Linda left the ranch, and while Ava had talked to her mother a few times, they hadn't actually made up. Linda had confessed that Dane's uncle was behind the offer and claimed she'd backed out. Still, neither Jameson nor Ava knew whether to believe her.

"Only if you want to," Jameson said.

Ava answered the call and placed the phone against her ear. "Hello."

Jameson stood close to Ava, hoping she felt his silent support as her mother talked. The cheerful Christmas scene around them didn't match the sudden tension in the air. Lights and garland were hung around every storefront, and the dusting of snow only added to the wonderland.

"I'll have to talk to Grandpa, but I'm sure that's fine." Ava paused before continuing. "I'm sure you could stay at the ranch if you wanted."

It sounded like the call was going okay, but he could tell from Ava's stance that she was nervous. One hand held the phone to her ear while the other wrapped around her middle, shielding her from the cold and the uncomfortable nature of the call.

Ava only contributed a few more words here and there before ending the call with a neutral good-bye.

Jameson waited until the phone was back in Ava's pocket before asking, "How did it go?"

Ava shrugged. "Fine, I guess. She wants to come

for Christmas. I offered her a room at the main house. Should I have done that?"

He wrapped his arm around her and pulled her close. "That's up to you. I think it could help by giving the two of you more chances to talk things out."

"That's what I was thinking too. I'm still angry with her, but I've been reading a book on forgiveness, and it's a little convicting. I should be able to forgive her, right?"

"Ideally, yes, but it's never easy." He'd gone through the same struggle with his own mom, except she hadn't been apologetic or cared if he forgave her or not.

Ava slid her gloved hand into his and started walking down the street. "It's over now. The offer is out there, and she said she'd like to stay at the ranch."

"I guess that's a step in the right direction. She's been pretty against the place for half of her life."

"You're right. It's a good thing she wants to come. I shouldn't give up on her completely." Ava turned to him and smiled. "I told Tracy I was finished with my Christmas shopping, but I still don't know what to get for you."

"I can't think of a single thing I'd need or want." It was true. He'd never been so content in his life. He was more than content; he was overwhelmed by the state of his life.

"I'm still getting you something. I'm just not sure what yet," Ava said as she ran her finger over a display of brooches. "I guess I should get my mother something if she's coming for Christmas."

Jameson watched in awe as Ava began browsing the booths with a watchful eye, looking for something Linda might like. "You amaze me sometimes," he said quietly. "Actually, a lot more often than I admit."

Ava looked up at him, confused. "Why?"

"Your mom did something horrible to you. She did a lot of horrible things by treating you badly for years. Yet, you're set on forgiving her."

She turned her attention to a display of crocheted scarves. "I'm not sure I could have done it had you not led me to the Lord. I've learned a lot about how to forgive, but only because I've seen how God forgives us for our sins."

It was a lesson he'd been taught in church since he was a kid, but it was rare he saw it play out in life. He hadn't considered forgiving Linda yet, but Ava had.

She ran her fingers over a brown scarf and pulled it from the hanger. "I think she'd like this." Ava handed it to the seller and kept browsing the booth. There were small, wooden plaques with Bible verses burned into the wood. She read every one of them before picking one up. "I think I need this one."

Jameson reached for it, and she handed it over.

"Judge not, and you will not be judged; condemn not, and you will not be condemned; forgive, and you will be forgiven. Luke 6:37."

Ava took the plaque from him and handed it to the seller. "I have a feeling we need this one in the main house office," she said as she pulled her wallet from her purse. "You have one in your office. I think it's fitting."

Jameson took the bag from the seller and added it to the handful of bags he'd been carrying. When they stepped out of the booth, he guided her into a narrow alley between shops and pulled her close.

Ava giggled. "What are you doing?"

He slid the bags up his arm and cupped her face in his hands. "Hiding in the shadows to kiss my woman."

She didn't wait for him to take the kiss. She met him with the same intensity he felt building inside him.

Every time Ava showed innocent kindness or did anything selfless, a surge of something big and uncontainable welled inside him.

Love. It was love. He was still getting used to the effects, and it caught him off guard every time.

He rested his forehead against hers and whispered, "I love you."

"I love you too." She smiled, clearly entertained by his adoration. "But we better slip out of here before your sister finds us making out in an alley."

Jameson chuckled and took her hand in his, leading her back out into the busy streets of Blackwater.

Ava hadn't asked him what he intended to get her for Christmas, and he was glad. It was hard enough keeping the ring tucked in his pocket when he wanted it on her finger now.

He could wait a few weeks until Christmas, right? At least he hoped he could.

CHAPTER 29
AVA

Ava looked up from her stitching to see Vera yawning. They'd been stitching and chatting for hours, but Ava wasn't ready to head back to the main house yet.

"You calling cows?" Stella asked.

Vera smiled sweetly. "It's been a long week."

"It's Tuesday," Ava said with a chuckle.

"Yeah, but I baked sweet potato casseroles for four different Christmas parties this week. Those extra hours add up fast."

Ava was the last of the Tuesday evening gang still hanging around, so she packed up her stitching. "I should head out anyway."

"You don't have to rush off," Stella said.

"I know, but Vera won't go to bed until I leave because she's a good host."

Vera's cheeks reddened. The woman was too soft spoken for her own good.

"I'll drive you back," Stella said as she laid her stitching on the end table.

"I drove. Jameson had something come up, so he said he'd meet me back at the main house later."

As if on cue, Ava's phone dinged.

Jameson: I'm heading your way soon. You think there are any leftovers?

Ava typed out a response and picked up her purse. "He said he'll be on his way soon, so I better run. Vera, is there anything I can do to help you out with the extra baking?"

"Oh, no. I can handle it. I enjoy it, really. I don't have any more Christmas party orders, so I'll be back on schedule soon enough."

Ava wrapped Vera in a hug. "Call me anytime."

"Thank you, sweetheart."

Stella opened her arms for her own farewell hug. "Don't let the snake bite you tonight."

Ava chuckled. "She's been pretty good so far." She held onto Stella a little longer so she wouldn't have to face her friend when she asked the next question. "I was wondering if I could invite her over here for our next stitching."

Stella groaned and sagged. "Are you pullin' my leg?"

"No. Maybe," Ava said.

Stella leaned back and straightened her shoulders. "Fine. But she better be on her best behavior. One wrong word and she's getting laxative in her coffee."

"Deal," Ava agreed. "I'll see you two tomorrow."

Stella and Vera both walked Ava to the door and gave her another hug before she ran into the snowy evening. Winter was in full swing, and the temperatures had been brutal all week.

Ava started her car and huffed warm breath into her gloves. She could see the lights from the main house in the distance. The ranch hands had gone all out with the lights and decorations for the few guests that braved the harsher weather. The activities schedule was minimized, and half the workers had gone home for the season, but the ones left seemed to enjoy the cheer of the holidays.

Ava parked in front of the main house and took a few deep breaths. The mad dash to the door required a pep talk. The freezing wind hit her hard when she stepped out of the car, and she made sure to keep her footing on the snowy steps leading to the porch.

She barged inside and closed the door quickly behind her. Before she could take a relieved breath, she heard shouting coming from the back of the house. More than one raised voice clamored for attention.

"Would you two stop it!" Grandpa shouted.

Oh, no. If Grandpa was upset, it couldn't be good.

She sprinted toward the voices coming from the office, but a man stepped out as she rounded the corner.

Ava tried to recall the bravery she'd used to stand up to her mother, but the man standing in front of her was tall and broad shouldered, making him seem three times her size. Besides that, his expression was stern and cold in a way that would strike fear in anyone.

He stopped to size her up, and Ava felt her blood run cold.

"Is that her?" he asked in a gruff and demanding tone.

Linda stepped around him, putting herself between the man and Ava. "Leave her out of this."

The man gave a short and sinister laugh. "Leave her out? She's the reason I'm here!"

"What's he talking about?" Ava asked in a low voice.

Her grandpa pushed his way out of the office. His expression was angrier than she'd ever seen. "None of this has to do with Ava."

The man rounded on her grandpa. "If she wasn't around, you'd have no reason to keep the place. She can't run the ranch anyway."

Ava narrowed her eyes at the man who must be Dane's uncle—the one who wanted to buy the ranch. "He said he's not selling. That should be the end of it."

The man's gaze bore into her, pushing her to back down with his size and power. "If you weren't around, he'd have no reason to hold onto the place, and it would be mine."

He took a step toward Ava, but Linda took a quick step to the side, blocking the man from Ava's view.

"I said leave her out of this," Linda said boldly.

"Not a chance," the man said as he grabbed Linda by the arm and jerked her out of the way.

Without her mother in front of her, Ava stood toe-to-toe with the angry man.

Linda's back hit the wall, knocking the breath out of her and making her gasp for air.

Ava turned on the man, summoning all her courage. "Don't touch her!"

The way his eyes narrowed to her, she had a feeling he wasn't interested in her mother anyway.

"Ava, get out of here," her mother said quickly.

The last of her sentence was cut off as the man lunged for Ava. His big hands reached toward her with the promise that he could easily overtake her.

She ducked to the side and barely escaped from the narrow hallway. Running toward the front door, she pushed a decorative end table over behind her, hoping to slow him down until she could get outside and scream for help. Glass shattered, but she couldn't worry about it now.

Ava looked over her shoulder and only saw the big man running after her. She said a quick prayer that her grandpa and mother were out of harm's way. When she had a second to think about her own safety, she started a prayer for herself.

"Ava!"

She was a mere three feet from the door, but she turned quickly at the sound of her mother's voice. The layout of the main house made a big circle on the main floor, and her mother and grandpa were racing toward her from the living room to her left.

Linda was running toward Ava, but her attention was glued to the man with a look of terror on her face.

The man had stopped running, and he held a gun pointed at Ava.

A heavy force crashed into her, knocking her off her feet. An ear-splitting noise came with the pain, wrapping her in a confusing daze.

Her grandpa's voice was muffled and far away as he screamed her name, and the world faded to black.

CHAPTER 30
JAMESON

Jameson turned off the light and locked the door to his office as he stepped into the hallway. Everly and Stella were long gone, and the check-in office was dark and quiet as he made his way out.

He locked up the check-in office and glanced toward the brightly-lit dining hall. Most activities moved inside during the winter months, but a few people scurried around outside, bundled up in thick coats and layers.

"Hey, you packin' up?"

Jameson pocketed the keys and turned to offer Paul his hand. "Callin' it a day."

Paul jerked his head toward the main house. "You heading over there?"

The main house was a few steps away, and Ava

waited inside. Of course he was headed that way. "You know it."

"Mind if I join you? I haven't said anything to Linda since she got here, and I thought I should at least stop by."

Jameson shook his head. "You're a better man than I am."

"Don't nominate me for sainthood yet. I just don't want to stay on her bad side. I'm not ready to exchange Christmas cards yet."

"I really do think she's trying to be better—for Ava."

"And for that, I'm glad," Paul said.

"Let's get over there. I'm freezing."

A scream came from the main house followed by the unmistakable bang of a gun firing close by.

Jameson was running before he had time to register what was happening, and Paul was right beside him.

The front door opened, spilling orange-tinged light into the dark night, and a man sprinted from the porch toward a truck parked at the corner of the house.

Jameson pointed at the man. "Get him! I'll see what's going on inside."

Mr. Chambers appeared in the open doorway, shaking and pale. "Stop him!"

Paul did as ordered and tackled the man to the ground. The fall looked painful for both of them, but it was a good thing Paul was in good shape. He wrestled the man on the ground as Jameson reached the door.

"He has a gun!" Mr. Chambers yelled to Paul.

Jameson felt the blood drain from his face. The man had shot that gun inside the main house where Ava probably was right now.

Then Mr. Chambers turned to Jameson and confirmed his worst fear. "We need help."

Jameson pushed past his boss into the house. Ava and Linda lay tangled in a pool of blood that crept slowly outward as it seeped into the rug.

"Ava!" He slid to his knees beside them and brushed the hair from her face.

Linda lay on top of Ava, and bright-red blood covered her mother's shirt around the hole in her back.

"Get the fire department on the phone. I have to let them know what we need."

He jerked his coat off and pulled his outer shirt over his head. Placing it on Linda's wound, he applied pressure and reached for the carotid artery on Ava's neck. There was a faint but steady pulse.

His shaking hand moved to Linda's neck where he detected an even weaker pulse. It took every ounce of his emergency training to remain calm while Ava lay unresponsive on the floor.

"Noah Harding is on the phone. What should I tell him?" Mr. Chambers asked.

"Put it on speaker."

Mr. Chambers did as he was told and held the phone out toward Jameson.

"Jameson?"

"I have one gunshot wound to the right lumbar region. Pulse is unstable, and bleeding is profuse. Unresponsive." Jameson turned his attention to Ava and brushed a hand through her hair again, afraid to assess her for fear her condition would be worse or equal to her mother's.

His fingers tangled in a section of hair, and he noticed the blood. He felt over her head and found the source of the bleeding. "Another victim with an open head wound. Unconscious."

"We'll be on our way soon. I'll alert the hospital," Noah said.

Jameson had worked as a paramedic for the Blackwater Fire Department alongside Noah for years before accepting the foreman job at Wolf Creek. He knew his friend would do everything he could to give Ava and her mother the best care possible.

Jameson remembered Paul, who was hopefully still hanging on with the shooter outside. "Call Asa and get the police department here. The shooter is still on site, and as far as I know, he's still armed." He turned to Mr. Chambers and ordered, "Call someone to help Paul."

Mr. Chambers looked at the phone he held for

Jameson.

"Call now. Noah knows what we need."

Mr. Chambers shakily held the phone to his face as he made the call, and Jameson turned his attention back to Ava and her mother. He pushed the fear out of his mind as he relied on his training to help keep both of them as stable as possible. With Linda's wound so close to her spine, he didn't want to risk moving her without backup.

Ava finally regained consciousness, but she was barely responsive when he saw the emergency lights through the window.

"Ava, I'm here. It's me. You're gonna be okay." He kept talking but refrained from mentioning Linda. He wasn't sure he could give the same assurances for her. Gunshot wounds were always ugly and stabilization was never easy.

Mr. Chambers held the door open, waving the emergency workers toward them. "In here!"

Jameson had never been so happy to see his old friend, Noah, in his life. With a team of trained EMTs, they were able to move Linda and get her loaded into the first ambulance and on her way to the nearest hospital. Minutes later, they had Ava on a longboard and in the other ambulance.

The police had apprehended the shooter, and Stella and Everly were doing crowd control around the scene with Thane pacing beside them. Mr.

Chambers stood out of the way, while Vera fussed over him.

Jameson waved his boss over. "You want to ride in the front?"

"Yes." Mr. Chambers' answer was quick. He'd want to be at the hospital where they were taking his daughter and granddaughter.

Remi jogged up as they were about to leave. "I'll meet you there and stay with Mr. Chambers in the waiting room."

"Thanks. Call Felicity and tell her what's happening." There was a good chance she might have already heard the news since she lived on the same ranch as Noah, but Jameson's sister would want to know what was going on with Ava. They'd grown close these last few months since Ava moved here.

Jameson climbed into the back of the ambulance where the EMT was starting an IV on Ava. He'd worked with Travis a few times before, but they'd generally been on different crews back when Jameson worked for the department.

Travis carefully administered the saline drip and tracked Ava's vitals. "So, how have you been?"

Apparently, Travis was a master at managing high-intensity situations. His words were even and calm, though he didn't look up from his work.

"Been better," Jameson answered. He'd resolved himself to staying out of Travis's way and let the man do the heavy lifting. Right now, Jameson held Ava's hand and kept assuring her he was by her side.

His pulse wouldn't stop thrumming in his ears, and Ava needed him to be at his best for her right now. He blew out a heavy breath and started praying. "Lord, please be with Ava. Please give her strength and healing. And the people helping her, give them focus and clarity. Help me to be whatever she needs."

He kept praying, naming everything he could possibly think of that would calm the storm they were caught up in.

"And please be with Linda. I—I don't know. She needs help. Ava needs to fix things with her mother."

He wasn't sure where the words had come from, but they were true, stuttering and rushed as they were. They all needed help tonight, and Linda most of all.

CHAPTER 31

AVA

Ava jerked out of a restless sleep when the intercom beeped.

"Doctor Hansel, call 404."

Looking around, she realized where she was—Cody Memorial Hospital—and this was not a nightmare. She rested her head against Jameson's shoulder where she'd been dozing off and on.

"What time is it?" she whispered. More people were walking past the waiting room than in the past few hours, but she hadn't even checked the clock before she drifted off the last time.

"About seven. Shift change," he whispered back.

Ava sat up and stretched her arms above her head. "I think I want some coffee."

Everly stood quickly. "I'll get it. What do you want?"

Everly had traded places with Remi early this

morning when Grandpa needed to go home and rest for a few hours. Now, Everly was the most chipper of the waiting room crew.

Ava didn't have enough energy to adequately appreciate her friend's unending optimism, but she gave her a warm smile. "Coffee with two sugars. Bold if they have it."

"Anything for you?" Everly asked Jameson.

"The same," he said dryly.

Everly sauntered off in search of caffeine. Ava stood, trying to force her body to stay semi-alert.

She rubbed her eyes with the heels of her hands. "How are you still awake?"

Jameson gave her a half smile that was a little sympathetic. "I didn't gash my head open twelve hours ago."

"Right." Ava's hand slipped to the back of her head where she felt the rigid staples they'd used to close the wound. "They said it's okay for me to sleep?"

"They did. You're walking and talking fine, so you can sleep. Besides, I'm here to watch for any symptoms that we would need to worry about."

Ava smiled, but she felt more like crying all of a sudden. "Thanks."

Jameson reached for her, and she went to him, sitting on his lap and tucking her face in the crook of his neck like a tired child. He brushed his hand over her hair, and she tensed when he moved over the newly closed place.

"I'm sorry," he said quickly.

"It didn't hurt." Ava squeezed her eyes closed. She'd only been released a few hours ago, and she was still processing everything that had happened. "I just remembered they had to shave some of my hair, and that seems like a stupid thing to care about right now."

Without warning, the tears came. They were silent, but Jameson's arms tightened around her when she sniffled. It was funny and ridiculous that she'd made it almost twelve hours without falling to tears, and a three-inch patch of shaved head pushed her over the edge.

Her mother was currently in emergency surgery, and every emotion was overwhelming. She worried for her mother and grandpa, fought constant exhaustion, and the pain medicine they'd given her was beginning to wear off.

Ava looked up at the angelic statue that hung on the wall at the far end of the waiting room. The verse below it read, "Come to me all who are weary and burdened, and I will give you rest. Matthew 11:28."

She was weary, she was burdened, and she was here, but she'd yet to have rest. Her eyes fell closed, and she began praying. It didn't take long before she was fighting sleep again. Maybe praying wasn't the best thing for staying alert right now.

Ava lifted her head from Jameson's shoulder. "What are you thinking?"

Jameson adjusted his arms around her. "Just praying."

She smiled, knowing Jameson was the best man she could possibly have by her side right now. "Me too."

The police officer who had come by her room when the doctor was stapling her head earlier walked into the waiting room. He set his sights on Ava and Jameson, and she stood to greet him.

"How are you feeling?" he asked her.

"Much better. Thanks for asking, Officer Scott."

He grinned and stuck his thumbs into the front of his belt. "You can call me Asa."

Jameson stuck out his hand. "Thanks for everything."

Asa smiled. He had a genuine good-guy vibe, and Ava had been glad to have him on their case even before he told her Jameson was his good friend.

"Anytime. I actually came to give you an update. The man who shot Ms. Collins was Clayton Harrington."

Jameson frowned. "I've heard of him."

"He ran for city council a couple of years ago. He also confessed to shooting Ms. Collins."

Jameson huffed. "As if he was going to get out of that one."

Asa tilted his head from side to side. "I know what you mean, but he didn't even wait for an attorney. He was pretty vocal when we brought him in, and he spilled everything. That's not to say that things won't change in the courtroom after he lawyers up, but it's a good start for his case. He's looking at twenty to life."

Ava released a heavy breath. "Wow." It was big news, and she still didn't understand everything that went with it. "Did he say why?"

"He'd caught wind that there was a geological survey conducted near Wolf Creek Ranch in the early seventies that alluded to an oil field. The Bighorn Basin is dotted with them."

Ava gasped. "I wonder if Grandpa knows."

"He knows," Jameson said. "Lots of folks around here have sold out to people looking for oil and natural gas fields."

Ava looked up at him. "Why didn't you say anything when I mentioned the offer?"

Jameson shrugged. "It didn't occur to me until now."

Asa shifted nervously. "Looks like this wasn't Clayton's first offense. He had a charge for domestic violence that was dropped in the late nineties. There's a family connection too. His brother and dad died in prison serving sentences for various assault charges."

"His brother? You mean Dane's dad?" Ava asked.

Asa nodded. "That's the one."

A weight dropped in her stomach. No wonder Dane had jerked her mother around. She'd heard of kids who grew up in abusive homes and became adults who did the same to their families, but she hadn't knowingly met one until now.

"Thanks for letting us know. I didn't even know who he was," Ava said.

Asa gave them a sympathetic grin. "We'll need to get your statement soon, but I imagine you'll need some rest first."

"We'll come by the station sometime tomorrow," Jameson promised.

Asa turned back to Ava. "I hope your mom is doing okay. I'll tell the church, and we'll be praying for both of you."

Ava's smile turned genuine. "I really appreciate that."

The church had become another sanctuary for her. She'd accepted Christ as her savior soon after returning to Blackwater, and she'd been welcomed in every way possible. She'd come to know almost everyone in the small church they attended, and she had no doubt the members would be calling soon asking how they could help.

Everly walked in balancing three cups in her hands. "Hey, Asa. How's the family?"

Asa gave Everly a careful, one-armed hug. "Same as always. Everything good in your world?"

"Oh, yeah. Good as gold."

Everly always said she was good when someone asked how she was doing. Her tendency to look on the bright side of everything was only heightened by her upcoming wedding.

If Ava had to have any friend by her side at a time like this, she was glad it was Everly.

The doctor Ava and Jameson had spoken to earlier walked in. He wore scrubs as he had earlier, and the flecked gray hair peeking from beneath his scrub cap gave him a distinguished look.

"Miss Collins. Mr. Ford," he said in greeting as he extended a hand to Ava first, then Jameson. "Linda has come through her first surgery. We were able to save her lacerated liver and repair some of the other damage to her bowels. She'll need more surgeries to fully repair everything, but we've done enough for today."

"How bad is it? I mean, how long will she be recovering from this?" Ava asked.

"I want to be hopeful, but we can't predict how severe or long lasting the injuries will be. She is stable, and you should be able to see her within the next few hours."

A wave of lightheadedness washed over Ava as she listened to the report. "Thank you, Doctor."

"We'll wait here until she's out of recovery," Jameson said.

The doctor clasped his hands and asked, "Would you like for me to pray with you again?"

Ava nodded, unsure if she could trust her voice not to crack right now.

Everyone bowed their heads as the doctor prayed for Linda's recovery. Ava felt the faint presence of hope and knew that if her mother had been fighting for her life a few months ago, everything would be different. Their relationship would still be strained, Ava wouldn't have the comfort of the Lord, and she wouldn't have anyone to stand beside her during the uncertain times.

Once the doctor left, Everly kept everyone in good spirits, including the older woman in the waiting room with them whose husband had suffered from a heart attack. Ava opened her mouth to thank Everly for keeping everyone's chin up more than once, but a word of thanks didn't seem to be enough.

Over three hours had passed before Ava started pacing. Everly had gone to get lunch and bring something back for Ava and Jameson, and she was beginning to see how much she'd been relying on her friend's optimism.

Jameson stepped up behind her and wrapped

his arms around her. "I'm sure they'll let you see her soon."

Ava sighed. "I know. I'm just tired of sitting here with nothing to do except think about it."

"You can go somewhere. Walk around. I'll call you if they come looking for you. I could go with you, and we can leave Everly here to wait."

Ava turned and pressed her face to his chest. "No. Surely, they'll come soon. I'd hate to walk out the door and miss them by ten minutes."

The waiting room door opened, and Everly walked in holding a bag and two drinks. Close behind her was the doctor, walking with purpose and a neutral expression.

The doctor pointed to the nearby chairs. "Have a seat."

CHAPTER 32

AVA

The breath Ava had been inhaling stopped, gripping her chest in an involuntary spasm. Jameson held her hand and sat beside her. When the doctor took the seat across from Ava, Everly strolled to the other side of the room and pretended she was interested in the wallpaper.

Ava focused on Everly's long hair and tried to will her friend to come sit in the chair next to her. She had a feeling the doctor wasn't going to tell them her mother was going to be fine.

"Ms. Collins has been out of recovery for a few hours now, and we're monitoring her closely. She has regained consciousness, but she is still unable to move certain parts of her body. It's very early in her recovery, and we're still exploring the extent of her injuries, so there's a chance that the paralysis isn't permanent."

Ava stared at the doctor. With a hand covering her mouth, she focused on breathing in and out of her nose. Paralysis?

"Like I said, we're still trying to understand the damage from the wound. Bullets are destructive to the sensitive internal tissues and nerves, and she will have multiple surgeries before we know of every injury Ms. Collins has."

"Okay." The word was monotone as Ava tried to make sense of the doctor's explanation.

"Do you have any questions?" the doctor asked.

"No." She did have questions, but she couldn't string together a coherent thought right now much less understand anything else he might tell her.

"I'm sure you'll have questions later, and I'll have more updates for you as we continue to monitor her condition."

Ava nodded as the doctor stood. Jameson grabbed her hand, providing his silent support.

The doctor left the waiting room, and Ava stood watching the door. What had he said? She couldn't wrap her head around the news.

Jameson pulled her into his arms. "I'm going to pray, okay?"

"Okay," she said low.

She closed her eyes as Jameson pleaded with God on her mother's behalf. He prayed for understanding, healing, strength, and peace, and she wanted all of those things. She wanted them to wash over her right now because she was breaking in two.

"Amen." He brushed her hair from her face. "What do you need from me?"

"Just this." She rested her head against his chest and stood as still as possible, hoping that nothing would disturb the bubble she wanted to stay in forever.

"I wasn't very kind to her," Ava finally said.

Jameson's hold tightened. "Stop. Don't think like that."

"What if I don't get to tell her I'm sorry?"

Everly walked over, and Ava released Jameson to hug her friend. This was only a tiny part of the support system she'd come to know in the last few months, and she could never take any of her new friends for granted now.

Everly spoke sweetly as she rubbed circles over Ava's back. "All I can say is that we'll weather all of this together. We'll be here to help you and your mother."

"I know." Ava raised her head and wiped her eyes. Her chest still felt heavy, but she desperately wanted Everly's words to be true—that they would come through the storm together. Facing her mother's prognosis wasn't as scary when she had people who loved her beside her through it all.

Ava turned to Jameson and Everly, who both

looked worried and determined. "Can we just eat and watch *Family Feud*?"

Everly grabbed Ava's hand and pulled her to the small table where she'd set up their lunch. "Yes! I love game shows."

They'd eaten their lunches and cleaned up the mess by the time a nurse came to see them. Ava tried not to expect the worst, but her shoulders tightened instinctively.

"Ava? Your mother is waking up a little more now, and she'd like to see you."

Ava nodded and reached for Jameson's hand.

"Only one visitor is allowed in the ICU rooms at a time," the nurse said sweetly.

Jameson faced Ava, pulling her hands close to his chest. "I'll be right here if you need me."

She took a calming breath. "Thank you. I actually think I'm okay. Why don't you go check on Grandpa? I'm sure you have a lot to catch up on too. I can do this."

Jameson squeezed her hands. "I know you can. Call me if you need anything, and I'll come right back."

She pressed a quick kiss to his lips and whispered in his ear, "I love you."

"I love you too. We're going to all get through this."

"Together," she finished.

"Together."

Ava let her hands fall from his grasp as she followed the nurse down the hallway and through a set of double doors. She kept her attention on the nurse leading her as they walked past rooms with glass walls filled with patients in the most critical conditions. She didn't want to know how much worse things could be right now.

The nurse did a spin in front of one of the doors and pointed. "Here you are. Visiting hours end at seven this evening."

Ava didn't like the thought of having to leave her mother here, but it didn't seem as though they were an exception to the rule. "Thank you."

When the nurse smiled and walked toward the nurses' station, Ava took a deep breath and stepped into the room.

It looked a little different than she'd expected, but her focus didn't remain on the furnishings for long. Her mother lay on her back in the single bed. Her usually pristine hair was matted and pulled to one side, and her eyes were dark with smudged makeup.

Linda opened her eyes and looked at the ceiling. "Ava?" Her voice was hoarse and low like a timid child.

"I'm here." Ava stepped to the side of her mother's bed and picked up her hand. Her mother's skin was freezing.

"I can't move much," Linda said.

"I know. They told me there was some paralysis." She swallowed hard, unsure how to talk about the injuries that she still didn't understand.

"My throat hurts," Linda rasped.

"Don't try to talk then, just listen." Ava squeezed her mother's hand. "Can you feel that?"

"Yes."

Ava pulled a chair close to the bed and kept a grip on her mother's hand. When she settled, she took a second to pray—for words and understanding.

"Whatever problems we have between us, they can be fixed. I resented you, and I was mad at you, but I didn't stop loving you. And I see now that I let the anger overpower that love, and I'm sorry."

A tear fell from the corner of Linda's eye, snaking its way into her hair. "I'm sorry. I love you too. I was wrong so many times."

"I forgive you, and I hope you can forgive me too one day," Ava whispered.

More tears fell from Linda's eyes that matched the ones on Ava's face. She still had her mother, and that was a blessing.

"Mom, we're going to get through this together," Ava said with the determination Jameson and Everly had given her in the waiting room.

"I forgive you," Linda said. She sniffed and looked up at the ceiling. "This is my fault. Not yours. I wasn't good to you, and I really messed up."

Ava brushed a hand over her mother's hair. "Can we leave the past in the past and make a better future?" she asked.

"I'd like that more than anything."

CHAPTER 33
JAMESON

Jameson stepped out of his office and peeked into Ava and Mr. Chambers' new office across the hall. The lights were off, and no one was around.

When Linda was going to be released from the hospital, they'd needed a main-floor bedroom for her. Since neither Mr. Chambers nor Linda could climb the stairs, they'd turned the home office into a bedroom and Mr. Chambers had moved into it, leaving Linda the room with the en suite bathroom.

That meant Ava's and Mr. Chambers' office was in the check-in building with Jameson's now, and he liked being able to peek in and see Ava whenever he wanted.

Right now, he wanted lunch, and he went looking for Ava to see if she could sneak away with him. They'd missed the outrageous Christmas dinner Vera had cooked, but she'd made a smaller duplicate meal for Jameson, Ava, Linda, and Mr. Chambers to eat on this week. Jameson didn't mind a Christmas meal after the new year. Vera's food was delicious any time.

With Linda in the hospital for three weeks, Christmas had looked different this year. He'd eaten in the hospital cafeteria with Ava, but they hadn't gotten to exchange gifts or attend the Christmas service at church together. She'd been looking forward to both, and he was determined to at least give her his gift as soon as things calmed down around here. Ava spent so much time looking after her mother, and he understood her attention was needed elsewhere. He could be patient.

Jameson walked into the main house and toed off his boots at the door. He didn't hear any rustling around and decided to try the living room where Ava and Linda spent more of their time.

Linda sat on the couch alone with scraps of torn envelopes piled beside her. She looked up from the card she held.

"Sorry"—Jameson held up a hand—"I was just looking for Ava." He turned to head for the kitchen when he heard Linda.

"Wait."

Jameson reluctantly turned, dreading what Linda might have to say. He'd done a good job of avoiding her this week, but she'd finally cornered him.

She laid the card beside her. "Ava told me you built the ramp out front."

He had. The dining hall had a ramp on the far side of the building, but the main house only had stairs. He'd built a wooden ramp between the main house and check-in office while Linda was still in the hospital.

"I did. Paul helped."

It was petty, but he hoped the mention of Paul stung her a little. Jameson still couldn't wrap his head around the secret Linda had kept from Ava and her real dad.

"I wanted to thank you." Linda picked at her fingernails in her lap. The manicured nails were chipped—something he thought Linda would hate. "Ava said you saved me. Thank you for that, too."

"It wasn't just me," he said truthfully. "But you're welcome."

Linda kept looking down, and her expression was sad like he'd never seen from her before now. "These are get well soon cards from viewers in Denver."

Jameson took in the pile of opened letters and the huge stack waiting to be opened. "That's a lot of well wishes," he said.

She nodded slowly. "The station said I could come back, but they requested I resign. I'll have so many doctor appointments and difficulties moving around, even more so standing, until I get through therapy. It just wouldn't work out."

What could he say? He'd always disliked Linda, but he didn't want her to lose her job that she seemed to love. What if something happened and he wasn't able to do his job as foreman anymore? It would be devastating. "I'm sorry."

"I'm just not sure what my life is going to look like now. My job was my life. Now I'm confined to that chair for at least the next few months." She pointed at the wheelchair she was using until they could determine if therapy would be helpful.

Ava had told him the doctors seemed hopeful that she would walk on her own again one day, but they couldn't be sure or even give a timeline of how long it would take her to learn to walk again.

"Maybe you need a different life," he said. "Your old job at the news station relied on your physical appearance."

She gave him a confused look.

He huffed and rubbed a hand over his jaw, trying to think of the words he wanted to say. "Your worth isn't in your appearance or your ability to move. It's not in your physical body at all. I've felt sorry for you for a long time because of the life you were living —lost."

Linda kept her gaze glued to him as if listening.

Good. He hoped she was hearing what he had to say.

"Your job depended on your face, but you're more than that. The way you look and the way you hold your chin up like you're better than everyone else doesn't mean anything to your family and the people who care about you—the people who spend their lives with you."

"You mean the people who have to take care of me now?" Linda asked sadly.

"No. You don't get it at all. Ava needs a mom, and that's important to me because I love her." He pressed a fingertip to his chest. "Your dad could use a daughter who gives a rip about him because he's lost a lot lately."

Linda tucked her chin, and he wondered if he'd just kicked her while she was down.

"Do you even want to hear what I think?" he asked.

She hesitated before nodding slowly.

"Your face doesn't get you into heaven. Neither does the way you treat people." He crossed his arms over his chest. "I hear you've been running from the Lord for a while now. It's not too late to go back and fix it."

Linda let out a shaky breath. "I don't know how," she admitted, sounding defeated and tired.

He heard a door close, and Ava walked in with a smile on her face.

"Hey, I was looking for you." She planted a sweet kiss on his cheek before turning to her mother. "You need anything?"

Linda cleared her throat. "No, I'm just going to finish going through these cards."

"Keep them together, and I'll tie them into a book later. Stella showed me how to do it for Christmas cards and stuff."

Linda straightened the pile of opened cards. "That would be nice."

Ava leaned over her mother and kissed her forehead. "We'll be right back. Call me if you need me."

Ava strolled over to him and took his hand. "Ready?"

"Just a second. I'll meet you outside."

She grinned at him and went to get her coat and boots by the front door.

Jameson turned back to Linda. He could only hope she'd been listening, for Ava's sake and her own. "You want to know how to get right with the Lord? You want to know how to turn everything around and do things right in the future?" He jerked his head toward the door where Ava waited. "Watch and learn."

CHAPTER 34

AVA

Ava sighed as Jameson parked the truck in front of the church. They were already running late for the service, and she was hesitant to go in at all.

"Everything okay?" Jameson asked as he turned off the diesel engine, quieting the heavy roar.

"Yeah. I feel like she was so close to saying yes this morning." Ava had been cautiously nudging her mother to come to church since she was released from the hospital, but she'd yet to succeed.

Jameson picked up Ava's hand and kissed it before threading his fingers between hers. He found new ways to adore her daily, and each look and touch sent her heart racing.

Right now, his dark eyes held understanding. "She'll come around. I think she's warming up to coming back, and you're doing all you can. Her decision will be just that—her decision. And it'll only happen when she's ready."

Ava squeezed his hand. "I know. I'm just so anxious. I want her to know the Lord like I do. It changed my life, and she needs Him. We all need Him in our lives."

"You're preaching to the choir, but I know what you mean. It's hard to see someone you love walking around lost."

"Is that what it was like with your mom?" Ava asked softly.

Jameson nodded. "Yep. It was like talking to a stump. She wasn't open-minded at all."

She still couldn't understand all that Jameson had gone through with his mom. The thought of a young Jameson being neglected by his own blood was heartbreaking. How many years did she ignore and belittle him? How had he grown into the wonderful man she knew today?

"I have a lot of people to thank today," Ava said. The church members had really gone above and beyond when her mother was released from the hospital. They'd made dinners, delivered cakes, and sent care packages. Hopefully, Linda would make it to church and thank them herself one day.

"Let's go. I'm right here with you," Jameson said with a smile.

Inside, they went straight to a pew on the right side where Remi and Jess were sitting. The pew in front of them was filled with wranglers, and her grandpa sat in the aisle seat.

Ava stood between Jameson and Jess as everyone sang hymns and praise songs. While the preacher delivered a message about the power of repentance, Ava's thoughts drifted to her mother.

She shouldn't be hanging onto the old hurts. Ava and her mother were on a good path, and dwelling on the past wasn't good for their future. Still, she couldn't help but think they were stuck right now, and a lot of Ava's worry hinged on her mother's disdain for the faith that Ava had recently embraced.

Closing her eyes, she prayed silently. *Lord, how do I lead her to You? How can I help both of us heal? Help me to understand what she needs.*

A creaking at the entrance behind her caught Ava's attention, and she turned. Stella held the wooden door open as Linda wheeled her chair into the sanctuary.

She'd come, and she'd convinced Stella, of all people, to bring her.

Ava scooted to the end of the pew where Linda pulled her chair to a stop. Jameson moved down to sit with them, and Stella sat in the pew behind them.

Every nerve ending in Ava's body hummed in excitement. Linda had gone through the trouble of getting ready, even with her limited mobility, and had gotten up the nerve to ask the person who blatantly despised her to bring her to church.

Did it all mean as much as Ava wanted it to? After hearing her mother put down religion at every turn, the fact that she was sitting in a church listening to a message on repentance was a miracle only God was capable of constructing.

After church, Stella invited some of the ladies over to stitch and plan Everly's engagement shower. Ava had contained her surprise when Stella had invited Linda, who'd accepted the invitation with only a moment's hesitation.

Once everyone was settled in the cozy living room, Vera showed up with pound cake, and Stella made coffee.

The winter season was slow, as far as guest capacity was concerned, but there were plenty of things to maintain around the ranch that kept the wranglers busy. Ava enjoyed the relaxed pace and the freedom to enjoy time with her friends, especially on Sunday afternoons.

Ava picked up the square she'd been working on and showed it to her mother. "You want one to work on?"

Linda held up a hand. "Oh no. I'll just watch."

Ava settled into her usual seat on the end of the

couch. Feeling bolder in the casual setting with her friends, she said, "I heard you used to stitch with Grandma Lottie."

"I did. A little. When I was young."

"Will you tell me what she was like?" Ava asked.

When Linda hesitated, Ava's heart sank. Maybe one day they'd be able to talk about the grandma Ava had missed out on knowing.

Stella plopped down on the couch beside Ava and draped her arm over the back. "I'll tell you a story about the time we got lost in Boogertown, Tennessee and had to call your grandpa for directions."

Vera burst into a cheerful laugh. "I remember that! We sounded like a bunch of clucking chickens on the church bus trying to figure our way out of the middle of nowhere."

Ava listened, and everyone laughed as they took turns telling stories. Each account that included her grandma filled her with a warmth and pride she'd never experienced before.

Eventually, Linda told a story about the time she'd smuggled a kitten and a chick into her bedroom and kept them hidden from Grandma Lottie for a week.

Stella's booming laughter filled the cabin. "Lottie was an animal lover, but she was not a fan of indoor pets."

"Did you ever have a dog?" Ava asked. She

hadn't been allowed to have pets growing up, and she'd grown fond of Paul's dog, Thane. The wolf dog was gentle despite his size.

"I had a border collie once. Her name was Sassy," Linda said.

"Are those the long-haired black-and-white dogs?" Everly asked.

"Yes. Like Lassie," Stella said. She turned to Everly. "You think you and David will get a dog?"

Everly scrunched her mouth to one side and kept her attention on the stitching in her lap. "Probably not. Even though our house will be here, we'll be gone a lot."

"Are you really quitting work when you two get married?" Stella asked.

Everly shrugged. "It's either that or stay here while he travels for half the year."

"I don't know why you're even buying the place here if you won't get to live in it," Stella said.

"I want to have a home," Everly said with little emotion. "We moved around my whole life while Ridge played football, and I want to at least have some place to call home."

Ava leaned over and took Everly's hand. "I'm sorry. It must have been hard for you growing up like that."

Everly's brother, Ridge, had been a high-profile professional football player until he slipped away from the stadium lights to the quiet ranch five years ago. The siblings had found a home here, one that they hadn't had growing up bouncing around to football camps and scouting events.

"It wasn't bad. It was just exhausting. I'd like to settle down one day, and maybe David would be more inclined to do that if we already had a home waiting for us."

Stella looked like she wanted to say something, but she pursed her lips instead. David was a sports agent, and his job was wherever the players and teams went. There wasn't a home base for that lifestyle. It was what Everly and her brother had gotten away from, but now she'd be going back to it.

"How's the house decorating going?" Ava asked.

Everly's shoulders sagged. "Not so good. I'm terrible at picking things out, and I don't know where to start." She rubbed her hands over her face nervously. "I haven't planned much of the wedding either."

Ava's eyes widened. "What? I thought you'd have everything settled by now." Everly and David had a long engagement, but the wedding was in three months.

"I know. I get so excited about all the colors and flowers and things, but it's overwhelming! I don't know where to start."

Seeing Everly obviously stressing was something Ava hadn't witnessed before, and she struggled for the words to help. "I'm sorry. I had no idea you were having a hard time. Do you have a wedding planner?"

"No. David said I could hire one, but I haven't yet. I guess I should just call someone."

"I could help you," Linda said matter-of-factly.

All the women looked at Linda, wondering if they'd heard her correctly.

Ava grinned. "I think that would be a great idea." She turned to Everly. "She has great taste, and she has an eye for design."

Everly looked startled for a moment before replying. "I would appreciate that. I could pay you to help me make the wedding decisions."

"Or decorate your house," Stella added.

Linda shook her head slightly. "There's no need to pay me. I've been feeling so useless lately. I need something to keep me busy."

Ava's brow furrowed. "I didn't know you felt that way. We could find some things for you to do around here."

Conversations about Linda's future here had been open-ended so far. She'd resigned from her position at the news station, and she'd yet to think about where things would go from here. Secretly, Ava had been praying her mother would find her place at the ranch, but only if this was where she was truly meant to be.

Linda picked up the mug of coffee beside her that had gone cold during their talk and lifted it slightly in Everly's direction. "I don't know what I'm going to do now, and helping you make some decisions would give me a purpose, at least for now."

Stella held up a rigid finger. "Just so we're clear, you're not the boss of anyone here. This isn't *Good Morning, Denver*, and you ain't in Kansas anymore."

Everyone laughed, including Linda, who seemed to be loosening up as the conversation went on.

Ava felt the pricking of the coming tears in her eyes. There was happiness inside her, but the emotion was overwhelming in the best way.

Reaching for her mother's mug, she stood. "Let me get you some fresh coffee."

She sped off toward the kitchen, thanking God for leading her through the day in a way she hadn't expected.

CHAPTER 35

AVA

Ava clicked send on an email and picked up her coffee mug. She clicked to the next email in her inbox and settled the cup at her lips as she read. Her nose scrunched at the stale smell, and she sipped the coffee. Cold.

It was nearly lunchtime. No wonder her six a.m. coffee was cold.

She checked her phone, wondering why she hadn't heard from Jameson. He usually sent at least a couple of quick texts throughout the morning.

Three messages were waiting, but her phone was on silent. She'd forgotten to switch the sound back on after they'd left the doctor's office.

Her mother's follow-up report had been a good one this morning, and the doctor was confident that she could be walking unassisted by spring.

Jameson: How did the appointment go?

Jameson: Remind me to never take a bet with Brett.

Jameson: Lunch?

Ava chuckled at the string of texts. She loved that Jameson texted her everything he wanted to tell her when they were apart. She usually did the same to him, but this morning had been a little different with Linda's appointment.

Ava: Lunch sounds great. Where?

She'd barely set her phone down when it chimed.

Jameson: Here.

She scrunched her lips to the side. Was that a typo?

Ava: Where is here?

Two knocks sounded on the open door of her office. Jameson stood in the doorway with a bouquet of flowers and a smile that had her heart beat skipping in her chest.

Ava stood and walked around the desk. "Hey. Have you been in your office? I thought you were out on the ranch." She pulled his cowboy hat off and laid it on the filing cabinet before running her hands through his dark hair.

Jameson wrapped an arm around her waist and pulled her in close. Pressing his lips to hers, he inhaled deeply and hummed low in his chest.

When he broke the kiss, he shook his head. "I'm sorry. What was the question?"

Ava laughed and swatted his chest. "Have you been in your office all morning?"

"No. I was in town." He held up the flowers. "These are for you."

She took the beautiful bouquet of pink and yellow peonies. "I love them. I had no idea there were so many beautiful flowers until you started bringing them to me." She picked up the tall vase she used for the flowers he brought her every other week and slipped them in. "I'll be right back."

She ran to the bathroom to fill the vase then arranged them on the small table she'd designated for the flowers. The color they added to the small office had kept her spirits bright during the long, cold winter.

With one last adjustment, she turned to Jameson, who waited patiently with his hip propped against the filing cabinet.

"I'm ready now. You want to grab a plate in the dining hall?" she asked.

Jameson wrapped his arms around her and trailed soft kisses down her cheek and jaw to the sensitive skin of her neck. "Can we bring it back here to eat?"

"Of course." She giggled as his lips brushed over a ticklish spot on her neck.

The familiar knocking of her mother's walker on the wooden floor echoed down the hall, and they took a small step apart. Ava ran a hand over her hair, and Jameson did a horrible job of looking innocent as he opened a drawer of the filing cabinet and started reading the file names.

Ava covered her mouth to stifle the laugh as her mother stepped into the doorway.

Linda's recovery had been to the tune of two steps forward, one step back for the months since she'd been released from the hospital. She was scheduled to have another surgery in two weeks, and she was in her eighth week of physical therapy. She'd only graduated out of the wheelchair last week.

Ava clasped her hands behind her back and smiled. "Hey. I didn't know you were out and about."

Linda gave her a tired smile. "I wasn't. Stella harassed me until I got up."

Pulling a chair over for her mother, Ava tried not to laugh. The relationship between Linda and Stella baffled almost everyone at the ranch. They'd all expected Stella to be assertive, but Linda's submission to Stella's demands had been shocking to everyone. Somehow, the two were stepping on each other's toes and learning the boundaries of what was shaping up to be a tentative friendship.

"You ready for lunch? We were just about to head over and get something. We can bring it back here and eat together," Ava said.

Linda slowly lowered herself into the seat. "I

already ate, but I wanted to talk to you about something."

Jameson grabbed his hat from where it sat atop the filing cabinet. "I'll meet you in the dining hall," he said as he stepped toward the door.

Linda held up a hand. "Actually, I wanted to talk to you too."

Jameson halted and turned, unsure what Linda might need with him. He'd been doing a good job of keeping his distance where Ava's mother was concerned, and she pitied him now. He was still wary of getting caught in Linda's cross hairs.

Ava rested her backside against the desk, and Jameson stood beside her. "What's up?"

Her mother looked uncomfortable, which wasn't unusual these days. She still had the look of a lost puppy most of the time, even after weeks of counseling. Ava wasn't sure if the injury or ending up here at the ranch instead of back at her job in Denver was the main cause of the sadness, but she hoped her mother was finally ready to talk about it with her.

Linda clasped her hands in her lap. "I'm getting around a little better, and I was wondering if you might have something I could do around here."

Ava tried not to react, but her mother's request had shocked the breath out of her. "Like what?"

Maybe that hadn't been the best response, but she'd been caught off guard.

"I've been helping Everly plan her wedding, and

I'm really enjoying it. I don't know much about weddings since I didn't have a real one myself, but I have lots of ideas."

Ava's chest tightened. She still couldn't believe her mother and father had started their marriage with a quick courthouse wedding because of her mother's pregnancy by another man. The old hurt was still there, but she'd forgiven her mother for keeping the secret from Paul and herself.

Linda sighed and blurted, "What if the ranch had a wedding venue?"

Ava's eyes widened, and she stood. "Weddings?"

"Yes, like a small chapel for ceremonies and a larger area for receptions. We could have an arbor overlooking the valley for outdoor weddings."

When Ava caught her breath, she whispered, "We?"

A look of concern flashed over Linda's features and she began to twist her fingers in her lap. "I know it's a far-fetched idea. I was just thinking. I'm so tired of sitting around. I want to be useful. I know you didn't like working with me before, but I want to do things better this time."

Ava thought for a moment before responding. "I'm sorry you're feeling useless, but you're healing. The down time is helping you rest and recover."

"I know why I'm supposed to, but I also hate being a burden to you."

"You're not a burden," Ava cried. "Stop thinking like that."

"I also want to be a part of your life. Here. I know I said a lot of things about this place, but I'm proud of you and what you're doing here."

Ava stuttered and looked to Jameson, who was gawking at her mother like she had two heads.

"Um, I love that idea," Ava finally said. "Let's talk about it more tonight after supper. We can write down some things we'll need and talk to Grandpa too."

"I'd really like that," Linda said. "And I wanted you to know that I'm glad you've settled in here. I see now that this place is good for you, and you're the best person to take over this place one day."

"Thank you," Ava whispered. She kept her voice quiet, afraid her emotions would get the best of her.

Linda turned to Jameson and lifted her chin. "And I'm sorry I judged you. I wanted something different when I was younger, but I shouldn't have taken that out on you and Ava. I know you're good to her, and you're a good worker. I owe you a lot of apologies, and it's been hard to know where to start."

Jameson swallowed and shifted his weight. "It's okay. Water under the bridge." He cut a glance to Ava before asking, "So, does this mean you're planning to stay here for good?"

Linda hesitated. "Well, I think I would like to.

I've had some time to think and clear my head, and I don't think I was as happy with my life as I thought I was. The counseling has helped me see a lot of things differently, and seeing the two of you working together here has been an eye opener."

Ava looked at Jameson, who stood strong and confident. She didn't know how they'd come this far, but it felt like only a drop in the ocean compared to what they could accomplish together.

Ava picked up her mother's hand and wrapped it in hers. "In that case, welcome to the team, Mom."

EPILOGUE

JAMESON

Jameson tightened the pack on a mule and patted its side. "Thanks for carrying the load, pal."

"Ah, you don't have to thank me. It's my job," Blake said.

Jameson picked up the next pack. "I was talking to Jonesey."

Blake rose up from the pack he was loading with a frown on his face. "Who?"

Jameson jerked a thumb toward the mule. "I gave him a name."

"When?" Blake asked.

"Just now."

"Um, I already named him. It's Bullwinkle."

Jameson checked the next pack and shook his head. "Okay, what about that one?" He pointed to the next mule in the line headed for the trails this morning.

Blake propped an arm on the fence post. "Jethro." He pointed at each mule down the line. "That's Leonard, Skynard, Elvis, and Paul."

Jameson quirked a brow. "Paul?"

Blake shrugged. "He doesn't talk much."

At the mention of his name, Paul walked out of the pack shed with a saddle pad draped over his arm and Thane at his side.

"What's he think about having Ava and Linda back at the ranch?" Blake asked.

Jameson inhaled a deep breath. "I have no idea, but it looks like Linda is here to stay." He still hadn't figured out what he thought about Linda being here all the time, but Ava was excited that her relationship with her mother was growing stronger now that they were planning to add the new wedding venue on the ranch.

Paul walked right past Jameson and Blake. "You replace the first-aid kit?"

Blake perked up. "You know it." He leaned toward Jameson and fake whispered, "He thinks I'm a dumb city boy."

"To be fair, you were a dumb city boy just a few years ago," Jameson said.

"Yeah, but I've got this cowboy thing figured out now." Blake tipped his hat and stuck his thumbs in his jean pockets.

Jameson rolled his eyes. He'd always appreciated Blake's initiative, and he'd gone from high-profile sports agent to mountain cowboy without a hitch. In fact, Blake was the best trail manager Wolf Creek Ranch had seen in the last twenty years.

"You done posin' over there?" Paul shouted.

Blake straightened and gave Paul a salute. "All done."

Jameson's phone dinged, and he reached into his jacket pocket. The screen lit up with a selfie he'd taken with Ava at the Christmas festival. So much had changed since then, and he was reminded again of the ring in his pocket. He'd planned to ask Ava to marry him on Christmas Eve, but they'd spent the holiday at the hospital with Linda. He'd been carrying it around ever since hoping he'd get some kind of a sign letting him know it was the right time to just ask her.

He answered the phone with a smile. "Hello, darlin'."

Ava laughed. "Good morning, cowboy. You busy?"

"Never too busy for you."

"Can you come to the check-in office?"

"Already on my way."

"See you in a minute. Love you."

He'd never get used to hearing Ava say those words. "Love you too."

"Catch you later," Blake said.

Jameson waved a hand over his head as he walked toward the check-in office.

"You and Ava coming to the party tonight?" Blake shouted.

"We'll be there." Today was Ridge's birthday, and Blake had planned a barbecue at their place to celebrate.

The cold March air pierced Jameson's lungs as he jogged up to the check-in office. He took the stairs in two long strides and barged in, closing the door behind him to keep out the cold.

Ava stood over the small table on the left side of the room and waved him over with a smile on her face. "Come look."

Blueprints for the new venue were rolled out with a mug holding one end down and her phone holding the other.

"This is it?" he asked as he wrapped an arm around her waist.

"This is it."

"Final answer?"

She chuckled. "Did I change my mind a few times?"

"Only thirty or so," he said as he pressed a kiss on her head. "I don't care. It should be exactly how you want."

"Well, Mom and Everly kept coming up with

good ideas, and I'd hate to miss out on adding something great when we have the chance to do it right from the start."

"I agree." He leaned over the blueprints. "Tell me all about it."

She pulled on his arm, turning his attention back to her. "First, I want to tell you how much I love you. I can't tell you what your support means to me. I don't think I would have had the courage to even start planning this if you hadn't been so sure that I could. I couldn't do half the things I do around here without you. You've taught me so much in the last six months."

Jameson's arms wrapped around her waist, and he drank in the smile on her face. In truth, the last six months with her had been the best of his life, and there were many times when he didn't feel worthy of the love she gave him so freely every day.

Ava looked at the lines and measurements on the table. "Do you know how many happily ever afters will start right here? I never thought I'd be a part of something this big. The ranch, the wedding venue, the friends I have here—I can see how this place changes lives." She tilted her chin to look up at him as she snuggled into his embrace. "This ranch is a great place for new beginnings."

Thanks for the sign, God.

"I'm glad you think so." Jameson knelt on one

knee and took Ava's hands in his. His heart thudded hard in his chest, but he couldn't wait another day to ask her.

Ava squeezed his hands, and her eyes widened with her smile.

Jameson looked up at her, trying and failing to wrangle his smile into a more serious expression. "I always knew you were the one for me. No one has ever held a place in my heart the way you do. I love your kindness, I love your selflessness, and I love your heart. The truth is I want to spend the rest of my life with you by my side."

Ava's cheeks were bright red, and her dark eyes were glassy with tears.

He was not getting choked up. No, he'd never been choked up before, and he didn't intend to start now. He cleared his throat to get rid of that pesky throat tickle.

"Will you marry me?"

Her answer was immediate. "Yes."

"Yes?" As many times as he'd played through this moment in his head, he hadn't actually gotten past his speech.

"Yes, yes, yes!"

He stood and wrapped her in his arms, letting her joyful laugh wash over him.

"I love you," he whispered against her hair.

"I love you too." She raised her head and looked

up at him with enough happiness to shine through the rest of their lives together. "I came here looking for the truth, and I found it. All of it. The greatest truth is that I want to spend the rest of my life here, loving you."

BONUS EPILOGUE

BLAKE

Blake buttoned his shirt as he raced down the stairs. He'd barely made it home in time to change before the guests arrived, and he needed to see if Brett needed a hand at the grill. The guy was easily distracted, and nobody wanted a burnt hotdog tonight.

Blake did a double take in the living room. The huge room with seventy-inch TVs, a massive fireplace, and top-of-the-line surround sound was where he and Ridge spent most of their time, and it usually looked like a bachelor pad. He'd planned to pick up a little before the party, but it looked like someone beat him to it. The place was spotless. He'd have to find the cleaning fairy later and thank them.

He heard the front door open and close. No one came in without knocking except—

"Blake! Ridge!" Everly yelled.

Blake jogged into the foyer to meet her. "Hey, you're early." Not that he'd ever complain about getting to spend more time with her. He'd just hoped to be able to put on his boots first.

But Everly always seemed to catch him off guard. He hadn't expected to fall for his best friend's little sister. He hadn't planned on harboring a crush on her. He certainly hadn't intended to miss his chance and have to watch her get engaged to someone else.

Yep. Everly never came into his life quietly. Tonight, she was wearing a navy sweater dress and burgundy boots, and the dark colors were a stark contrast to her blonde hair and fair skin.

She was gorgeous, which made it that much harder to keep his distance and his thoughts in check.

Everly's smile was so wide he could count the teeth in her mouth. She threw her arms in the air and shouted, "Jameson proposed!"

"To you?" Blake joked.

She laughed and threw her arms around him. "No! Ava. They're getting married!"

Blake swallowed hard and carefully wrapped his arms around Everly before releasing her quickly. Friends could hug, but it didn't work well when one of them wanted more than a hug. He was better off putting distance between them.

Everly stepped out of the hug and bounced on her toes. "Is she here yet?"

"No. You're the first."

"I'm so excited. We have another wedding to plan!"

Blake was happy for Jameson and Ava. Really. But he wasn't a fan of wedding talk these days. He didn't need another reminder of Everly's impending wedding. The looming date and the torturous countdown were a dark cloud over all his days.

Her eyes widened. "I left the cake in the car. I was so excited, I forgot it."

"You need help?" Blake asked.

"No, thanks," she said as she ran back out the door.

Now he really needed to check on Brett. The grill and smokers were out on the back patio, and Brett, Asa, and Colt were leaning against the rail.

"Get here when you can," Brett said.

Blake eyed the grill. "You burnt the food yet?"

Brett lifted the lid on the grill. "Not yet, but I'm working on it."

"You put the kabobs on last?" Blake asked.

Brett slapped his hand against his forehead. "I completely forgot them."

"I'll get them." Blake turned and headed for the fridge. Thankfully, he'd gotten them ready earlier, and they were ready to put on the grill.

Blake took over the cooking, and Brett didn't

object. Guests were starting to arrive, and more and more people crowded onto the patio.

This was exactly the kind of get-together Blake and Ridge had in mind when they bought the five thousand square foot house. Well, that, and they'd both agreed to the investment. When they both got married and moved out, they could sell this place for a pretty penny. They both had more money than they knew what to do with, so a house made for gathering was at the top of their lists when they'd moved out of the world of professional sports and into the quiet life of rural Wyoming.

Blake had just pulled the kabobs off the grill when Everly showed up beside him.

"Hey, I have something I want to ask you. Feel free to say no if you don't want to."

"Yes." His answer was immediate. He looked at her, knowing it was a bad idea.

She laughed. "I haven't even told you what it is yet."

"Does it matter?"

They both knew it didn't. He'd do anything for Everly. He'd been best friends with her brother for over a decade, and he'd become friends with Everly after he missed his chance to ask her out. He hadn't expected his cautiousness to lose him the girl, but here he was, stuck in the friend zone because he'd been afraid to ask her out.

"Can you give me a ride to the airport on Saturday? I'm flying out to Cleveland to meet David for a charity auction."

Blake stared at the kabobs, wishing for once that he wasn't the dependable friend. Driving the girl of his dreams to meet up with her fiancé sounded like pure torture.

Instead of backing out, he did the only thing he knew how to do when it came to Everly. "Sure. What time do you need me to pick you up?"

"Eleven would be great." She reached up and wrapped her arms around his neck.

This time, he didn't return the hug.

She whispered, "Thanks. You're the best."

Just as she released the hug, the crowd shouted a chorus of "Happy Birthday" as Ridge walked in.

Everly bumped her elbow against Blake's arm. "Thanks for throwing this party for him. It means a lot that his real friends are here for him today."

The thirty people here weren't much compared to some of the parties they'd attended when Ridge had been nothing short of a celebrity in the professional sports world, but Blake knew what Everly meant. That lifestyle blurs the lines of friendship, but they'd found something real here in Wyoming.

Seconds later, everyone shouted, "Congratulations!" as Jameson and Ava walked in.

Everly gasped. "I have to go. Save me a kabob!"

Ridge wouldn't mind sharing the celebration with Jameson and Ava tonight, but Blake wasn't too excited about the constant reminder of marriage that would be hanging over the rest of the evening.

Brett walked up holding a plate of ribs and shoved it toward Blake. "Want some?"

"No, thanks." He wasn't sure he could stomach food right now.

Everly laughed loud enough to be heard above the chatter, and Blake turned, looking for the source of the laugh instinctually.

"You're doing it again," Brett said.

"What?"

Brett pointed to Blake with a rib bone. "That thing where you stare longingly at Everly."

Blake looked back to the grill and grabbed the serving plate to take up the hotdogs. "Sorry. I can't help it sometimes."

"You should really get that checked out. It's not normal."

Nothing about the feelings Blake had for Everly was normal. She was taken. Off-limits. Not his to look at.

But that didn't stop him from silently wishing he was getting a happily ever after, and not with just anyone. He hadn't thought twice about another woman since he met Everly.

"Thanks for the advice, but I don't think there's a cure."

OTHER BOOKS BY MANDI BLAKE

Unfailing Love Series

Complete small-town Christian romance series

Just as I Am

Never Say Goodbye

Living Hope

Beautiful Storm

All the Stars

What if I Loved You

Unfailing Love Series Complete Box Set

Blackwater Ranch Series

Complete Contemporary Western Series

Remembering the Cowboy

Charmed by the Cowboy

Mistaking the Cowboy

Protected by the Cowboy

Keeping the Cowboy

Redeeming the Cowboy

Blackwater Ranch Series Complete Box Set

Wolf Creek Ranch Series

Truth is a Whisper

Almost Everything

The Only Exception

Better Together

The Other Side

The Blushing Brides Series

Multi-author series

The Billionaire's Destined Bride

The Heroes of Freedom Ridge Series

Multi-author Christmas series

Rescued by the Hero

Guarded by the Hero

Hope for the Hero

About the Author

Mandi Blake was born and raised in Alabama where she lives with her husband and daughter, but her southern heart loves to travel. Reading has been her favorite hobby for as long as she can remember, but writing is her passion. She loves a good happily ever after in her sweet Christian romance books and loves to see her characters' relationships grow closer to God and each other.

Acknowledgments

I owe enormous thanks to so many people. This book was years in the making, so my acknowledgments list is long.

First, I couldn't have completed this book without the fantastic beta readers who put up with me and my struggles day after day. They worked so hard to help me make this book better, and I can't thank them enough. Tanya Smith, Pam Humphries, Kendra Haneline, Laura de la Torre, Trudy Cordle, Ginny Roberts, Natasha Wall, Haley Powell, Demi Abrahamson, Jenna Eleam, and Stephanie Palmer Taylor, I really appreciate the attention you put into this book.

I also have wonderful friends and ARC readers who either helped me brainstorm or let me know about typos that made it through countless editing rounds. I appreciate everyone who took time out of their day to help me. It truly takes a village.

To my wonderful editor, Brandi Aquino, and my fantastic cover designer, Amanda Walker, you two are the bones behind every book. Thank you for lending your skills.

My family was understanding when I needed to sneak away and write. They cheered me on from the next room. There are countless people in my life who helped make this book possible.

Now that it's finished and out in the world, I hope you love the story. I write every book with you, the reader, in mind. I pray it brought you hope and peace. Thank you for giving this book a chance.

Almost Everything
Wolf Creek Ranch Book Two

Her fairytale ending turns into a disaster. Can her brother's best friend convince her that she was chasing the wrong happily ever after?

Everly Cooper had it all. A successful fiancé, a dream home being built, and the life she always wanted away from the spotlight.

And then it all crashed and burned... publicly, and her brother's best friend, Blake, was all too eager to race to her rescue.

Blake Lawson left the world of professional football for the small town life five years ago. His friend, Ridge, needed help, and being closer to Everly was more than just a bonus. He'd been silently in love with his best friend's sister for years. He had everything he could possibly want, except her.

Blake refuses to watch her cry over a man who didn't deserve her. He's ready to fess up to Everly and show her how a real man treats the woman he loves.

When Blake's plan to win her heart backfires, he'll have to figure out what loving someone really means before he loses Everly forever.

Almost Everything **is the second book in the Christian romance Wolf Creek Ranch series.**